STRIVERS ROW

During the 1920s and 1930s, around the time of the Harlem Renaissance, more than a quarter of a million African-Americans settled in Harlem, creating what was described at the time as "a cosmopolitan Negro capital which exert[ed] an influence over Negroes everywhere."

Nowhere was this more evident than on West 138th and 139th Streets between Adam Clayton Powell and Frederick Douglass Boulevards, two blocks that came to be known as Strivers Row. These blocks attracted many of Harlem's African-American doctors, lawyers, and entertainers, among them Eubie Blake, Noble Sissle, and W. C. Handy, who were themselves striving to achieve America's middle-class dream.

With its mission of publishing quality African-American literature, Strivers Row emulates those "strivers," capturing that same spirit of hope, creativity, and promise.

THE SHIRT OFF HIS BACK

VILLARD / STRIVERS ROW / NEW YORK

THE
SHIRT
OFF
HIS
BACK

A NOVEL

PARRY "EBONYSATIN" BROWN

Copyright © 1998, 2001 by Parry "EbonySatin" Brown

All rights reserved under International and Pan-American
Copyright Conventions. Published in the United States by
Strivers Row, an imprint of Villard Books, a division of
Random House, Inc., New York, and simultaneously in
Canada by Random House of Canada Limited, Toronto.

VILLARD BOOKS is a registered trademark of Random House,
Inc. Strivers Row and colophon are trademarks
of Random House, Inc.

This work was originally published in different
form by ShanKrys Publications in 1998.

ISBN 0-7394-1548-4

Printed in the United States of America

Book design by Jo Anne Metsch

Dedicated to all my girls . . .

*Nicolle, Michelle, Shanelle, Krystal,
Kendra (1998), and Krysten*

B ITS OF DILIGENT research were required before I began this foreword. Having been a student and teacher of African-American literature for a number of years, I sought a reference point for first-time novelist Parry Brown's volume of work, *The Shirt off His Back*. While there were many examples of great work—from James Baldwin, Chester Himes, and Toni Morrison to Ernest Gaines, J. California Cooper, and Terry McMillan—none has approached the issue of positive African-American male image with such sincerity as *The Shirt off His Back*.

Parry Brown has created a stunning work of simple eloquence. She pulls no emotional punches, but she delves into the intricacies of "ethnic" love so tenderly that her characters spontaneously emerge with both passion and restrained elegance. Kudos to Ms. Brown for this sketch of The New Black America. While this is a relatively fresh approach, she skillfully blends the more traditional black characters with a sexy mix of nouveau blackness that draws the most astoundingly inspirational portrait of African-American life I have ever read.

I look forward to her next work because *The Shirt off His Back* speaks historical volumes. Some might simply call it new fiction, but I would have to disagree. The present-day sociological truths within this work are so clear and bright and filled with hope, it will no doubt usher in the new millennium with the finest collection of shirtless black manhood this side of the twentieth century.

Indeed, it is a grand tribute to the men who have lived in the literary shadows of dogs, bastards, and hoodlums far too long.

'Bout time.
Judi Ann Mason

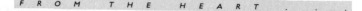
ABOVE ALL ELSE, I must give thanks and honor to my God, my Lord, my Savior. I thank Him for how He has seen fit to bestow the talent of the written and spoken word upon me. Me, who is nothing without Him. Me, who can do nothing without Him. All praise to my Lord and Savior, Jesus Christ!

Nothing but love for you all . . .

There are so many people who have helped make the dreams of a six-year-old, nappy-headed little girl a reality forty years later.

Nicolle, honey, you are the best press agent a mother could ask for. Thank you for the wonderful concept for the original cover. Michelle, my daughter and mother of my wonderful grandchildren, you would just put up with me no matter how outrageous I got . . . thank you, sweetie. Mary, Lorraine, Jackie, and Beatrice, thank you for the endless unconditional love and undying support! Being your sister is everything to me. Neville, you have brought such a wonderful balance into my life. Thank you for making my heart sing! Without question you personify the kind of brotha I characterize on these pages. Twania, you believed in me when I wasn't so sure about myself. My dear friend

Wanda, just thank you for loving me, gurl! Glynda, my friend, my sistah. You will never know what our early morning conversations did to keep me going. Then proofing when we were down to the wire, while juggling the twenty-seven other things you had going . . . you know I love you! Victoria, I so proudly have stepped in the footprints that you so expertly left for me. God is so awesome, and I am consistently amazed at how He brings His people together. Portia, my roommate, my manager, my agent, my friend! You are truly another example of God's perfect planning! Rico, your prayers and good wishes sustained me when it would have been so much easier to give up. Lloyd, you talk about a brother taking care of his sister . . . you are the best!

Judi Ann, thank you for sharing your knowledge with a beginner, my sistah. Phil and Dan, thank you for believing in me and putting your money where my heart is.

To my Internet family . . .

Thank you, Sabreen (ALSO BREE), for giving me an audience and encouragement with each chapter. Gerald (BlakCat), what can I say? You were my number one fan from the very beginning. Thank you for convincing me this could be not just another short story. Lisa (LvingSingl), I told you I was writing! Thanks so much for making me know I could do this. Jeralynn (LIGHT728), for your hours and hours of editing, just because you believed in me and this project. I love you! Thomas (IvoryBear), my friend, my cyber-confidant, thank you for knocking on doors, ringing up phones trying to get someone to read my work. James (CheesyB1), my cyber-godchild, you never let me get discouraged and constantly checked to make sure I was surviving all the stress. Howard (HONO), my friend who has always had my back! Others will never understand how close people can become through their cyber-association until their fingertips have tickled the keyboard through laughter and tears.

*To all who made this story a Blackboard Best Seller
the first time around!*

The grand book goddess herself, Emma Rodgers (Black Images Books). I will never forget the first time I walked into your wonderful store and those words that every author lives to hear were uttered—"You know you are on the best sellers list." To all my brothers at the International Association of Professional Black Fire Fighters, thank you for embracing me with open arms, and for your unwavering support and inspiration for my third novel, *Fanning the Flames.*

To the unsung (s)heroes of the African-American literary world—the book clubs: Los Angeles—Shades of Brown, Pages; Houston—The Good Book Club, Sister to Sister, Mahogany Minds; Hartford—Eden Book Club.

Thanks for the inspiration . . .

Last but certainly not least, to the men who inspired me to tell this story. The story that so desperately needed to be told! To the heroes that go unsung—the husbands, fathers, and boyfriends that just do the right thing even when no one is watching . . . Neville, Jerome, Lloyd, Robert Sr., Dan, Gene, Chuck, Larry, Don, Ed, and Kevin, and millions and millions of others—I salute you! Thank you for giving me such a rich storyline for my first novel.

Many brothers are good . . .

Some are even great . . .

Only a few will give you . . .

THE SHIRT OFF HIS BACK

TERRY RUSHED THROUGH the aisles of the supermarket, realizing the girls had to be picked up from school in twenty minutes. *Why weren't there ever enough hours in the day?* he thought. *Between work, Alisa, and Ariana, there is hardly time to breathe. But hey, breathing is an option, right?* The line was so long, he feared he would be late.

"How am I ever going to make it out of here to get to the school on time?" Terry wondered out loud.

Just then, a young woman with a warm smile pointed at him and said, "I can help you over here." Miraculously, Terry was soon out of the market and headed for the school.

With not a moment to spare, Terry pulled up at the usual pickup point. Alisa pulled Ariana by the hand as she ran toward the car. "Daddy, Daddy, I got second place in the essay contest!" Alisa said breathlessly.

Terry popped off his seat belt and sprang from the car. He ran to the passenger side of the car to hug his older daughter as she leapt into his waiting arms. "Congratulations, baby! I am so proud of you!" Terry turned to his other daughter, "How did you do with the artwork you presented with the story, Ariana?" Terry asked as he let Alisa slip from his arms.

"I won first place," she stated simply as Terry looked into her big, brown eyes.

He hugged her tightly and shouted, "Alright! My girls, the superstars! I am so proud of both of you. I was going to make meat loaf tonight, but this definitely calls for tacos."

Both girls yelled, "YES!" and high-fived each other.

As he stood in front of the elementary school, Terry felt so full that tears welled up in his eyes. "Get in the car, my superstars. Let's stop at the bakery and buy a cake to celebrate!" The happy bunch scrambled into the black Ford Explorer and sped away singing along with their favorite old Temptations song, "My Girl."

The girls were identical twins, yet so unique. Their physical features were the same, down to the birthmarks on their right forearms, but their personalities were quite different. Alisa was outgoing and vibrant, while Ariana, who was only four minutes younger, was quiet and even-tempered. Since Terry had brought them home from the hospital nearly eleven years before, he had never regretted his decision. Catherine, their mother, was a woman he had dated for three years on and off right out of high school. When she became pregnant, she announced she had no intention of keeping the child. Catherine was in her third year of college and felt she had no time for a baby. She threatened to abort the baby every time she was angry at him, but through some miracle she never followed through. He had pleaded with her not to kill his baby and said that if she delivered the child, he would raise it. Then, four weeks earlier than her scheduled due date, she called him from the hospital. She told him that she had given birth to twins and that if he did not want them, she would sign the adoption papers in two hours. He rushed to the hospital, and while looking through the glass at the two screaming baby girls, he fell in love.

The girls chattered all the way home and into the evening, and although on occasion the giggles were a bit much to handle, Terry so much enjoyed seeing these two very special young females in his life so happy that the noise hardly bothered him.

Toward the end of the evening, the phone rang, and Alisa leapt for it as usual and sang, "Helloooo?"

The look on her face told Terry exactly who it was.

"Hi, Catherine, you want to talk to my dad? . . . Oh, we're doing okay. We won an essay contest that required artwork today, and we were about to have cake to celebrate. When are you coming back to Texas to see us? . . . Oh. Well, we'll write you to let you know what we want for Christmas."

It was their mother. Alisa's gaze shot toward Ariana, who got up from the couch and headed for the upstairs bathroom as soon as she realized their mother was on the other end of the phone.

"No, Ari is in the bathroom. You want to talk to Dad?"

Anger welled up in Terry's chest as he slowly walked toward Alisa to take the phone. *How dare she disappoint them again,* he thought. "Hello, Catherine. How's it going? It's been a while. How's life treating you these days?" Terry struggled to keep his tone even. His internal voice was screaming and cursing. He had to remain civil for the girls' sake. "Very glad to hear it . . . Oh yes, I get the child support checks on time every month. You are very generous . . . So you won't be here for Christmas this year? I thought it was all set." Terry could feel every beat of his heart in the palm of his hands as he tightened his grip on the receiver. "No, they haven't really expressed what they want. You would really have to know them in order to shop for them, especially for clothes . . . Yeah, you could send a check, and I'll be glad to pick the gifts up for you . . . Of course, they will know it comes from you." Terry spoke the words through clenched teeth. "No, she hasn't come down yet . . . Okay, I'll tell her. If it isn't too much of a bother, let us know when you'll be back in the States." His words dripped with sarcasm. He hung up the phone without another word.

The hurt on Alisa's face was undeniable as she stared at her dad, but she only said, "Can I cut the cake?"

"But Dad, she did it last time!" Ariana whined as she descended the stairs.

"She's right, Lisa, but I'll tell you what—you can scoop the ice cream," Terry said with a broad smile, knowing that would please his older daughter.

The remainder of the evening was quiet, and as the girls were about to climb into bed, Ariana called to her dad. "Can you come in and tuck us in, Daddy?"

"Tuck you in? Now, that is an unusual request. Wasn't it you who said you were too mature for that?" Terry said with a chuckle.

"What we really want to do is talk to you, Dad," Alisa volunteered. "We've been talking and we know that Catherine is sending us a check for Christmas, *again*, and you want to know what to buy us with the money, right? So we were thinking that this year we want you to buy two airline tickets."

"Oh, and where do you two plan on going? Do you want to go see Catherine in Spain? Her checks are considerable, but I am not sure it will cover two international airline tickets," Terry said, a little sad that they wanted to be away from him during Christmas vacation.

"Oh no! Daddy, we would never leave you for Christmas," Ariana interrupted.

"We want you to buy tickets for you and Ms. Rogers to go to the Bahamas or Hawaii or somewhere romantic," Alisa chimed in.

"Neither one of you ever goes anywhere without us or Michael and Michelle," Ariana chirped.

"We want you to go alone, but there is one condition: you can't go for Christmas, you have to go for New Year's," Alisa concluded.

"Or Valentine's Day would be even better," Ariana said, looking at her mirror image for confirmation.

Terry didn't know what to say, but as emotion constricted his throat, he managed, "Girls, that is very nice of you, but that money is for the two of you, and I could never do that. But thank you and I will be sure to tell Jackie about your most generous offer."

"But Dad, if it is *our* money, why can't we spend it how we want? If you don't buy the airline tickets, then we will send the check back. Catherine doesn't love us. She moved to Spain three years ago and promised to come home every Christmas but hasn't. We didn't even see her for Christmas when she lived in Oklahoma because something always came up. She never even made it here for Ari's surgery. Daddy, we love you, and we know you love us, and we just want to say thank you for being the best dad in the world. You have given up everything for us. You didn't even date until you met Ms. Rogers, and she has twins, too. *Please*, Dad, don't turn down our gift." Alisa finally took a breath as tears ran down her cheeks.

Terry grabbed both his daughters in his arms and buried his face in their hair. "Okay, my princesses, I'll think about it. But there's no need to thank me. I should thank you for giving me the richest life any man could wish for."

It was all he could say. The rest was in his heart.

2

TERRY CLOSED THE door to the girls' room, taking in a deep breath. He had not let on how much he had been touched by their gesture. This was his favorite time of the evening—the quiet time right after the twins turned in for the night—even though he could still hear their muffled voices through the door.

Terry hit the speed-dial button on the phone and fell on the bed in one motion. It felt good to let his five-foot-ten frame sink deep into the mattress. The only thing that could make this moment better was Jackie being there in person, rather than picking up the phone to say hello.

"Hey, baby," Terry said as the distinctive warmth flowed through his body at the sound of Jackie's voice. She was the kind of woman that every loving mother would want for her son. She was smart, beautiful, kind, funny, and an excellent mother. And she was also what every father would wish for his son—strong, supportive, and sexy. His woman had it all.

"How are ya, sugah? I was just about to call you. I finally got the kids to sleep. I took them to Chuck E. Cheese's. I must be a masochist," Jackie said, almost catching her breath.

"You will never guess what Lisa and Ari did tonight," Terry

began. "They offered to buy us a vacation with the money Catherine is sending them for Christmas. Of course, I told them they couldn't do that, but I was so touched by their benevolence."

"Wow!" Jackie responded. "Lisa and Ari are two very special girls, honey. We've talked about that so many times. But you know, they're onto something. We *should* take a vacation, just the two of us. Not a long one, just a weekend. Would your sister be willing to watch the girls for a couple of days? My mother would be thrilled to take Mikey and Ikey for a weekend."

Up to this point Terry had only focused on the twins' gesture of kindness. He had not even considered how badly he needed some time away. "You know, that would be a great idea, Jackie. Maybe a trip to Vegas. The girls had suggested New Year's or Valentine's Day. But that's a little soon, and I heard that it is pretty wild there on New Year's Eve and it is really crowded on Valentine's."

Jackie smiled to herself as she listened to the man she loved so very much, always so considerate, but also so cautious. "Honey, you know we could use a little 'wild' for a few days, throw caution to the wind. You know, feel the wind on our faces. We don't have to decide right this second, but please tell me you'll think about it, and we can talk about it right after Thanksgiving."

"Yes, I promise I'll give it lots of thought," he said enthusiastically.

"So tell me, how was your day?" Jackie asked, delighted at the prospect of some quality uninterrupted time with Terry.

Terry and Jackie talked for more than an hour, discussing the day's activities, including the essay-art contest and Catherine's call. They ended with the usual "I love you." Terry regretted not preparing for bed before making that call. He was exhausted.

Jackie, on the other hand, lay on the bed relishing the quiet and thought about how lucky she had been on that fateful December day almost four years before. She had finished grocery shopping and was struggling to get Michael and Michelle into their car seats, which were next to each other in the backseat of her silver BMW 525. A sudden, driving, Texas-style rainstorm was assaulting them horizontally when she heard a deep warm voice that made her freeze momentarily, despite the downpour.

"Hi, can I give you a hand?" Terry's voice had sounded like that of an angel. He continued, "I'm not a weirdo. I have twin girls there in the car," pointing to the backseat of the Explorer.

"You get her, I'll get him. Come on, we're all getting drenched."

Jackie didn't know what to say, other than "Thank you."

The handsome stranger buckled Michael in as she placed Michelle in the rear seat on the driver's side. She had never felt more unattractive as she leaned over the seat with her hair plastered to her face. The stranger with the million-dollar smile looked at her and said, "There you go," as he turned to his car, which was parked next to hers. She was sure he thought she was some pathetic woman who should have known better than to venture out with two toddlers with the threat of a rainstorm in Dallas.

"Thank you very much," she said, waving.

"No problem. I remember those days myself. All too well." They both waved as his car slipped out of the parking space.

Jackie collected herself and buckled her seat belt. His scent lingered in the car. *Whew, my handsome stranger, you smell so gooood,* Jackie thought to herself, looking at him through her rearview mirror.

More than two weeks had passed, and Jackie could not stop thinking about the kind man who helped her or forget his scent. Christmas was less than ten days away, and she still had shopping to do. Her mother had agreed to watch the twins for her while she embarked on a late-night shopping expedition to Toys "R" Us. As she pulled into the parking lot of the toy store, she could not believe how many people had the same plan.

The lot was full, and as she circled looking for a spot, she noticed a black Ford Explorer. She immediately thought of the stranger from the grocery store parking lot. But she was soon distracted and got on with the business at hand.

As she entered the store, Jackie thought to herself, *They must be giving away gubment cheeze up in here,* laughing aloud. At the sight of all the people in the store, she knew shopping was going to take more time than she had thought. "Nothing to it, but to do it," she said audibly.

Much to her surprise a warm and vaguely familiar voice responded, "I see I am not the only glutton for punishment tonight." As she turned around, she inhaled that glorious, manly fragrance that she could not forget—it was him, the kindly stranger.

"Hi," Jackie said. She was glad that she was still wearing the black designer dress she had selected for the Dallas *Herald* staff writers meeting that day—and that she had checked her hair and makeup before leaving the house. Her trench coat was open, and she felt at least presentable that night, unlike the last time he had seen her. *If only I had not worn flat shoes,* she thought, imagining she would appear slimmer in her three-inch heels. *Oh well.*

"Well, hello yourself. You left before I had a chance to properly thank you the other day. I can't believe how fast that rainstorm came up. We were getting drenched! By the way, my name is Jackie," she said, extending her hand.

"Hi Jackie, I'm Terry, and it was no problem. We were caught by surprise, too. Fortunately, Ari and Lisa are old enough to run and jump in the car without any assistance from me.

"Shopping kind of late, aren't you? I guess we had the same idea. I do hate this place at Christmas, but what's a dad to do?" He hadn't released her hand, and he was staring into her eyes.

What am I sensing? Jackie wondered. Was he attracted to her? What was he thinking? His manner was more than just polite, that was for sure. She was secretly flattered but also disturbed. *Is he married?* she thought. *I have enough problems without being attracted to someone else's husband. I wish I had a man who was willing to brave Toys "R" Us for me and my children . . . damn!*

"I should let you get started shopping. Very nice seeing you again." Jackie couldn't help but smile to herself as she walked away. Jackie found herself smiling and humming to herself as she pushed her way through the very crowded aisles. She had been unprepared for this trip. Normally, she was armed with a list and coupons, but tonight she had left with the intention of simply getting a start on the shopping. But after seeing Terry, she couldn't concentrate.

She finally picked up two items that she thought Michelle would like and headed for the quick checkout when she saw him again.

"Are you done, too? I only came in for two things, since no other store had them in stock," Jackie lied, feeling as if she had to make an excuse for running into him again.

"Yes, I guess I am just too tired to really get into this tonight. Perhaps early on Sunday morning would be better," he said as he looked at the mob of people with their carts overflowing. Jackie followed his line of vision, and they both laughed.

The conversation naturally veered to their children and the endless requests for gifts as they waited in line. Jackie was happy that she had at least another year before her kids started being influenced by Saturday morning commercials, which could seriously affect her wallet.

"It was a pleasure seeing you again, Terry. Merry Christmas to you and your family," Jackie said, as she started to walk away.

"Oh, please wait! I'll only be a second, and then I'll walk you to your car. After all, it *is* rather late," Terry said with a pleading look in his eyes.

Jackie didn't know what to make of his request, so she simply agreed to wait. They were out of the store in minutes. As he walked her to her car, she realized that the Explorer she had seen earlier *was* his! He placed her packages in the trunk of her car, and she thanked him once again, realizing that this was a genuinely kind man. She extended her hand, but this time he didn't take it. He looked down at the ground. Jackie felt awkward as she let her hand fall.

Terry faltered as he began to speak. "Jackie, I am way out of practice with this, but may I call you sometime?"

"Aren't you married?" Jackie asked as she tried to temper her elation. "I don't get involved with married men, ever."

"Oh no, I haven't even been on a date in longer than I can remember. I'm a single dad, and there hasn't been time. But I've thought about you constantly since that day at the grocery store. I noticed you inside and followed you out, only to be pleasantly surprised to find you parked right next to me. I've been kicking myself constantly since that day for not giving you my number at that time. But of course it was raining with hurricane force, and it just didn't occur to me at that moment." He finally stopped to take a breath.

"How do you know I am not involved with someone?" Jackie asked, trying to hide her amusement. It had been a long time since someone had tried to *pick her up.*

"If any man would allow you to come out here tonight alone, he is a fool. Besides, I checked your ring finger when I first saw you," Terry said, worried that he had come to the wrong conclusion.

"I *am* single, very single, and the mother of two-year-old twins, and believe me they are called the terrible twos for a reason!" They both laughed.

"I thought they were twins, but I wasn't really sure. What a coincidence—my girls are twins, too."

"I would like very much for us to talk further. Do you have a business card or a pen?" Terry wrote her home number on the back of her business card. They said good night as he closed her car door. Little did Jackie know that Terry was smiling brightly all the way home, just as she was.

3

TERRY NEVER THOUGHT he would need to engage the services of Roland's very successful family law practice, but when an International FedEx letter arrived from Catherine on Friday, he found himself in a twilight zone. Catherine wrote that she felt it was time she took a more active role in Alisa's and Ariana's lives. She said she had admittedly not been as accessible to them as they needed. Especially now that puberty was approaching, they needed a mother, and she was ready to be just that. She wanted joint custody. After reading her letter, Terry was stunned. *How could she think she could waltz into their lives after all this time?* he thought.

Terry's day had started off much too harshly. In stark contrast to the sunny Dallas day, he felt only doom and gloom as he walked quickly toward the forty-story office building. His longtime friend from college, Roland, had agreed to meet with him that evening.

Unable to focus on work, he had left early without explanation. When he told his boss, Valerie Sharpton, that he was leaving for the day, she had started to question if everything was okay, but she knew by the ashen look on Terry's face that things were far from alright.

Terry knew how fortunate he was to work with Valerie. When

she was hired as the head of their design team, most of the guys had screamed affirmative action. His architectural firm was a heavy government contractor, but they had virtually no women in management. Even the brothers had moaned and complained they would not work for a *skirt*. Nevertheless, Ms. Sharpton had won over most of the designers in short order. She was strong, fair, but most of all, a *very* talented architect. She was a third-generation designer, second-generation *female* designer. In fact, she had designed her first dollhouse when she was six.

Valerie was a great boss; she had been more than understanding over the years when it came to his duties as a single parent. Her ability to read the body language of those she dealt with was just one of the things that made her a superior leader. She made a mental note to check with him on Monday to see if she could be of assistance.

Terry didn't remember the drive home, or pouring the glass of chardonnay. The burning in his chest as he drank without stopping brought him back to the present. Less than a day earlier, his life had seemed so in order. He had finally found a woman who loved him, he had a promising career in one of the top design firms in the country, but most important of all, he had his girls. They were his life. Now Catherine wanted to step in and change everything. How could they have joint custody with her living in Spain? With her villa in Spain, her housekeepers, her cruises, and of course her lovers, how could there be room for Ari and Lisa in her world?

"Roland!" Terry said, as he snapped his fingers, breaking the deafening silence in the house. "I'll call Roland. She can't do this to us!"

Roland and Terry had met on the first day of registration their freshman year at Texas State. Roland—president of the African-American student union, captain of the basketball team—had had coeds of every hue at his beck and call. But behind the dashing smile and charismatic personality was a man whose heart was deeply troubled. He had grown up in an abusive home. A home where his father beat his mother, and his mother beat him. When he would beg his mother to leave his father, she would only say that he didn't mean to hurt them. He had feared for his mother's safety when he left on a full basketball scholarship. But she had assured her only son that she would be fine and that he had to be the first Carpenter to go to college. He had cried the first time he told Terry that story.

Roland was all that Terry wanted to be—tall and extremely handsome, with a smile that showed at least twenty-eight of his thirty-two perfect teeth and a voice that caused women to think of polished gold. He never seemed awkward in any situation, so his decision to go on to law school didn't surprise anyone. They had remained close friends throughout the years. Roland was constantly telling him about this woman or that who wanted to meet him, but Terry never had the charm with the ladies Roland always displayed. He had consistently used his daughters as his *excuse* for never following up on any of the leads, as Roland called them. Terry secretly wished he could be more secure in his looks. He was average . . . average height, average weight, brown hair, which was thinning on a daily basis, brown eyes . . . average. He worked out three mornings a week, and his body was okay . . . and Jackie was always telling him how perfectly his well-rounded butt felt in her hands, but she loved him, for goodness' sake.

Terry pressed the speed-dial button below Jackie's, and the phone was answered on the first ring.

"Carpenter, Pickford, and Harper," a congenial, mature voice sang out.

"Roland Carpenter, please," Terry said, bypassing his normal pleasantries with Roland's longtime receptionist.

"May I say who's calling?" Margaret queried with an assurance in her voice, already knowing who was at the other end of the line.

"Sorry, Margaret. It's Terry Winston, and let him know it is business, serious business," Terry said, as he paced in his kitchen.

Roland picked up, "Terrence, my brotha, you need me to draw up a pre-nup so you and Jackie can finally get married? No fee—

on one condition—I'm the best man," Roland said as he started to chuckle.

"Catherine wants joint custody of Ari and Lisa," Terry said, almost screaming.

Roland's tone changed instantly, and he was no longer Terry's best friend, but rather the man who had earned the reputation as the best litigator in family court, not only in Dallas, but in all of Texas. "Did she have you served, call you, or what?"

Terry took his first deep breath since he had read Catherine's letter, fully believing Roland would make this thing right. "No, she wrote me a letter of intent. Didn't even type the damn thing herself, had her secretary do it. She's got balls, man."

"Okay, first thing we need to do is talk, but man, I am headed up to Aspen for the weekend with Monique, so it will have to wait until Monday. Hang on, let me get my calendar." The moments seemed forever to Terry.

"How about ten-thirty?" Roland finally asked, with some warmth returning to his voice.

"Man, can we do it after work? I just walked out today, and I probably need to stay at the office Monday." The urgency in his voice rang loud and clear to Roland.

"Not a problem. How's five-thirty, Monday? Can you get your sister to stay with Ari and Lisa? I don't think it's a good idea for them to know anything about this just yet, unless you've already told them."

"No. I am not saying a word to them about this, because I will not let this b— I mean their mother—affect them," Terry said through clenched teeth.

"Good. Now, speaking of you leaving work today, how is that foine ass Valerie? Lawdhamurcy, if that girl wasn't married!" Roland quipped, trying to lighten the mood.

"Valerie? I thought you were heading to Aspen with, what's her name, Monica?" Terry smiled to himself, as Roland's tone became that of his best friend again.

"Monique, man, Monique. Well, I am, but she did the inviting.

Met her in Cancun when I was on vacation. She seems to think she has what it takes to settle a brotha down and plans on proving it this weekend. She has a house in Aspen, but lives in Seattle. But she is just a little too thin for this brotha, though. You know how those size-six women think they are all that. I like a sistah more like Valerie, looks like she eats corn bread with her greens, you know what I mean." They both laughed hysterically, something Terry needed desperately.

By the time Monday came, Terry had spent an anxious weekend unable to focus on much. Even the Cowboys and Forty-niners game couldn't hold his interest. His first stop Monday morning was Valerie's office. As he stepped in, he could see why Roland thought she was so foine. She really knew how to accent her five-foot-six, pleasingly thick frame. She wore a black designer jacket—which she would probably shed by mid-morning, exposing the true shape of her firm, curvaceous body. The entire office smelled of her soft, sensual scent, and her smile lit up any room she graced with her presence.

Terry brought her up to date with what was going on with Catherine and the girls, and she listened intently. "Let me know what I can do. I know some people as well. I play tennis with a judge, and she's rough on these Janie-come-lately mothers," Valerie offered.

The day seemed to drag on as he awaited his meeting with Roland. As Terry rode up on the elevator to the picturesque twenty-ninth floor, he knew Roland would fix this mess . . . he had to.

"Terry, my man," Roland said, as he shook his best friend's hand and embraced him. Roland loved Terry like a brother, and the pain on Terry's face cut him to the very core of his soul. "So sit, let's get right to business. Did you bring the letter?"

"Yeah, man. I'm just sick about this mess, and the thought of losing my girls even part-time makes me crazy," Terry began with a glazed look in his eyes.

"Well, my brotha, until now you've only heard about my work.

Now you are about to find out firsthand why I make 'em quake in their knee-high boots. Remember, I was there when Catherine was so adamant about giving the babies up for adoption. I was the one who was there when you brought them home from the hospital. I was the one who helped you assemble their cribs—man, these girls are my goddaughters and don't think for a minute I'll let this woman do anything to hurt them."

Roland's confidence began to make Terry relax, if only a little. Roland and Terry discussed the particulars of the letter. All of the legal jargon had his head spinning, but Roland assured him that no judge would even entertain the notion of joint custody with one parent out of the country, especially with Catherine's track record.

"So how much is this going to cost me, Roland? I know you come with a pretty sizable price tag," Terry questioned, his face reflecting the serious look he had when he walked in. Terry would pay anything to keep Ari and Lisa, even if it meant taking out a second mortgage on the house.

Roland sat back in his chair and brought his fingers together, pausing for what felt like hours to Terry. Terry knew this was going to cost more than he had ever even imagined it would, especially if Catherine was truly willing to fight him. "Well, Terrence, my brotha, you know we go a long way back, but business is business. I would have to crunch some numbers to get you an estimated total, and if I end up in Madrid on this one, we could be talking about hundreds of billable hours. You know, I am a senior partner and my billing rate is the highest of anyone, right?"

"Of course. I also know that you are the best. Just tell me how much you think it will be," Terry said holding his breath.

"I figure this will be about a hundred hours. So do you think you can handle one hundred dollars?" Roland said, flashing his stellar smile.

Terry was sure he had not heard him properly or that Roland had made a mistake with the dollar amount. "Okay, so one hundred hours at your billing rate is what?"

"I just told you—one hundred dollars. And this cannot leave these four walls, you understand, man," Roland said, trying to look serious.

Terry still couldn't comprehend what his friend was offering. Was he saying he would do it pro bono? "Are you saying that you are doing this for free?"

"Hell no, I don't work for free. I'm charging you a dollar an hour, and you can make payments over the next five years if that will make it easier on you," Roland stated, leaning forward over his desk.

The realization finally hit Terry as he spoke slowly. "I don't know what to say, man . . . I never expected you to do this for free. I mean, a dollar an hour?"

"You don't seem to understand. These are my goddaughters we are talking about, and I will be damned if I will allow anything or anyone to hurt them. Even if that person's name is on their birth certificate."

Terry was a jumble of emotions. He was relieved, happy, sad, excited, and apprehensive all at the same time.

"Now that that is settled, you got some time for dinner? I'm starving. Besides, I gots to tell you about Monique. How do you let me get into these messes? I thought you were my boy, damn!" They both laughed as they put on their coats. Terry knew Roland would make this thing right.

Roland and Terry walked into the crowded restaurant and the maître d' immediately acknowledged them. "Mr. Carpenter, a pleasure to see you as always. How many this evening?"

"Just two this evening, André. How long is the wait?" Roland spoke using the charisma that charmed even men.

"Oh, for you, Mr. Carpenter, we have a table available now," André replied, and he gestured for them to follow him.

The foyer of waiting, anxious customers immediately became quiet as they wondered aloud who this black man with so much clout could possibly be. Terry overheard one say, "He must be an athlete." Terry smiled to himself and shook his head. *They will never get it, will they?* he thought.

Roland ordered wine and an appetizer. After Terry took two large gulps of wine, Roland saw his friend relax finally. This pleased him. He knew that the tale he was about to share would definitely lighten the mood. "Are you ready for the Monique story, my brotha? You know, I envy you and Jackie. You know what to expect because you love each other. This dating is for the birds, and I don't mean the falcons, more like the buzzards," Roland remarked as he began to eat the escargot.

Terry smiled. He had heard all of this so many times before. Roland had no intention of changing his lifestyle, but he always amused Terry with tales of his not so pleasant experiences. Terry leaned back in his chair and sipped more wine.

This was going to be a long one; he could feel it.

4

JACKIE LOOKED THROUGH the men's fashion catalog, unable to decide what to get Terry for Christmas. She had been laboring over this for weeks. She had given him suits, ties, shirts, robes, slippers, CDs . . . What was left? What could she possibly buy for him that would show exactly how special she thought he was?

She slipped her reading glasses off and lay back against the leather high-back chair. Thinking of Terry always made her feel so secure; just the thought of him made everything right. Michael and Michelle had gone Christmas shopping for her at the mall with her mother, who was a saint, except when she was nagging her about marrying Terry.

Why was she so hesitant to broach the subject of marriage? Terry was almost perfect. She had never met a more gentle, sincere man. She knew beyond a shadow of a doubt that he loved her and the twins. She loved his girls as well. And they had even talked about having a child together one day . . . *Lawdhamurcy!* she thought. *Five children, or six!*

But whenever it seemed as if Terry was close to popping the question, she would grow distant, pick fights, or look for reasons not to see him. *What the hell is wrong with me?* she wondered.

As she sat in the quiet of the den, she thought back to the time shortly after their meeting in the Toys "R" Us store. They had exchanged numbers, but only after a few awkward moments. She had called it once to see if it was a pager number. So many men give only their pager number, but of course they want your blood type, your mother's maiden name, and a copy of your father's credit report.

When she dialed the number and a very pleasant woman answered the phone, Jackie was stunned. She stuttered and apologized, "I'm sorry, but I must have the wrong number." She moved quickly to return the receiver to the cradle when she heard the voice at the other end yell, "Wait! Are you looking for Terrence Winston?"

"Yes, I am," Jackie answered slowly.

"He's out Christmas shopping, and he may not be back until after midnight. May I take a message?" The woman volunteered, almost singing.

A little taken aback Jackie responded, "Please tell him that Jackie called."

"Oh, I sure will, and you have a nice holiday!" the animated female voice responded.

Three days went by and she still had not heard from Terry. Like the many who had gone before him, Mr. Winston—so handsome and seemingly kind—had disappointed her.

She was outside stringing lights on the tall hedges that framed the front of her house two days before Christmas, when she heard a familiar voice from below.

It was a voice she had never expected to hear again. "Jackie, it is you!" It was Terry. *What is he doing here, and how did he find me?* she thought to herself.

"I lost your phone number, and when you called, you didn't leave your number with my sister. I've been heartsick about it. As I drove past, I saw a car that looked like yours, and when I saw you up on the ladder, I thought it was you. I am just so glad that it *is* you!" Terry rambled on without breathing.

Jackie stepped down the ladder slowly and looked at him suspiciously. "How did you find out where I live?"

"I didn't. I was passing by. I only live a block and a half from here, and I recognized your car. When I saw you up on that ladder, I knew no other woman could grace a ladder quite like that." Terry held both her hands as if he were afraid to let her go.

"I am so sorry I lost your number. I was just so damn happy that you had given it to me that I can't remember what I did with it." He took a breath, then said, "Jackie, you have occupied my every thought since that night at the toy store. I thought I had let you slip through my fingers again." He moved to hug her, but stopped short, not knowing just how receptive she would be. But to his surprise, she moved toward him as well, and they embraced like long-lost friends.

"I'm really glad to see you, too, Terry. I had all but given up on ever seeing you again.

"It is freezing out here. Would you like to come in for some tea or hot cider? My mother is here, and we have the fire going," Jackie said, pointing toward the house.

"I'd love to, but I have to do something important first. I hope you don't mind." Terry smiled broadly, while walking away. She was more disappointed than she cared to express as she watched him appear to leave. But to her amazement, he had gone to his car to get his gloves.

As he ran back up the walkway, his smiled melted her heart. "Okay, I will make you a deal. You make us some coffee, and I'll finish these lights. It's a health hazard for you to be up there on that ladder like that."

"Oh, but I am really careful when I'm up on that ladder," Jackie interjected, matching his broad smile.

"Miss lady, it is the health and safety of all of the men passing by here while gazing up at you and *your assets* on that ladder that concern me, 'cause you gonna cause someone to commit some kind of traffic violation. Now, you go inside and get warm and make a hardworking, absentminded brotha some coffee. This will only take a second," Terry told Jackie, flashing a Denzel Washington smile.

Jackie almost protested, but she was so glad to see him, she just turned and ran up the four steps to the porch.

"And Jackie, I am not losing you again," Terry uttered without even looking up from the tangled string of lights.

"Chile, why are you grinning like that?" her mother said, looking up from the sweet potatoes she was peeling. "You couldn't be finished wit dat tangled mess of lights you took outta here a few minutes ago. And why you grinnin'? You probably don't 'member, but there was a TV show back when you was a baby called *Da Millionaire,* and dis man would come to da door and just hand you a million dollars, but you had to keep it secret. Now baby, I'm yo' momma. You can tell me if dat is what done put the grin on yo' face."

"Oh Momma, of course not, but there is someone outside. Remember the man I told you about who helped me with the twins in the rain? The one that I saw again in the toy store? He's outside putting the lights up! Can you believe it?" Jackie told her mother, amazed at believing the words coming out of her own mouth.

"Wait a minute . . . the one who never called you after you gave him yo' number, and you called and some woman answered the phone? Dat's the man outside? Well, I sure hope you tol' him where to go!" her mother retorted, shifting her weight in the chair.

"But Momma, he seems—" Jackie began, but her mother cut her off abruptly.

"Well, I guess you was right to wait 'til he put up the lights, smart chile. I did raise you right."

"As I was trying to say, Momma, he seems like a nice man. He said he lost the number, and I didn't leave my number with his sister when I called—yes, that's right, his sister. I told you she was overly friendly, and it just didn't seem that would be the case if she was his woman, now would it?" Jackie kept talking, despite her mother's attempts to interrupt. "And Momma, I invited him in for some tea, so you be nice. You hear me?"

"Umph, I just won't open dese here lips, 'cause if you can't say nuthin' good, then say nuthin'."

Jackie smiled to herself, knowing that they would hold the Winter Olympics in hell before her mother would sit in silence. She began making a pot of coffee while her mother started again.

"I thought you invited him in for tea. Oh lemme guess, you offered him tea, but he wanted sum'in' different. Hmmph, just like a man."

"I thought you were not saying anything else," Jackie said, good-heartedly. Her mother rolled her eyes and started slicing sweet potatoes with a vengeance while mumbling to herself. They spent the rest of the time in silence.

Jackie could feel a song stirring in her soul. *Calm down, gurl. Don't get excited; he's only stringing lights,* she told herself silently. When the doorbell rang about ten minutes after she had skipped into the house, her heart beat loudly in her chest. She wiped her hands, checked her face in the reflection of the toaster, and headed for the door, thinking, *I should have used that time to change . . . dang.* "Hi there, Terry, you need some help?" Jackie smiled despite herself.

"Well, yes and no. I got the lights untangled, but only one string works. Do you have any extra bulbs?" Terry asked, staring into her eyes.

"No I don't. I guess I'll have to buy some tomorrow, or maybe I just won't put up lights this year. I've waited this long, and tomorrow is Christmas Eve, so what's the point?" Jackie said, purposely avoiding his gaze. "Please come in out of the cold. I'm sorry you spent all that time out there for nothing. Now that the coffee is ready, please let me take your coat. My mother is in the kitchen cooking. If you will wait in here, I'll get the coffee."

"It would be rude of me not to say hello to your mother. Besides, I want to meet the woman who is responsible for the smells coming outta there," Terry said, flashing her a smile. "Unless of course you're the one responsible for the aromas reaching even the air outside."

"Not at all. If it were not for the microwave, I don't think we would eat. I'm so glad that Mikey and Ikey don't care," Jackie volunteered, blushing.

"Mikey and Ikey?" Terry inquired, once again looking into her eyes.

Jackie explained how her father had named them when he visited the hospital to see them. He had not been there when they were born because he said there was no way he could bear to see his baby girl suffer. When he arrived at the hospital, he did not go see the babies for hours, and instead sat by Jackie's bed and watched her sleep. She had been in labor for thirty-three hours before a C-section was finally performed. When she awakened, her mother was holding Michelle and her father was holding Michael. Terry didn't ask about their father. Her father said, "You done good, baby girl. Ikey and Mikey are just beautiful." The names stuck.

"Jackie, baby, where can I find yo'—Oh, I'm sorry, I didn't know you had company," her mother interrupted, standing in the doorway wiping her hands on her apron.

Jackie and Terry looked at each other and exchanged a knowing smile. "Mother, this is Terry Winston. Terry, this is my mother, Clara Rogers."

"Pleasure to meet you, Mrs. Rogers," Terry said extending his hand.

"Oh, call me Momma C. Everybody does. Why don't you come on in da kitchen, Terry? We just made some fresh coffee. You look a little chilly."

"Momma, I was going to serve Terry coffee here in front of the fireplace," Jackie said, trying to give her mother the evil eye.

"I would love to join you ladies, but can I make one phone call to let my mother know that I will be home shortly? She's here from Northern California," Terry said, looking at Jackie admiringly.

Jackie showed him the phone in her office, and as she was leaving to give him privacy, their arms brushed. Jackie was not certain, but she believed that an electrical current must have shot through her body. She almost ran from the room. She had to get to her mother and warn her to keep her cool, as if her mother would listen.

Terry came from the office and sat at the kitchen table for more than an hour drinking coffee and sharing his life story. Jackie noticed that even Momma C was captivated by his charm, but it wasn't a slickness as with most men she had encountered. Not at all like Lawrence, the pretty boy who had promised her the universe and then disappeared like lint up a Dustbuster when he found out she was pregnant. No, Terry Winston's charm was fueled by kindness and genuine concern.

As Terry prepared to leave, Momma C wiped her hands and extended them. She took his right hand in both of hers and said, "Son, you a good man. I hope ta see ya again soon, real soon."

"Thank you, Momma C. I would like nothing more," Terry replied, looking directly at Jackie.

That had been the first day of what Jackie knew was the rest of her life. A life that would hopefully include this man forever. She shook her head and wondered how long she had been reminiscing, because now the fire was burning low.

The fourth anniversary of what was affectionately known as "the light stringing" was in two weeks. The thought of four years with Terry made Jackie feel warm and secure. But what was she going to get him for Christmas? The stereo was playing low and Anita Baker's voice made Jackie sit upright in her chair. "That's it! Concert tickets to see Anita Baker!" Terry loved Anita, and she was appearing in early January for the first time in more than four years. Jackie would make it an occasion—limo, dinner, the whole nine yards. There was nothing too good for the man who had strung new lights over all of her hedges while she slept on the day before the first Christmas Eve of the rest of her life. Would the new year bring her and Terry together for the ultimate . . . *marriage?* She sat back and hugged herself.

She must get over her fear of getting too close.

5

THE TABLE WHERE Terry and Roland were seated was se-
cluded from most of the restaurant noise. The two old friends enjoyed the atmosphere, the food, and, most of all, the company.

The wine warmed Terry from within; he hadn't realized how
tense he had been all weekend. *What must Jackie be thinking?* he
wondered. His actions were very out of character. He made a
mental note to call her from his car after dinner. He knew how
blessed he was to have her in his life, and he planned to let her
know that really soon.

"Man, I couldn't believe this woman!" Roland said, breaking
into Terry's private thoughts.

"So what did Monique do that was so bad, man? You had spent
time with her in Cancun, right?"

"First of all, there is *no* house in Aspen. She got a rental. This
was evident because she couldn't find anything. I found the wine-
glasses before she did. Why sistahs think they gotta perpetrate?
But that is not the worst part. Nothing on her was real: hair,
eye color, nails, *nothing* . . . and let's just say I now know why
they call it the *Miracle* bra," Roland said, finishing off the last
of the escargot, something Terry could never understand anyone
enjoying.

Terry tried hard to keep a straight face. "But Roland, my man, you didn't know all this when you were with her in Cancun?"

"Heeelllll naw! We just kinda kicked it on the beach, went dancing. I tried to make that move, but she played hard to get. She was kinda thin for me anyway, so it was no big deal. We exchanged numbers, and we talked for three months. She had me wanting her so bad, man, I would have walked to Aspen." Roland laughed as he recounted his weekend. "Then to make matters worse, when we get there she has no conversation; everything was 'Whatever you want.' I left on the first thing with exhaust yesterday morning, and told her I had to prepare for a big case. When am I going to wise up and get smart like you, my brotha?" Roland said as the waiter placed an appetizing pasta dish before him.

Terry's free-range chicken smelled wonderful. He realized he hadn't had a good meal since lunch on Friday. "Yeah man, I am lucky. Jackie is all that any man could hope for. You know, I really want to marry her, but I think she is afraid for some reason. Every time I start to talk about it, she pulls back from me or finds reasons not to be together. Mikey and Ikey's father really did a number on her."

"You know, you never talk about their father, and you know me, I don't pry," Roland said.

"I know, man. It took Jackie almost a year to talk about him. They had worked together for three years at the time they started dating. Man, you know how beautiful Jackie is, and she thought he didn't like her because she was thick. Lawdhamurcy, just the thought of her—oh never mind. But you know what I am saying. So she was thrilled when he asked her to the company picnic. They started dating casually after that, but he was such a player. Kinda like another pretty boy I know." They both laughed. "She was just so happy that this *pretty boy* was willing to share some of his time with her. Of course, I think it should have been the other way around, but nevertheless she tolerated whatever he dished out. They dated off and on for more than a year. Then somehow, she got pregnant despite being on the pill. When she told him she was pregnant, he split, even quit his job. Blamed her for trying to trap him. A real *man*, huh?" Terry said, with a look of disgust on his face.

"Man, I'll be the first to acknowledge that I *play*, but don't ever think I am so low as to pull some weak stuff like that. And why is it that sistahs like Jackie think that they have to put up with that shit from a man? You're right though. She *is* beautiful, and as for her size, that's what I'm looking for in a woman. But the sistahs are so insecure. Maybe I need to read some books or something. *How to Meet and Marry a Thick Sistah*. Women always think they are the one who can't find the right O-N-E," Roland sighed while rolling his eyes, taking another sip of chardonnay.

"I know. Jackie still has issues about her size, and she feels lucky I love her anyway. Why can't I make her understand that her size is one of the things that attracted me to her in the first place? When I saw her walking down the aisle in that super-market that day—*dayum*." They slapped hands and laughed out loud, causing the Anglo folks to turn and stare.

"So, are you going to ask her to marry you, my brotha?" Roland leaned across the table for emphasis.

"Yes, I am, Roland. On New Year's Eve, actually, right after I kiss her at midnight," Terry said with his voice trailing off. "I love her more than life itself. Next to Ari and Lisa she is the reason I breathe. After this mess came up with Catherine, I had thought of postponing it because I couldn't afford the ring and legal fees, but because of your *discounted rates*, I don't have to wait. Besides, won't it look better to a judge if I'm married?"

"Let me worry about what makes you look good to the judge," Roland said. "Besides, man, you know all you have to do is ask. I can help you with the ring, if need be. Do you know anything about diamonds? One of my former clients is a jeweler. I got his daughter back from his ex-wife in a custody battle, so he would swim the English Channel as a paraplegic if I asked him. I know you can get it at cost, maybe below."

"I don't know what to say, man. You always seem to be doing something or giving something to me. But I never give you any-thing." Terry thought back to the extravagant gifts Roland had given both him and his girls over the years. He even bought them clothes and supplies for school one year when Terry had had to replace the roof on his house and was low on funds.

"How can you say that you don't give me anything? You give me something no one else has ever been able to give me, even my own parents. You love me, man. When my parents would get drunk and embarrass me in front of our friends, you always took care of me. I only wish you had been around when I was growing up. After my mother would beat me, I'd sit in the closet, listening to my folks argue about who was getting the most vodka, wishing I could be invisible. If I could've been around you and your mother and sister, I think my life may have been different. I've told you this so many times before. And by having you, Jackie, Ari, Lisa, Mikey, and Ikey in my life now, I have a family. Money can't buy that." Roland started to get choked up, giving Terry a rare glimpse of emotion. He loved Roland with all of his heart, and he wanted him to find the happiness he had.

Roland cleared his throat, sat up straight, and asked, "Want some dessert?" The waiter seemed to magically appear as if he knew Roland needed his services. *How does he do that?* Terry wondered. After ordering dessert and coffee, the good friends chatted lightly and laughed about some of the woes of dating.

Roland picked up the check, arguing that it was a business expense since Terry was now his client. Terry knew this action was also about retrieving his ego after the emotional display.

They picked up their coats from the young woman in attendance. Terry observed in amusement how she just gazed up at Roland and blushed crimson when he pressed a five-dollar bill in her hand and said in that liquid gold manner, "Thank you, beautiful."

Oh yes, Roland had recovered quite nicely.

6

Terry had really enjoyed the time he spent with Roland. They were such good friends and loved each other like brothers. Their busy schedules didn't allow them to get together as much as they would like, which made times like this evening very special. He also knew in his heart that Roland was going to handle this mess with Catherine. He had felt a peace wash over him during dinner, and his anxiety was almost totally gone. Now he had to talk to Jackie. He had been distant and short with her all weekend. He needed to make it right.

"Hello there, miss lady." It felt so good just hearing Jackie's voice, which reminded him of satin being pulled over his skin. "How's my baby?"

"Hi, honey. Is everything okay? We've hardly talked in the past three days," Jackie responded as she settled in her favorite chair. "I was beginning to get a little worried." It was one thing for her to pull back from him, but she just didn't like it when she thought he was the one getting cold feet.

"I'm sorry, baby. This weekend has been kind of rough for me. May I stop by for a few minutes so we can talk about something?" Terry felt like such a jerk for not telling Jackie what was happening with Catherine. He had worried her unnecessarily, something he promised himself and her that he would *never* do.

"Of course, you can stop by. You know you don't have to ask. I'll put another log on the fire. How long before you get here?" Jackie could feel her heart beating faster.

"I should be there within twenty minutes. I'm just leaving downtown. I'll see you in a few, baby."

As Jackie started to stack the wood for a fire, she had a sense of foreboding. Terry had never spoken to her as little as he had this past weekend. He had not called her all day, and most of all, she had not seen him in four days. She could not remember the last time she had not seen him for an entire weekend if they were both in town. Something was definitely wrong.

She thought of all the possible scenarios. She had pulled back over Thanksgiving because she was afraid he was going to propose at the annual family dinner. Momma C had thought so, too. Jackie had picked a fight with him on Thanksgiving Eve, and they hardly spoke when they sat down to the dual family dinner. She had started another diet in September announcing she was going to lose twenty-five pounds by Christmas, and her regimen had lasted all of three days. She felt she had no discipline, unlike Terry, whose life seemed to be so structured. But her worst fear was that he had found someone else. Someone younger, thinner, and with no children. She knew he loved her, but what would a good man like Terry want with her, considering all her problems, shortcomings, and lack of discipline?

Yet, he was always so kind to her, telling her how beautiful he thought she was. He told her constantly that she was *the* most beautiful woman he had ever encountered. It always made her happy to hear this, but she also had a mirror. She had seen all those beautiful women that worked in the office towers in downtown Dallas. She felt she knew what Terry was coming to tell her. He never *asked* if he could stop by. He was being far too polite. He wanted out of this relationship. What was she going to do? She loved him so much, and the kids loved him and Ari and

Lisa. *Oh my God, what would their lives be like if Terry and I broke up?* she thought, panicking.

Jackie hadn't realized that her thoughts had occupied every moment since she had hung up the phone until she heard Terry slipping his key in the door. She quickly wiped her face and dashed into the bathroom just off the den to check her makeup. She hadn't even known she was crying.

As she stepped out of the bathroom, Terry stood before her looking so strong and handsome, but there was something behind his eyes. A look of worry, deep worry. He was concerned about hurting her. He interrupted her thoughts—not with words, but with a hug that lifted her three inches off the floor and a kiss so deep it touched the center of her soul. "Honey, I'm so sorry if I caused you worry this past weekend. I was distant, and I don't even know if I called you. I realized driving here that I haven't seen you since Thursday. I don't know what you must be thinking, but I am sorry," he said, kissing her again.

"Oh, I wasn't worried," Jackie lied unconvincingly.

Terry lifted her chin and looked into her eyes, and before he could say anything, they both started laughing hysterically. Jackie's laughter was out of relief that her concerns were unfounded. Terry laughed because he knew she was not telling the truth. They kissed again, this time filled with all the passion that they had known for the past four years.

Terry took her by the hand and sat in her favorite chair in front of the fire and pulled her on his lap. "Jackie, I have a really serious problem. One that is bigger than anything we have faced so far. I don't even know where to begin," Terry said, breaking their locked gaze.

During the silence, Jackie's imagination returned with a fury. *Oh my God, he has AIDS. He has been unfaithful to me, and now he has AIDS, which means I have it, too . . . Oh my God! They found it just like they did with Magic Johnson, when he wanted to increase his life insurance last month . . .* Maddening thoughts raced through her head.

When Terry finally looked back in Jackie's eyes and saw raw

fear, he panicked. *What is she thinking?* "Honey, are you alright? What's wrong?"

"I just want to know what it is that you have to tell me, that's all. You have me a little worried," Jackie said, her voice cracking.

"Oh, baby, I am soooo sorry," Terry whispered, pulling her closer and burying his face in her breast. "I got some pretty startling news on Friday. I have been wrestling with it all alone over the weekend, and now I know that was not the right thing to do." Jackie's heart was pounding so hard Terry could see it through her sweater.

"What is it?" Jackie could not hide her anxiety.

"I got a letter from Catherine," he began, "and she's suing me for joint custody." He cried for the first time since any of this had happened. Being with Jackie made him realize that he could handle anything as long as he had her. Then he noticed tears falling onto his coat that were not his own. "Jackie, baby, what is it?"

"We will never let this happen. She will never win," Jackie said with conviction, not adding that the tears were also induced by the relief she felt. "How can she even think that you would allow this to happen? Has she lost her mind or finally found her conscience?"

Terry filled her in on what Roland told him would happen and that they may end up in court. She assured him that weathering the hurricane together would not be all that rough. She would be there every step of the way. They agreed that they would turn to each other first, no matter how insurmountable the problem appeared on the surface. Jackie also promised to try to control her imagination, and they both laughed. He was so overcome by her sincerity that he couldn't speak any longer, and began kissing her. He knew now more than ever that he had to marry this woman. Their passion was so intense that he lifted her as he stood up. He gently laid her on the couch in front of the fireplace, removed his coat, and knelt down over her. They made love until the fireplace held cold embers.

And what a sweet promised land it was.

7

S ISTAH-GURLFRIEND!" THE VOICE on the other end of the phone bellowed.

"Cedes, my gurl, when did you get back?" Jackie said as she was jolted wide awake.

Mercedes Harper Marshall was her oldest, and most definitely dearest, friend. Their friendship had literally begun at birth. Their mothers had been hospital roommates after their children were born. The five days during which they had shared the hospital room had bound them together for life.

Jackie was born at seven minutes past midnight on June 4; Mercedes was born exactly two hours later. Their mothers kept in touch after they were discharged from the hospital, and Jackie and Mercedes had grown up more like cousins than friends.

Momma C and Mercedes's mother, Margaret, had been like sisters until Margaret died suddenly just eight months earlier. Jackie felt almost as if her own mother had died when she received a frantic call from Mercedes that Momma Margaret, after suffering a massive stroke, had died before the paramedics could transport her to the hospital.

"Gurl, I got in so late last night, my jet lag got lag." They both laughed. Jackie had so missed Mercedes while she was away this time. She was a public relations representative for the Dallas Cowboys and had been on the road for more than three months. It sounded like a plush job, and Lord knows she made tall dollars, but she was always living out of a suitcase and could never keep a relationship for more than a few months at a time.

"I am so glad to hear your shrieking voice, gurl. I have missed you so much. We have so much to catch up on. How long are you home for this time?" Jackie was trying to fit all of the missed conversations with Mercedes into the next three minutes.

"I am home until, are you ready, January twenty-first!" Mercedes said in her signature high-pitched voice. "I am on a long-awaited, and even more deserved, vacation. Most folks go away for vacation, but I come home. And you know the first thing I want to do after I hug your neck is eat some of Momma C's greens. What is on your agenda today?"

Jackie stretched and thought about how Terry had made love to her last evening until the wee hours of the morning. She was not tired, but it would be more than easy to stay in bed. However, she knew she had a deadline at the newspaper and not only was she not finished, she had yet to write the first syllable. "Cedes, I have to work today, and you know I will meet no deadline before its time. My column is due by five o'clock, but I am free after that."

"Does that mean you and Mr. Wonderful are not seeing each other tonight? I can't believe it!" Mercedes said with the slightest hint of envy. "Oh no, you aren't on the outs are you?" Mercedes said knowing this couldn't possibly be the case. She would turn in her platinum-status frequent flyer card faster than a press and curl reverted in a rainstorm if she could just feel the contentment that was apparent in her best friend's voice. But she just never seemed to attract the stay-faithful, go-to-work-every-day, pay-his-bills-on-time, love-you-no-matter-what kind of brother. *Oh well*, she thought. When Jackie didn't answer, she added halfheartedly, "Okay, let me buy you and the kids dinner tonight, say at six-thirty?"

"No way! You have eaten out for the past three months. I'll call

Momma C as soon as we hang up and tell her you're home, and you know she'll start cooking before Al Roker puts on his ear-muffs," Jackie said, knowing what Mercedes had really wanted to hear.

"I need to sleep all day, have a stiff drink and a good meal, and make love until I can't string a sentence together—and not nec-essarily in that order." Mercedes laughed.

"Well, the first two I can definitely help you with, but that third one—you are on your own," Jackie quipped, smiling to herself as she had a brainstorm. "I love you, gurl. I'm so glad you're back. I'll see you here tonight at seven."

"I loves you, too, Jackie. I've missed you and them children something terrible. I can't wait to see all of you." Mercedes seemed choked up as she said her good-byes or her "until next times," as she called them.

Jackie pressed the reset button and then dialed Terry's number. He picked up on the first ring, obviously still sleeping. "Hey, sexy," Jackie said, unable to control the smile that spread across her face as she thought of the previous evening.

"Good morning, my love," Terry managed to say in a voice still weighed down by sleep. "What time is it?"

"Time for you to get up, mister man. Think I'm just gonna let you sleep because you put me in an altered state last night, huh? Wrong!" They both laughed.

"Listen, Cedes is back in town, and she called this morning. I can tell by her voice she's feeling really alone. How about joining us for dinner and bringing Roland if he can make it? You know how those two are together." Jackie's voice was low and sexy, working it so that Terry would be unable to resist.

"I'll check with him, but you know how busy he is," Terry said as he was thinking, *Oh Lord, Roland just does not like Mercedes. She's just too hyper for the man.* But he decided he would try be-cause it would make the love of his life very happy and her hap-piness meant the world to him.

Terry showered and dressed quickly, glad that Lisa and Ari had stayed with his sister last night. This way only he was running late. He hummed as he dressed. How could a woman satisfy him so completely? Jackie fulfilled his very soul. "Man, I'm lucky—no, correct that . . . I am blessed." Terry heard his own voice and was astounded that he had said the words out loud. In less than thirty minutes, he was out of the house.

The ringing car phone startled him. He was deep in thought about how he was going to convince Roland to join them for dinner, especially once he found out that Mercedes was the guest of honor. "Terry Winston here," he answered.

"Terry, my brotha, good morning. I am glad I caught you. There is one question I failed to ask you, though I believe I know the answer. Would there be any chance that Ari and Lisa might want their mother to have joint custody?" Roland asked, sounding so on-the-record that Terry hardly recognized his voice.

"No way, Roland. They don't want to visit her, let alone live with her. Why do you ask?" Terry was glad that Roland was already working on the case.

"Well, Texas law states that if the child has a preference and there are reasonable grounds to effect a change, the court may entertain the motion. Catherine living in Europe will almost guarantee this would not happen. However, what are the chances that she may move back to Oklahoma, or anywhere in the U.S. for that matter?" Roland queried.

"She would do anything to get what she wants, and now almost eleven years later she wants her children. She can't have them, Roland. If I have to, I will leave Texas with them and no one will ever be able to find me. The only thing that will separate me from my girls is death. Have I made myself clear?" Terry never yelled at his best friend, and this manner of speaking was so foreign to him that he had to check the car to see if there was someone else talking.

"It is going to work out. Trust me, Terrence. I need you to stay calm and not let anyone else ever hear you talk that way. She's going to hire the best attorney her money can buy, and according to you that means a damn good one. But there's something that no matter who she hires won't have going for them." Roland paused.

"What is that, Roland?" Terry said, left weak by his previous outburst.

"Whoever she hires doesn't love Ari and Lisa, never changed their diapers, never had them throw up on an Armani suit, never paced the floor in a surgical waiting room because of them. You know what I mean, man?" Roland said, his voice almost trailing off.

"I know, man, I know. I'm sorry that I lost it a minute ago. I do trust you, implicitly. By the way, what are you doing for dinner tonight? Momma C is cooking, and it is going to be family night. Can you make it?" Terry asked, trying to take advantage of Roland's vulnerability.

"Man, you know I can't resist Momma C's cooking! I was just doing some research tonight, but I can do it later. What time?"

"Seven, and by the way Mercedes is back and she is coming, too. Gotta go!" Terry said, trying to escape Roland's wrath.

"Damn, man, you tricked me, didn't you?" Roland laughed. He always pretended he didn't like Mercedes, but in all honesty, he thought she was an alright sistah. Just needs to tone down her voice a couple octaves, and maybe get another forty or so pounds on those hips. "I'll be there, my brotha."

8

MS. MARSHALL, ALWAYS a pleasure," Roland said, kissing Cedes's hand.

"Roland, the pleasure is all mine, believe me," Cedes said, trying not to blush as she looked up into Roland's strikingly handsome face.

"So how is the exciting world of the NFL, Cedes? Think your 'Boys are going all the way?"

"Why do you *insist* on calling me Say-dees, instead of C-deese?"

Though busily preparing for dinner, Jackie and Terry looked up simultaneously. First, looking at Roland and Cedes, then at each other; it had taken less than half a glass of wine for the two of them to be at each other's throats.

"I just pronounce it the way it is spelled. You have a problem with that?"

"And I suppose you call Sade Say-dee or perhaps Said?" Cedes said, crossing her perfectly formed legs so that her thigh showed almost to her hip.

"Since we have this same conversation every time we are together, I will work on calling you C-deese. It just doesn't flow off my tongue."

"Oh *paleeze*! You are one of the most eloquent speakers in the continental United States! You just do this to aggravate me, don't you? You don't really like me, do you?"

"What would make you ask me that, C-deese?" Roland asked, stunned by her sudden outburst.

"May I freshen your drink, Roland?" Terry inquired as he stepped into the living room area where the situation had become potentially volatile.

"No man, I am fine. Perhaps *C-deese* could use another glass of wine." Roland sat back and smiled. He did actually enjoy getting a rise out of her. She was truly beautiful, with deep, dark, rich chocolate skin that was flawless, and makeup that was always perfect. Her closely cropped hair was so meticulously shaped, he often wondered how she found a hairstylist to keep her "natural" so fastidiously manicured when she was on the road two to three months at a time. Her bone structure was perfect, and her statuesque five-foot-ten-inch frame made it evident that this woman truly descended from African royalty.

"Yes, I *will* take some more wine, Terry, thank you," Cedes said, rolling her eyes at Roland.

"Okay, I'm sorry. I will pronounce your name correctly, and I do like you. I respect any woman who can make it in the NFL world. Back to my original question, you think your 'Boys are going all the way?"

"Respect is not *like*! Of course you respect me. I command that! I respect you, too, but I'm not so sure I like you at this moment."

"Cedes, can you help Momma C and me here in the kitchen?" Jackie said, poking her head out into the dining area.

"I will be right there, Jackie," Cedes said, never taking her eyes off Roland.

As Cedes walked toward the kitchen, Roland watched her every move, and Terry watched him watch her. Terry handed Cedes a freshly filled glass as they passed each other.

"That was not the look of a brother who doesn't like what he sees," Terry teased, sitting opposite Roland on the emerald green Italian leather sofa.

"Why is everyone saying I don't like her? I do like her. She is a really nice sister. A little high-strung, but aiight."

"But you don't really *like* her, do you?"

"Like I said, she's aiight, but she's like family. I've known her for as long as I have known Jackie, and you know I think of Jackie as my sister-in-law."

"Okay, I'll leave it alone. You sure you don't want me to freshen that cognac?"

"No, man, I'm fine."

"What in the *hell* is wrong with you?" Jackie said, with her hands on her hips and her neck working in her best sistah-gurl stance.

"What do you mean?"

"You know what I mean. You were down Roland's throat within ten minutes of him walking through the door. I know how you feel about him, despite what you say! Is anything wrong? You're acting strange."

"Nothing is wrong," Cedes said, averting her eyes.

"Now, y'all stop dat bickerin'," Momma C began. "You don't want dem men out dere to hear you, do you?" She sat down at the table and looked at Cedes. "Come 'ere, baby, tell Momma C what's wrong. And don't be tellin' me nuthin' 'cause you kno' I knows you as good as I knows my own baby here."

"Nothing is . . ." Cedes started and broke into tears before she could finish.

"Oh, baby, it's alright. Come on, tell Momma C."

Cedes sank to the floor and put her head in Momma C's lap.

Roland and Terry appeared in the kitchen within seconds of hearing Cedes wail. They stopped short in the door when Jackie put her hand up and motioned them away. They looked at each other, and Terry asked if they could help, before reluctantly turning to walk away.

"No, wait," Cedes said, looking up from Momma C's lap with mascara running down her face.

"I am sorry, Roland. I had no right to attack you like I did. I don't know what is going on with me. I even slapped a reporter who said I must be sleeping with one of the players to have gotten this job. The only reason he didn't sue me is because he wants the panties himself. Sorry, Momma C. My boss told me that if I didn't get ahold of myself, I would lose my job. Under normal circumstances there is no way I could have time off this late in the season. This vacation is anything but voluntary, and I realize now that I need to put myself back together."

"That's alright, baby. I tol' you dat you went back to work too soon after Margaret died. You been blamin' yo'self 'cause you was outta town. Baby, look at me. Da only thing you coulda done was call the paramedics instead of yo' brotha callin'. There ain't a damn thing you coulda done. Nuthin'. When it's yo' time, it's yo' time."

Everyone was stunned because Momma C never swore. Jackie began to cry, and Terry was by her side quickly. Roland moved slowly toward Cedes. He had never seen her like this. She was vulnerable, and the pain was evident on her face and in her body.

"Momma C, I'll take her into the den," Roland said softly, taking Cedes's hand to help her up.

As Cedes raised herself from the kneeling position, her legs betrayed her, and she felt herself falling. Roland caught her and picked her up as though she weighed nothing. Without a word, he carried her to the den and laid her on the couch.

Cedes had cried softly at her mother's funeral, unlike her brothers, who literally threw themselves on the casket. Momma C and Jackie had escorted Cedes to see her mother for the last time. Cedes had bent over, kissed her, whispered something in her ear, and walked back to her seat.

Everyone was amazed at her composure, except Momma C and Jackie, who were very troubled by this apparent display of courage. Cedes and Margaret, like Jackie and Momma C, had been inseparable. They had always referred to themselves as the four musketeers.

The mood in the house was somber, and Alisa startled those in the kitchen when she asked, "What's burning and why is everybody crying?" The children had been playing video games while the last preparations for dinner were under way. Everyone had forgotten about them after all the commotion.

"Oh my Lord, thank you, baby! I plumb forgot 'bout the pies in the oven!" said Momma C.

"Why is everyone crying, Daddy? Uncle Roland is in the den with Miss Cedes, and she is really crying loud," Ariana said, moving close to Terry and Jackie.

"Miss Cedes is not feeling well, so we won't be eating right away. You kids want some cheese and crackers?"

"I don't, but I'll ask Ikey and Mikey . . . Why is Miss Jackie crying, Daddy? Did someone else die?" Ariana asked.

Momma C put the pies on the counter, wiped her hands on her apron, and called to Lisa and Ari. "Come ovah here, babies. 'Member when Cedes's momma died awhile back? Well, she nevah really cried like da rest of us did then, so she's doin' her grievin' now."

"What's grieving?" Lisa spoke up, looking quite intense.

"It's when yo' heart hurts 'bout much as it can possibly hurt, 'cause someone you love has gone 'way from ya."

"Is that like a heart attack?" Ari asked.

"It is a attack on yo' heart, but not on da part that makes yo' blood flow. It's on da part of yo' heart that makes yo' love flow."

"Is it like being really, really sad because someone is not with you all the time, like Catherine not wanting to live with us?" Ari said.

The adults in the room looked at each other in total shock.

After a few moments, Terry finally said, "What makes you say that, Ari?" breaking the pregnant silence.

"My heart hurts because our mother doesn't love us enough to want to live near us. She always says that she does, but she's not telling the truth."

"What makes you think she is not telling the truth?"

"You always tell us that it's not what we say that counts, but what we do that really matters."

Terry looked from Momma C to Jackie to Lisa, who had moved closer to Ari. "That's very true, my princess, very true." Lisa spoke up for the first time. "Daddy, we just don't understand why we don't have a mother like our friends do. We talk about it all the time. We don't know why she never comes to visit. She just sends money. We know the money is nice, but you take good care of us and you make a lot of money and Ari cries about it sometimes."

Terry pulled a chair away from the kitchen table and sat, looking at Lisa and Ari at eye level. "I can't explain why Catherine doesn't come to visit and breaks promises to you. I do know that you will never ever have to wonder if I love you or want to be with you. Do you understand what I am saying to you?"

"Yes, Daddy," they said in unison as they put their arms around his neck.

Terry looked up at Jackie, who mouthed the words "I love you" as tears fell from her eyes. "I had better go check on Cedes as well as Mikey and Ikey—they are too quiet," Jackie said, brushing the tears away.

Momma C busied herself with the dinner preparations, humming a hymn that Terry couldn't remember the name of, but that soothed his soul nonetheless. He held Alisa and Ariana very close and silently vowed to do whatever it took to shield them from pain.

9

H OW IS EVERYTHING in here?" Jackie inquired as she walked cautiously into the den.

"Oh, Jackie, I am so sorry," Cedes muttered as she leapt from the couch and threw herself into Jackie's arms.

"Gurl, you know it's okay. I just want you to be better. I've known something was wrong for the past few weeks, but I couldn't put my finger on it. I should have been more insistent when you kept saying nothing was bothering you. The first thing tomorrow morning you are calling a counselor," Jackie informed her best friend, as though there were no other options. She then pulled Cedes close to her and held her as they both cried.

Roland eased his way past the two of them, not wanting to intrude on this moment between two women who very obviously shared a love for each other rivaled only by the love he felt for Terry.

As Roland started toward the kitchen, the sound of tumbling from the direction of Michael's bedroom caught his attention. The door was slightly ajar, and as he peeped in, he could only laugh. Michael and Michelle had pulled the mattress off the bottom bunk and were taking turns jumping from the top bunk onto the mattress on the floor.

Jackie wasn't going to like this. Then Roland asked himself if he really wanted his lifestyle totally changed by a woman and children. Did he want to give up the weekends in Aspen, weeks in Cancun, trips to Paris on the Concorde? And for what? Waking up with the same woman every day for the rest of his life, screaming kids, braces, PTA meetings, Cub Scouts, ballet lessons? He sure did.

"Alright, dis here pity party is ovah." Momma C came barreling out of the kitchen. "Cedes, baby, 'morrow mornin' you gonna see so'body to hep you git ovah this thang wit yo' momma up and dyin' like she did. But fo' rat now we gonna sit down and have us a fam'ly dinner. I ain't worked all day fo' nuthin'. Now y'all two go wash yo' faces. Roland?"

"Yes, ma'am?"

"Roland, since you standin' dere by Mikey and Ikey, git 'em ready for dinner. I done tol' Terry and da girls to finish settin' the table. We gonna eat in ten minutes. Is dat clear?"

"Oh, yes, ma'am." Roland smiled to himself, warmed by the love in this family. If only his family could be more like these people.

"We're heading to the bathroom, Momma C, before you get the ironing cord out for us." Cedes smiled, wiping tears away. She felt such relief from just being with the people she loved so much.

True to Momma C's word, they were gathered around the table and holding hands to say grace within ten minutes. The spread was magnificent. Baked capon chicken, dressing, candied yams, mustard greens, macaroni and cheese, complete with homemade crescent rolls.

Momma C offered the blessing. "Lord owah God, I thank you fo' bringin' my fam'ly t'gether one mo' time. Thank you fo' bringin' Cedes back safe and sound. Ease her heart, Lord. Fill that empty space wit yo' love and comfort. Bless dis here food prepared for the nourushmen' of dese here bodies. In Jesus' name I pray and we all say—"

The family sang in unison, "Amen!"

The conversation was light throughout dinner. Lisa and Ari wanted to know all about Cedes's travels with the Cowboys and if they went to Disneyland after every game. The laughter was as plentiful as the food.

Momma C could not have been any happier than to have all of her children around her table. She had adopted the philosophy many years before that any table that she dressed with food became her table. Cedes had always been like her own daughter. She had never had any other children after Jackie, because an illness left her late husband unable to produce sperm.

Willie had been stricken with mumps when Jackie was six months old. His fever had reached 104 degrees, and the doctors said that he would not live through the night. Clara had promised God that if He spared her Willie, she would serve Him for the rest of her days. He had and she did. Willie came out of the coma at sunset on the following evening, asking for some of his Clara's greens, but they were unable to have any more children.

God had really blessed her when He sent Terry into Jackie's life, and he quickly became her son. Of course there were Cedes's three brothers—Robert and Charles, who lived in other parts of the country, and Marcus, who had been a drunk since his mother had died in his arms. Terry was there all the time loving and taking care of her baby. She could go and join her Willie anytime and not have to worry a second about Jackie.

Terry, Roland, Ari, and Lisa had come as a package—one of those big packages you see under a Christmas tree and can't wait to see what wonderful surprise is waiting inside. Yes, Momma C was truly a happy woman.

Jackie looked around the table at all the people she loved in one place. She felt so blessed to have a mother who was supportive, loving, and still living. Four wonderful children and a man who loved her as much as, if not more than, she loved him. And she felt as if she had known Roland all of her life.

Terry could not help but wonder what he had done to have such a rich life. Momma C had almost filled the void he felt with his mother, Teresa, so far away. Roland was the peanut butter to his jelly. *Jackie, oh Jackie, is going to be my wife,* he thought. He would convince her or die trying.

Cedes looked around the table and thought to herself, knowing somehow that her mother could read her thoughts: *If you had to leave me, you left me with the best.*

Without knowing the thoughts of the others around the table, each one knew they had all they needed right there in that room.

H EY, GURL! ARE we still on for shopping and lunch this afternoon?" Cedes shrieked into the phone.

"You know it! I still have to shop for Roland and pick up a couple gifts for people at the office. You'll be finished with the therapy session at two o'clock, right?" Jackie was fishing to make sure that Cedes was keeping the appointment.

"Yes, actually at one-fifty. And *yes*, I am still planning to go. If I don't, I would have to answer to all of you, and Momma C really scares me." They both laughed. "Thank you so much for loving me the way you do, Jackie."

"Okay, enough of that. Let's have a late lunch at Dick's and then head out to the Galleria. My copy editor loves Godiva, and I can always find something for Roland in Nordstrom," Jackie interjected quickly to avoid the flood of emotions she had experienced the night of Cedes's welcome-home dinner.

"I need to stop by Black Images Books, too. Emma ordered some books that I need to pick up for my sisters-in-law. I'll pick you up at two-fifteen, and please let me help you plan this night out on the town for your Mister Wonderful. Until two-fifteen, my sistah." With that Cedes was gone.

As Jackie headed to the kitchen to make some coffee before

starting on her article, she couldn't shake the feeling that she should call Terry. She had talked to him until two o'clock that morning and felt silly wanting to call him again. She knew he was getting ready for work, and he left little or no spare time for early morning conversations. She shook it off and put her energy into the feature story that was due in less than ten hours.

Terry couldn't shake a sense of foreboding that came over him. Though he knew it was an old wives' tale, his left eye had been twitching for the past twenty-four hours. He just didn't like this feeling.

Roland told him that he had made preliminary preparation for the parental custody filing, but until he heard from opposing counsel, there was little else to do. Catherine could just be blowing smoke. Every now and then she would get a pang of conscience where the girls were concerned, but she usually eased that with a sizable check.

"Daddy?" Ari interrupted his thoughts as he adjusted the beautiful silk tie the girls had given him for his birthday that year.

"Yes, Miss Winston, how can I help you this morning?"

"Oh Daddy!" Ari began giggling. "Lisa and me want to go shopping this afternoon. We saved up our allowance for gifts for Mikey and Ikey and Miss Jackie and Momma C."

"That should be 'Lisa and I.' Oh, so I'm not getting a gift this year? I am crushed!" Terry was hanging his head pretending to cry.

"Daddy, you know you can't be with us when we buy your gift! Auntie Veronica is taking us to buy it on Saturday," Lisa piped in from the bedroom.

"Why not?" Terry teased. "I promise I won't look."

"Daddy!" they sang in unison. The phenomenon of identical twins never ceased to amaze him. There were times when they finished each other's sentences without thinking about it. He was never "my" dad, always "our" dad. When Ari had surgery, Lisa became violently ill. Whenever you saw one, you knew the other was not far away.

They were beautiful in every sense of the word. As much as he hated to admit it, they were the spitting image of Catherine. He had tolerated Catherine's behavior throughout college because she was the most beautiful woman he had ever seen. Now with twenty-twenty hindsight, he fully understood the saying "Beauty is only skin-deep."

Even with all of his insecurities as a teenager, he knew what he liked physically in a woman. Catherine was almost six feet tall and Rubenesque. She had that "If you don't like me as I am, that's your problem" attitude. His friends teased him mercilessly at the time as he pursued her, and she treated him as if he had an eye in the middle of his forehead throughout their relationship. None of that mattered because he felt that he was with a goddess. *Damn, what a fool I was.*

Ari and Lisa were going to be tall like Catherine, and even more beautiful. They had her outward beauty and his values. They would never treat anyone with the disrespect their mother did. She treated people as if they were paper cups. She just tossed them away when she was done.

"Well, since I see you two have planned my afternoon off, let's say I pick you up from school and we shop, then have a little dinner to celebrate the beginning of our Christmas vacation," Terry said, following Ari into his bedroom.

"We love you, Daddy." They both hugged his neck. These were the moments Terry lived for, and Catherine was not going to take them from him, even part-time. A chill came over him again as that unshakable feeling of consternation loomed over his head.

"Let's get out of here so this day will end quickly," Terry said, grabbing his jacket from the closet. Just as he reached for the door, the doorbell chimed. As he opened the door, he was startled at the sight of the small, unassuming Barney Fife–looking man.

"Can I help you?" Terry asked, a little annoyed someone would make a visit at this hour.

"I am looking for Terrence Winston," the man said sheepishly.

"You got him. What can I do for you?" The man said nothing. He simply gave him a stack of papers and walked away. "Excuse me?" Terry yelled after the stranger, who practically ran to the station wagon parked in his driveway with the engine running.

Totally mystified by the actions of the stranger, Terry realized it was futile to pursue him. Then he turned his attention to the document in his hand. His knees buckled under him when he read the heading "Petition for Child Custody."

"Daddy, who was that man? Daddy? Daddy! DADDY!" Lisa's voice escalated into a scream before Terry realized she was even speaking.

"Oh, I am sorry, princess. He just brought me some papers I need for work." Terry was not a good liar.

"Then why do you look so upset?" Ari said, questioning his response.

"I just wasn't expecting him to bring them to the house, that's all." Terry heard his own words, but felt as if someone else was speaking.

Lisa and Ari exchanged glances. "Okay, are you ready to go, Daddy? We want to get to school early so we can give our Christmas cards to our friends. We made a different one on the computer for each person," Ari said, her excitement apparent.

"Daaaddddyyyy! Are you okay? You look really funny, and you're not answering us," Lisa said, looking up at him intently.

"Yes. Yes, I am fine. You guys ready?" Terry said, stepping onto the porch.

"Daddy, you left your briefcase," Ari said, looking again at Lisa, perplexed.

Terry had no idea how he drove to the school. He realized he was there when the girls kissed him and jumped out of the car, yelling to a group of their friends gathered in front of the school. He reached into his pocket to retrieve the petition and was startled into the present by a horn honking behind him. He realized that he was obstructing the drop-off circle. He needed to get someplace quickly to read this hellish document. He drove to the corner and parked in the first available space.

As he stared down at the document, he again saw the words "Petition for Child Custody, State of Texas, County of Dallas. Petitioner: Catherine Marie Hawkins." Terry could not believe his eyes. She was filing for custody. The words all ran together. It was as if he was reading a foreign language; he saw the words, but could not comprehend them.

He needed to take action, but what? He should call someone, but who? He should go someplace, but where? He needed to be somewhere, but when? He was unaware of how long he had been parked at the curb and was jolted when the crossing guard tapped on the window.

This woman had protected the children at the corner for as long as Terry could remember. She could easily be someone's great-grandmother, but she possessed the energy and the spirit of someone much younger. "Is everything alright, sir?"

"Oh, yes, I'm okay. How long have I been sitting here, Miss Prescott?"

"A long time. I just wanted to make sure you weren't sick or something. One time a man had a heart attack sitting right over there and we never even knew it. So anytime one of my parents sits for too long, I just make sure they are okay," the friendly crossing guard rambled on.

"It's not one of my better mornings, Miss Prescott, but I am not having a heart attack or anything." Terry tried to force a smile.

"Well, you have a good day, and you can sit here as long as you like. You look a little pale; you sure you're alright?"

"Yes, Miss Prescott. Thank you for your concern." Terry prepared to leave, and again tried to think logically. What should he do next? Call Roland! That's what he needed to do. He pressed the speed-dial number on his car phone. "Carpenter, Pickford, and Harper," the unfamiliar voice answered.

Terry realized that the office wasn't open. He just hung up, having no patience for the answering service. He then speed-dialed Roland's home. No answer. He followed it with Roland's car phone and voice mail. Terry could not breathe. He lowered the car window and felt a rush of cold air against his face. It helped to clear his head, but did nothing to relieve the sense of panic that gripped him. He had to get to work. Today was his last day of work this year. He must at least make an appearance. The drive to the office was no different than the journey from his home to the school. He had no clue how he got there.

As he pulled into his parking space, he noticed Valerie struggling with packages. She looked like Mrs. Santa in designer wear. Her white wool coat was open to show her red suit. Terry ran over to assist her. "Good morning, Mrs. Santa." Terry managed a smile.

"Good morning. How is my favorite architect who is going off on vacation and leaving the rest of us to slave?" Valerie asked, flashing that stellar smile.

"I'm okay, and how about you?" Terry said unconvincingly.

Despite struggling to balance the packages as she passed them to Terry, Valerie stopped and looked into his eyes. "Everything okay, Terry?"

"Yeah, why do you ask?"

"I just thought I heard a little something in your voice. It must be my imagination." Valerie greatly respected Terry and made a mental note to inquire again later. There was a problem. She was certain of it.

As Terry settled into his work area, he dialed Roland's office again. This time he was greeted by the receptionist's warm and friendly voice: "Carpenter, Pickford, and Harper."

"Good morning. This is Terry Winston calling for Roland. Please tell me he's in."

"Oh, I'm sorry, Mr. Winston. He's in court all day today, but he'll check in for messages. May I have him call you?" There was a pregnant pause. "Are you there, Mr. Winston?"

"Yes, yes, I am. Please have him call me as soon as he can."

Terry hung up the phone without giving her a chance to ask any further questions. He felt the presence of someone in his area and turned to find Penny, the firm's receptionist. She was a young, attractive college student who had been with the firm since her junior year in high school. "Good morning, Terry. FedEx just dropped this off for you."

"Thank you, Penny. You all ready for Christmas?" Terry attempted pathetically to exchange pleasantries.

"Pretty much. I'm going to see my boyfriend in Los Angeles this year, so I finished early. I'm leaving right after the gift exchange and luncheon today. I can hardly wait."

"Well, I'm sure you'll have a great time. How is he doing at UCLA?" Terry was delaying looking at the FedEx envelope as long as he could.

"He pulled a four point oh this quarter. He's doing great. We just miss each other a lot, is all. Well, I had better get going. I have to help with the party decorations."

Terry watched Penny until she disappeared. Without looking down at the envelope, he knew it was from Catherine; he could just feel it. He slowly turned the package over. His suspicions were confirmed, but it wasn't from Spain. It was from San Antonio, Texas.

Promptly at two-twelve, Cedes pulled the shiny black Mercedes into Jackie's driveway and honked the horn. Jackie grabbed her coat, kissed Momma C good-bye, and instructed her not to let Mikey and Ikey convince her that she said they could have ice cream as their afternoon snack.

Jackie thought of what her life would be like without Momma C. She quickly dismissed her thoughts; she couldn't imagine life without her mother. She fully understood why Cedes needed counseling.

As Jackie slid into the passenger seat and hugged Cedes, she was painfully aware that her best friend had been shedding a few tears at her first grief-counseling session. She had promised herself she would only go there if Cedes brought it up.

"*Diva!* We sure look foine to be going to a mall. Now you know I gots to have my mackin' garments on, but you got that wonderful man already, and you know I don't be needin' no competition."

"Gurl, *paleeze*. How can I be competition for a diva with a twenty-six-inch waist?" Jackie said laughing, but feeling a slight pang of envy.

"Here we go again. You need to get yourself some of this counseling. You are one of the most beautiful sisters I have ever encountered. I have told you that beauty comes in all waist sizes: twenty-six, thirty-six, forty-six, it does not matter. It is the attitude that matters, and, diva sistah, we both got plenty attitude!" Cedes reassured her friend.

"Yeah, yeah, whatever you say, but I sure see how the men look over me to look at you, so you can say whatever you want, my diva sistah."

"I don't believe we are having this conversation again. Who in this car has a man? Not just a man, a *good* man?"

"He is wonderful, isn't he? Lord forgive me for being so insecure. He loves me no matter how much weight I don't lose," Jackie said more to herself than to Cedes.

"Thank you. Now please, I had enough heavy crap for one afternoon. Let's go to Dick's and let them abuse us." They both laughed heartily.

Cedes warily reflected on her session that afternoon, and Jackie did her best not to pry. She was so relieved that Cedes was getting the help she so desperately needed to deal with the death of Momma Margaret.

The conversation turned light, and they began planning the evening out for Terry. Jackie had purchased front-row tickets for Anita Baker's concert. Cedes decided that they needed to spend the night at the Adam's Mark hotel in a suite, be picked up by a limo an hour before sunset. Jackie and Terry would watch the sunset from the Ball high above Dallas over champagne and dinner before they went to the concert. The evening would end with lovemaking until sunrise. The two friends left no detail unattended as Jackie made notes over lunch.

Dick's was a fun place. First-timers were always shocked by the apparent blatant rudeness of the staff until they realized it was all a part of the restaurant's charm as much as the picnic tables and sawdust on the floor.

Jackie and Cedes were having a great time catching up on all the National Football League happenings and the woes of single parenthood. They had been together for hours and were having the time of their lives just being in each other's company.

The trip into Godiva had been hilarious. Jackie pretended she was having an addiction attack being around all the chocolate and that it was like offering an alcoholic a shot of Jack Daniel's. Cedes, the clerk, and all of the customers were in stitches over her witty exchanges.

The sun had long since set as they strolled up to the men's fragrance bar at Nordstrom. Jackie was so perplexed when it came to buying gifts for Roland. The man had *everything*, except a good woman. She sure wished she could hook him up with Cedes, but there just didn't seem to be any magic there . . . *none*. They were as platonic as she and he were. *Oh well*, she thought.

Just as she thought she had found the perfect gift ensemble for Roland and turned to ask Cedes's opinion, she noticed her friend staring intently at something. She followed her line of sight and almost gasped audibly at the object of her attention.

Standing on the other side of the fragrance bar was a strikingly attractive man. He displayed the poise of Denzel Washington, the rugged handsomeness of Wesley Snipes, and the confidence of Michael Jordan. Even Jackie was mesmerized. "Gurl! Look at that man," Cedes whispered, never averting her gaze.

"He *is* foine. Damn."

"I want to meet him. Excuse me for a moment."

"What are you going to do? Just walk over there and introduce yourself? This I gotta see!" Jackie watched as Cedes made her way to the other side of the fragrance bar. She saw her body language switch to that of a predator in a matter of seconds. She was standing next to him pretending to sample displayed fragrances. He looked at her politely, and they exchanged smiles. His smile made the department store lighting pale in comparison.

"May I assist you with a choice?" the well-dressed black woman asked her.

"Yes, I do believe I am ready. The full line of Façonnable,

please," Jackie said, looking past the sales associate to where Cedes was working her charm.

"Would you like to see what the full line consists of, ma'am?" the clerk asked with a hint of sarcasm in her voice.

"That won't be necessary. If it is a part of this line, I would like to purchase it, and if there are multiple sizes, I would like the large one of each. And please have it all arranged very nicely in a gift box for me."

"You will have to pay for the items before we will be able to do that." Now the sarcasm was blatant. Jackie turned her attention fully to this woman who obviously thought that she was not aware of the cost of what she had requested.

"I am well aware of that, Melissa." Jackie strained to see the name tag attached to her very smart black suit. "I shop here quite regularly, and I assure you that I can afford these items; but perhaps you are not in need of the commission associated with a purchase of this magnitude." Jackie did nothing to mask her annoyance at this woman on the other side of the counter.

"I am sorry, I just thought . . ."

Jackie leaned in close so that no one could hear her except Melissa. "Please do not assume that all of us are sales associates with mediocre incomes and cannot give lavish gifts to the men we love. Okay, my sistah? And I will make sure that your supervisor never finds out that one of my own discriminated against me."

The woman's almond complexion was flushed red as she busied herself with the task at hand. Jackie once again focused on the action on the other side of the counter. Cedes was now chatting with the man dressed in the gray pin-striped Armani suit.

Jackie laughed to herself and wished she had that kind of confidence. She walked over to join Cedes and said, "It'll be a while before the box will be ready. I'm going to the shoe department to check out shoes for my New Year's Eve dress."

"Okay. Charles, this is my friend Jackie—Jackie, Charles. It was very nice chatting with you. Happy Holidays to you and yours." Cedes extended her hand.

"Very nice chatting with you as well, and same to you and yours. Nice meeting you, too, Jackie," Charles said, extending his hand to Jackie this time.

As the two friends walked away, they were almost giggling. The man's voice matched everything about him, reminding one of ebony satin.

They shopped and chatted. Jackie shared her experience with the sales associate at the fragrance counter. They laughed about how African-Americans discriminate among themselves. No matter what direction the conversation took, it always came back to Cedes's brief encounter with Charles. She was truly moonstruck. "I must talk to him again."

"Did you get his number?"

"No, I had no idea I was this affected. What am I going to do?"

"Well, Cedes, you missed your opportunity; he's gone. If it is meant to be, then you'll encounter him again."

"God helps those who help themselves," Cedes said as she reached for her cellular phone.

"Who are you calling?"

"He is the regional manager for Nordstrom, so I'm calling the store. They'll know how to get a message to him."

"You are serious, aren't you?"

"Of course, I am!" After three phone calls, Cedes had found his office. She left an urgent message including her home and cellular numbers. They laughed as Jackie looked on in awe. This woman was truly a master at the dating game.

They decided to stop for gourmet coffee, and just as the waiter brought them the cappuccinos they had ordered, Cedes's cellular phone rang.

1 2

ELLO, THIS IS Mercedes," Cedes answered the phone, her fingers crossed.

"Why yes, Charles, thank you for calling me back so quickly. I was wondering if perhaps we could chat a little more sometime in the near future?" Cedes was silently screaming and pretending to stamp her feet, while all the time remaining very calm on the phone.

"I didn't realize you live elsewhere. I am on the road a lot as well . . . Public relations. How long before you leave? . . . Ahhhh, I was hoping that we could get together for coffee or a little holiday libation, but since you are leaving in the morning, I guess it'll have to wait until your return. Just when will that be, Charles?"

Jackie stared in absolute amazement. It was no wonder the Dallas Cowboys did everything they could to keep her happy.

"I would like very much to stay in touch with you during the holidays . . . Yes, I'm writing as you speak . . . Well, we'll just see about that now, won't we, Charles? I'll talk to you soon." Cedes touched the End button on the phone. Both women screamed. They were laughing so hard neither could speak for several minutes.

"Tell me everything, you brazen hussy!" Jackie was still laughing.

"Gurl, he lives in Seattle, manages all the stores in the western region. He's heading home for the holidays. He *said* he had thought of me often since our brief encounter and he likes a woman who goes for what she wants. Now, if I had a dime for every time I have heard that one."

"Don't I know that is *correct*! They make the claims and talk the talk, but they damn sure cannot walk the walk. So what was the 'we will just have to see about that' all about?" Jackie regained her composure, though a chuckle escaped occasionally.

"He asked me if I had a date for New Year's Eve. I was not about to tell him that I was dateless in Dallas *again*!"

"Now, you know you have a standing date with Roland." Jackie tried to look serious.

"Have you ever thought that perhaps the *standing* date is the problem? Once before menopause sets in I'd like to have a *laying* date for New Year's Eve."

Jackie lost it. She spit cappuccino across the room. "Gurl, you are a fool!"

"You've had a steady diet of good lovin' for the past four years. I, on the other hand, am suffering from malnutrition, so of course, I'm a fool. I'm suffering from delirium." The two best friends continued to laugh and enjoy the evening together. They had done the Galleria proud and officially proclaimed they were finished Christmas shopping.

On the ride back to Jackie's house Cedes was unusually quiet. "Cedes, are you alright? You've been quiet ever since you got in the car."

"Jackie, how am I going to make it through Christmas without Momma? This was her favorite time of year. She would have started bugging me to let her open at least one gift because she always said 'Tomorrow ain't promised to you, baby.' I never knew just how right she really was."

Jackie could see tears forming in Cedes's eyes as she tried to find the right thing to say. "I am not going to pretend that I know what you're going through. I just want you to do whatever you need to do to get through this season."

"I never told you this, but I was planning to give our mothers a cruise for Christmas this year. I teased Momma something terrible when she hinted that she wanted to take a cruise. I told her she just wanted to get on board to chase those young men in white pants around the boat. She told me that I had her confused with Terry's mom." They both laughed as tears fell from Cedes's eyes. "I would still love to give Momma C a cruise. How would you feel about that?"

"Oh Cedes, what a gift! But who would she go with? There's no one Momma C would spend seven hours confined with, let alone seven days, besides Momma Margaret."

"I know, I know. I just need to do something really special for Momma C this Christmas. I've bought her gifts, but it just doesn't seem to be enough. I can't explain it."

"When do you see your counselor again, sis?" Jackie was whispering.

"Next week. Why do you ask?"

"You need to talk to her about this."

"Yeah, I guess you're right. I'm sorry, I didn't mean to bring you down. We had such a wonderful day. I did meet that foine brotha Charles, didn't I?"

"'Chased Charles' is more accurate!" Jackie gave Cedes a high five, and the laughter once again filled the car.

As they pulled into the driveway, Terry's and Roland's cars were parked in front of the house. Jackie and Cedes looked at each other, but said nothing. *Why are they here?* Jackie wondered. *Has something happened?* Jackie bolted from the car, leaving her purse and all the packages. She ran up the steps of the porch. The door flew open, and Mikey rushed into her arms. "Mommy, what did you bring us?"

"Nothing, Michael. Is everything alright?" she asked, rushing into the house with Michael in her arms.

Momma C met them with the news. "Well, yes and no, baby. Terry is in da kitchen wit Roland. I made them some tea and they eatin' some of mah pineapple upside-down cake. Terry is a mite upset. Ari and Lisa are in da room wit Michelle. Dey don't know, yet."

"Don't know what, Momma?" Jackie never stopped walking toward the kitchen.

"Hey, baby. I am so glad to see you." Terry rose from the table and took Jackie into his arms.

"Will someone please tell me what is going on?" Jackie pulled out of Terry's embrace reluctantly.

"Catherine has moved to Texas"—Roland was speaking almost in a defeated tone—"and she filed for joint custody."

"Oh my God! She's really going through with it?" Jackie fell into the kitchen chair just as Cedes stepped through the kitchen door. Momma C had brought her up to date.

"It really does appear that way. We put our best private investigator on it this afternoon. If Catherine has any skeletons, we will uncover them." Roland was glad to offer some encouraging news.

"Baby, look at me," Jackie said, and took Terry's face into her hands. With her face just inches from his, she said, "She will not win. Do you hear me? She will not win!"

Terry said nothing. He only drew her nearer to him and held her for what seemed like hours to Roland and Cedes. "With friends and family like this, I can't lose," he finally sighed. "And if your momma feeds us, everything will be just fine." His words were spoken with no confidence, but they all laughed anyway.

Momma C entered the kitchen as if on cue. "Alright, Roland, tell Momma C what the plan is. 'Cause I knows you got one, baby. And speak so Momma C can fully undastan'."

"Well, Momma C, we will file a cross-complaint, which means we will file for full custody. We will meet with her attorney and try to reach a settlement out of court, which, if she is serious, will not happen. In the meanwhile, we're buying time. We're investigating her background now, and by the time we're done, we will even know what kind of dental floss she uses. Howard—that's our investigator—is doing the work for expenses only. Which means we only have to pay if he has to travel, develop film, 'encourage cooperation' from a few folks, that kind of thing."

"Well, y'all know I don't have much money, just my dear Willie's pension and a little income from mah real estate, but I will give you every dime I got to make sho' dat woman don't get dem babies. You undastan' Momma C, Roland?"

"Yes, ma'am, but we got that part under control. Everyone connected with the case is working for free. All they need is expense money. We're all on the same page with this one."

"Well den, I say it is time for some dinner. What y'all say? 'Cause I done prayed so dis here mess is finished. And little Miss Catherine betta watch her step 'cause she may just stumble and fall. You know God sits high and looks low. Terry here done been a good daddy to Ari and Lisa, and God is not blind or unjust."

Everyone in the room felt the same surge of power that Momma C did. All of a sudden, they too knew it was goin' to be alright. Only, they just had no idea how turbulent the storm was going to get.

DESPITE THE DARK cloud that Catherine cast over the holiday season, Terry felt blessed. He had a woman he was going to make his wife, two—no, make that four—beautiful children, a mother-in-law who satisfied the longing in his heart to see his own mother, his sister Veronica, who was wonderful and supportive, and a best friend who would run through hell in a gasoline jacket for him. Yes, he was truly blessed.

He dressed for church and hummed as he thought of the wonderful evening he had spent with Jackie. Momma C had watched all of the children while he took her to André's, one of their favorite restaurants. It was the first place he had taken her after he knew it was love.

After he had strung the lights early that morning four years before, she had called to thank him. She was so warm and genuine, and their conversation lasted for three hours. She laughed at his lame attempts at humor, and there was a gentleness about her voice that warmed him all over.

He had only dated casually since Catherine had ripped his heart out, slow-broiled it, and served it back to him on a dirty paper plate. There had been no one who understood his dedication to his girls. He fully understood the plight of single mothers. After one or two dates, potential girlfriends would just fade into the sunset. One woman actually told him he was too nice. He had asked her to explain her statement, but she couldn't. She just kept repeating "you are too much," which was another statement she couldn't quite explain.

Jackie had agreed to have dinner with him after some tall talking on his part. She kept trying to explain away why he thought she was so attractive and wonderful. She was so unaffected by her beauty that she could not even imagine how beautiful he thought she was. He thought she was the most sensual creature God had ever created.

He could not be certain, but he thought her personal life had been as "exciting" as his own. If she would give him half a chance, he would surely change all of that. He was getting out the Kirby because he was going to sweep her off her feet.

Jackie had agreed to dine with him on Saturday night, two days after Christmas. She had never been to André's, but had heard great things about it. She was really looking forward to an adult evening out.

He was sad that he would not see her for three whole days. It was Christmas Eve, and he really wanted to see her again *now*. He was awkward at dating as he had proven quite well when he met her. He thought to himself, *What would Roland do?* but quickly dismissed those thoughts and relied on his own instincts.

"Jackie, I realize it is Christmas Eve, but I would really like to see you this evening, if only for a few minutes. We're having a family dinner and the girls will be in bed by nine, so perhaps coffee and dessert after that?"

"Thank you very much, but I couldn't possibly leave the twins on Christmas Eve, even if they are sleeping."

Terry detected a hint of regret in her voice, but it in no way matched his own. "Would you object to having coffee and dessert here? I'll make a nice fire, and we can listen to Christmas carols." The words rushed out of her mouth so quickly they had amazed even her. She didn't want him to think she was brushing him off, which was truly not the case.

Terry felt like leaping up and clicking his heels. That would be perfect. It would be the first of many Christmas Eves together, he could just feel it.

Terry was so glad to have his mother, Teresa, home for the holidays. He really missed her after she had moved to California right after he graduated from college. It was hard to believe that the woman in his kitchen with the sassy haircut, wearing leggings and an oversized T-shirt, was his mother. She was so vibrant and alive. It was rumored that she was dating a man three years younger than his older sister Veronica. The thought sent a chill up his spine. More than a few fathers had warned him about sitting on the porch with a shotgun when Alisa and Ariana started dating, but no one had ever mentioned how a son felt when his mother was dating. She was always carded when she attempted to use her senior citizen discount. What a hoot! His mother getting carded.

Veronica had been visiting since their mother arrived three days before. She had been in the Middle East for almost six months. He was really happy that she had decided to spend a couple of days with him.

As an international photojournalist, Veronica spent a lot of time out of the country. She loved her job, freelancing for all the major magazines, but it was a rough life and she had not had a serious relationship since college. Terry also worried about how much she drank. She seemed so troubled since she had returned from this trip.

Veronica was a senior in high school when their father decided that the next-door neighbor's grass was greener. What Terrence Senior didn't understand at the time was all he needed to do was fertilize his own lawn. The breakup caused them all tremendous pain, but Veronica internalized hers. Veronica took her first drink on graduation night, when dear ole Dad was more concerned about his own embarrassment than his daughter's disappointment.

Terry wanted so much for her to find a man who could love her for all of her strengths and weaknesses. She always seemed to pick those who were certain to disappoint her.

Teresa and Veronica had prepared a feast for two hundred and fifty people, each of whom could take a doggie bag with them. The spread was magnificent, but Terry could hardly eat. Teresa asked him several times if he was feeling okay. He assured her he was fine as he glanced at the grandfather clock for the eightieth time in an hour.

Ari and Lisa were excited about Christmas. They had asked for a computer, and they were sure that the big box under the tree was just that. Terry had fooled them. It was actually a Barbie dream house. He had heard the horror stories about assembling that masterpiece and had started on it right after Thanksgiving. He had spent many hours in Roland's garage listening to his tales of dating, drinking Coronas, while trying to figure which piece went with which. His college minor was in engineering—*My God, what must other people experience while trying to assemble this thing?* he had thought. Ari and Lisa chattered on and on all evening, but it seemed so far away to Terry. He kept watching the clock.

He phoned Jackie twice that evening, and he could hear the same type of activity at her place. They had had dinner, complete with Christmas Eve chatter, and Momma C was spending the night as she had every Christmas since the twins were born. She assured him that he wasn't bothering her by calling so often and that she too was looking forward to seeing him that evening.

After much persuasion, Ari and Lisa finally settled down. Terry kissed his mother on the cheek and told her he would be back in an hour or so. She smiled up at him and asked, "Baby, who is she?"

"Just someone I met at the supermarket."

"She's the one, isn't she?"

"Oh, Momma, we haven't even had a date. I am going over for coffee."

"A momma knows these things, baby ... a momma knows these things. You mark my word."

"I love you, Momma." With that, he picked up a package from the table and was out the door, but as he got in the car, he changed his mind about driving. He wanted to walk. It was cold, and the air was crisp and clean. The walk would give him time to relax. His heart was beating so fast he thought he might have some sort of attack. As he walked, he deliberately took his time and enjoyed the elaborately decorated houses in his neighborhood. There were carolers singing in the distance. Afterward, his head was much clearer and he could breathe, or so he thought.

She took his breath away when she opened the door. She wore a white jumpsuit with a gold belt, gold and white pumps, and a smile that could light up a city block. Her hair was pulled back and highlighted her beautiful face. Her scent enveloped him and took him to a place he had never visited before, but he knew he wanted to live there forever.

"Hello Terrence, please come in." Her voice was melodic. "Oh my God, you brought me a gift?" Her words finally broke the spell she had cast over him.

"It is only a little something; please don't be upset."

"I'm so shocked. You've given me so much already, and now a gift. Please, let me take your coat. We will have coffee and dessert in the den. The fire is wonderful tonight, and the tree is beautiful. Momma and the kids did it."

Jackie was right; the tree was unbelievably decorated. All of the trimmings, including the packages, were gold and white, and Jackie looked as if she was a part of the trimming. Terry smiled to himself as he thought that she was all the gift he would ever need.

Momma C came in and said hello, then excused herself, saying how tired she was after all that cooking. She was going to bed and would be sleeping before her head hit the pillow. Terry laughed, because she was overexplaining, which he thought was awfully cute.

Jackie returned with dessert and coffee on a silver tray. Terry marveled at her beauty. They spoke with the ease of old friends, and it seemed as if they were catching up on old times. As the fire burned low, Terry added more wood. Jackie refreshed the coffee, and they continued to talk.

Terry heard four soft bongs in the distance, and it registered somewhere in his brain that it was four in the morning. Oh my God, four in the morning on Christmas day, and there were still things that needed to be placed under the tree from Santa Claus.

It was as though Jackie had the same thoughts, and they both laughed.

"Let me help you with your toys, Ms. Claus." Terry resisted his desire to lean over to kiss her.

"It will only take a few minutes. They're only two, and it's the simple things in life that please them."

"Just wait, that will change." They both laughed again, this time so loudly they thought they would wake Momma C.

"Before we do that, I bought you a little something, too. It's not much, but I really wanted to express my gratitude for your kindness."

Terry was stunned. No woman other than his sister and mother had ever given him a Christmas gift before. "I don't know what to say, but thank you. Can I open it now?"

"Only if I can open mine, too!"

"And you thought I was leaving before you did?" She gave him an exquisitely wrapped box. It was almost too pretty to open. She picked up her gift from the coffee table. Like two children they tore into the packages. She stopped short as she recognized the Victoria's Secret box. Terry noticed her hesitation.

"Oh, it is nothing like that. Please just open it."

Inside was a collection of shower gel, lotion, after-bath splash, and a mesh sponge that was the same color as the other items. It was her favorite fragrance from Victoria's. How had he known that? She was truly moved. No man had ever taken the time to choose such a gift for her.

As he looked down at his gift, his heart was touched. It was a sterling silver photo album, and it had been engraved:

ARI AND LISA
THE WONDER YEARS

Without even realizing what he was doing, he reached over and kissed her. She kissed back. Her kiss delivered him to a place he knew deep in his soul he belonged. The kiss was passionate, but filled with warmth and kindness. The kiss said, *Please join me at this special place and stay forever.* Terry was not sure how long it lasted, or when he walked home. He only knew that it had confirmed what he felt since that moment they met in the parking lot. This woman was special. His momma was right—she was the one.

The sound of Jackie's voice brought him back to the present. "Honey, is this suit okay for church this morning? The skirt is a little short. I don't have anything else here. Momma C has the kids ready. We should hurry."

As Terry turned to look at Jackie, she once again took his breath away. Even after four years, she had that effect on him. Oh yes, he was truly a blessed man this Sunday morning.

ON THE DAY before Christmas Eve the scent of the holiday tickled Terry's nose. The pine tree in the living room was decorated in Christmas colors—*all* of them. His mother and sister were in the kitchen, and the aroma of sweet potato pies and homemade cakes filled the house. The familiar smells took him back to a time when everything in life was simpler. His mother always baked for days before Christmas—cakes, pies, cookies— and she had brought the dreaded fruitcake with her from Fresno.

This was the first year that the two families would break tradition. They both were spending Christmas Eve at his home and Christmas at Jackie's instead of having separate celebrations. If Terry had his way, this would be the last year this decision would have to be made at all. He wanted to marry Jackie this summer in the garden of Roland's palatial estate. She just had to say yes—she just had to.

"Daddy?" Ari came skipping into the room. "Can Mikey and Ikey spend Christmas Eve here?"

"Well, they are spending the evening here. We're all having dinner together and singing Christmas carols, but they'll be going home because they have to wait for Santa."

"I know they still believe in Santa, but why can't they believe that Santa brought their stuff here? They could camp out in our room, and Grandma and Momma C can sleep in the guest room and Miss Jackie and Aunt Veronica can sleep in your room."

"I see you've really thought this through, but you left off someone very important . . . *me!*"

"Oh Daddy, you can sleep on the couch. That way we can be one big family. *Pleeeease!*"

Terry pulled her onto his lap. "You're such a sweet child, and I love you so much. How does Lisa feel about this, and where is she anyway?"

"We talked about it, and she went to talk to Grandma and Aunt Veronica while I came to talk to you."

"Oh, so you're double-teaming us?" Terry was laughing now.

"Honey, this sounds pretty important to you. Why did you wait until today to bring it up?"

"Well, we weren't sure how to ask so we waited and waited and then decided that we'd better do it today if we were going to do it at all since tomorrow is Christmas Eve. And there's something else . . ." Ari dropped her head.

Lifting her head so their eyes met, Terry gently inquired, "And that is?"

"Well," Ari began very slowly. "We know you love Miss Jackie and she loves you."

"And just how do you know this, Miss Winston?" Terry interrupted.

"Oh Daddy, we're not babies. We know all about love. We want you to marry her, Daddy. There, I said it!" Relief washed over her face.

"You're right. I do love her, very much, and I want to marry her, too."

"So why don't you? We don't want to live in separate houses anymore. We love Mikey and Ikey, and we want Jackie to be our mother." The words stabbed Terry in the chest. He was lost for a moment. There was nothing he wanted more than to have Jackie be mother to Ari and Lisa. They had talked about it countless times, but they had no idea how the twins felt about it. Apparently, they had done some talking on their own.

"Well, Little Miss Thang, all in good time. But I will talk to her about the Christmas Eve thing right away. However, I make no promises. We should go into the kitchen to see how Lisa is doing with Momma and Veronica. You two are too much, you know that?" Ari looked at him and smiled with Catherine's eyes and mouth. The same smile that had made him so weak for Catherine so many years ago.

Meanwhile in the kitchen the three generations of Winston women were chattering away. Lisa had won them over pretty quickly, and they were all talking about staying up most of the night to make it a real party. "So I guess you two are in agreement with their little scheme," Terry said knowing he was outnumbered on this one.

"I think it is a fabulous idea!" Veronica chimed right in. "We have spent four Christmases as separate families, and we really aren't. Now we just need Cedes and Roland to make it complete."

"Yeah baby, Roland got any plans this Christmas Eve after dinner? And poor Cedes needs to be around as many people as possible this year. We can make do for space—the important thing is being with family." Teresa never looked up from picking greens.

Teresa had very strong feelings about family being together on holidays. Veronica and Terry's father had walked out on her when Terry was twelve, and she pledged that she would make every day as special as she could for her children. That went double for holidays. It took a lot of convincing from her children before she finally accepted a prestigious position with the school board in Northern California shortly after Terry graduated from college. Now she came home to Texas every Christmas. Roland had been a part of her family for the past fourteen years and was like a second son. Since Terry had brought Jackie into the Winston family, their holidays had been richer and fuller. What a wonderful idea the twins had . . . *Out of the mouths of babes,* she thought.

"You know this idea is growing on me. I'll call Jackie and see what she says. It would be nice to have all the people I love in one house on Christmas morning." Terry was so incredibly moved by the love his family felt for Jackie and her family.

"Then it's all settled. You think we have enough food, Momma?" Veronica was peeking into the refrigerator, which could not accommodate another slice of bread.

"Oh, baby, yes. We were preparing dinner for everyone already, so we just need more breakfast stuff."

Terry shook his head and headed for the bedroom to call Jackie. Everyone was so excited by the idea, and he hoped Jackie would be as enthusiastic. It would be her routine and the children's that would be most affected by this turn of events. He secretly prayed that she would say yes.

Jackie picked up on the first ring. "Hey, baby, you busy?"

"Never too busy for you, you know that," she said in that wonderful voice of hers. "What's wrong? Has Catherine done something else?"

"Oh, please don't talk about her. No, the twins came up with a request, and quite frankly, I would like it very much, too. Momma and Veronica agree as well." He was procrastinating.

"Well, what is it, honey?" Jackie was losing patience.

Terry explained the whole scenario, including the sleeping arrangements, and held his breath.

"You know, that is not a half-bad idea. Then the whole crew can come here for Christmas dinner, and we can open the other gifts then. We would have to make a few trips and move some presents, but we would love to. You know if you are sleeping on the couch, I'm sleeping on the couch, don't you?" They laughed, both feeling the immense love flowing between them even over the telephone.

"I'll talk to Momma C. Mikey and Ikey would like nothing more than a sleepover, and I'll explain that we'll leave a note on the fireplace for Santa." They continued talking for a few more minutes and agreed to call Cedes and Roland. If they came, that would make the event complete.

Everyone busied themselves with the duties of the season while the Temptations, Nat "King" Cole, Patti LaBelle, and the Chipmunks played in the background. Terry had planned to propose to Jackie at the New Year's Eve bash they attended every year given by the Black Legal Eagles, but with this turn of events, perhaps he would do it tomorrow.

It was the fourth anniversary of their first date, after all. *What could be more appropriate?* he thought. He went to his drawer and pulled out the black velvet box and held it in his hands awhile before opening it. He had looked forward to this day his entire adult life. He wanted a complete family, and now he was about to have one.

As he opened the box, he stared down at the almost perfect 2.53-carat stone set in platinum and gold. Once again, Roland had come through for him. Because he had put him in touch with his former client, Terry paid one-fourth the appraised value of the ring. She would be the envy of all her girlfriends. He smiled to himself and decided that he must get champagne for this occasion.

"Terry. Telephone," Veronica yelled from the kitchen.

Terry picked up the extension and sang, "Hello, Terry Winston."

"Merry Christmas, Terry." The sultry voice responded on the other end of the connection.

Terry's tone was as cold as the iceberg that brought down the *Titanic*. "Hello, Catherine."

"No Christmas greeting?" Catherine's laugh could be so evil.

"Merry Christmas. What can I do for you?"

"In case you haven't noticed, I have not yet sent a Christmas gift for Ariana and Alisa."

"Yes, I have noticed. I was sure you would come through with a rather large check by tomorrow."

"Well, surprise! I'm buying them gifts this year. I am living in San Antonio, but I'm *sure* you know this by now."

"Of course, I'm aware of it. I'm also aware you've been in San Antonio for more than two weeks and you haven't called or come to see Ari and Lisa. Catherine, it has been more than a year and a half since you've seen them. That shows a wealth of maternal instinct."

"Well, I had to get settled and get my new office set up, but I'm on vacation now and I'm flying into Dallas tomorrow. I want to spend time with them on Christmas."

"You are really a piece of work, Catherine. Do you think that we don't have *family* plans already?"

"I *am* their mother, Terry, and I want to see them on Christmas!"

"Humph! Their mother, now that *is* funny. They're perfecting a method for test tubes to do what you did. You disappointed them already this Christmas. You told them you couldn't make it back to the States to see them and now less than a month later, you've moved here. And of course because you changed *your* warped little mind, the universe is expected to pause in reverence. Well, think again, Catherine. We have plans for both tomorrow and Christmas, and those plans do not include you."

"You cannot stop me from seeing my daughters, Terrence Winston. Do you understand me? I'll get a court order, if I have to!"

"You just do that, and I hope you can get it by tomorrow because that's the only way you'll see them on Christmas."

"I want them to have my Christmas gift on Christmas, and I am bringing it to them. You cannot stop me."

"Why don't you FedEx them a check? It'll get here by tomorrow."

"I bought them computers, one for each of them. And I am getting them their own phone lines so they can surf the Internet. That way we can send e-mail back and forth."

"Catherine, they already have computers with Internet access. They've had them for three years now. They told you when they got them, but oh that's right, you were busy laughing with Miguel at the time. Did he come with you? Oh, that's right, you have had several lovers since Miguel."

"You're full of yourself, aren't you, Mister High and Mighty.

Well, I'll have your ass in court, and my lawyer assures me, I will get joint custody."

"Well, my lawyer, their godfather, assures me that you won't."

"Be prepared for the battle of your life, Terrence."

"No, Catherine, you haven't seen a fight. This is not one of your corporate mergers or hostile takeovers. These are my children! And, yes, you heard me right, I said *my* children. I'm in full battle armor and ready to go to war with you."

"You can't compete with my financial power, Terry. I'm a millionaire, and everything and everyone can be bought!"

"Catherine, Catherine, I have a power you know nothing about. I have the power of love. Love power. You should try it sometime."

There was silence on the other end of the line and then a distinctive click as the connection broke. Terry stared at the phone. There is no power like the power of a black man who loves God and his family. Catherine was totally unarmed.

ALL THE BLOOD in Terry's body seemed to rush to his head. He felt dizzy. His legs gave out on him, and he fell to the bed. He could feel the presence of someone else in the room and turned to see Ari, Lisa, and Veronica standing in the doorway.

"Daddy, why were you yelling at Catherine?" Lisa moved closer to the bed with Ari in tow.

"We had a disagreement about her visiting tomorrow," he said, ashamed he let Catherine make him lose control of his temper.

"She's coming from Spain tomorrow?" This time Ari spoke up as Terry's and Veronica's eyes locked.

"Well, not exactly, Ari. She no longer lives in Spain. She lives here in Texas, down in San Antonio. She moved here a couple of weeks ago."

"Why didn't she come see us when she got here?" The anger was apparent on Ari's face. "She hasn't seen us in a long time."

"She's been busy," he lied, but even Terry didn't believe the words he said.

"So what! You're busy all the time, too, but you would never *not* see us if you were in the same state. You would have come to see us first. I hate her, I *hate her*! Why can't our mother love us?" Ari ran from the room crying.

Terry started to follow her, but Veronica motioned for him to talk to Lisa, who stood transfixed, staring after her sister. Veronica disappeared down the hall into the girls' room. "Come over here, Lisa. Are you okay?"

"Yes, Daddy."

All of Lisa's vibrant personality seemed to have abandoned her. Terry became even angrier. *How dare Catherine cast such a dark cloud over their holiday?* he thought. "Why aren't you saying anything? You're usually the one with all the opinions."

"Daddy, I don't understand either. I want to scream like Ari, but I can't. My chest hurts too much. Why does she treat us like strangers? You're a grown man, and Grandma sees you more than Catherine sees us."

Terry was stunned. "Honey, I don't know how to explain it. I've known for a few days she came back to the States, but I wasn't going to say anything until she was ready to visit. I didn't want to upset you. I'm so sorry I lost my temper and that you heard me yelling."

"I'm going to see if Ari is alright," Lisa said woodenly. How could one person drain the spirit from an entire family with just one phone call?

"I will go with you," Terry managed.

"No, Daddy, let me take care of her. I know exactly how she feels. I'll call you if we need you." Terry was taken aback by her maturity and pained by the faraway look in her eyes.

"Okay, honey, I'm going to call Uncle Roland. I'll be in to check on you both in a little while."

"Okay, Daddy. We love you." Lisa's eyes filled with tears.

An indescribable pain shot through his heart as he smiled at her. He called Roland. "Happy Holidays, the Carpenter residence," his longtime live-in housekeeper answered in her heavy accent on the first ring.

"Hello, Marguerite. Is Señor Carpenter in?"

"Si, Señor Winston, and Feliz Navidad."

"Feliz Navidad, Marguerite."

Moments ticked away before Roland picked up the call.

"Terry, my man! How ya livin'?" Roland was in a fantastic mood. Terry hated to lay the Catherine thing on him and deflate yet another balloon filled with the happiness of the season.

"Hey, man! Sounds like Christmas cheer is flowing all through château Carpenter." Terry tried desperately to lighten his tone, but felt he was failing miserably. "Listen, Ari and Lisa came up with a hell of an idea, and we want you to participate."

"So what is this splendid idea?"

"Having Christmas Eve dinner turn into a party that ends with Christmas morning breakfast with a serious family gathering in between."

"Hmmmm. Well, I do have a date after dinner. Let me check with her to see if she would like to join us at your place. She's a snob, but damn, she has a walk that should be patented."

Terry managed a weak laugh. "When are you going to learn to choose women for what is in their hearts instead of their panty hose?"

"Some of us brothas are not as fortunate as you, and we are shallow." They both laughed, but Roland picked up on the weakness in Terry's chuckle. "What's wrong, my brotha?"

"Man, you know me too well."

"Let me guess. Catherine?"

Terry relayed the whole story. There was silence at the other end of the phone, which worried Terry. "Why so quiet, Ro?"

"I'm thinking we could use this, Terry. But we have to be more cooperative. Instead of telling her emphatically no, compromise. Let her come by, briefly, drop off her gifts and see the whole family together. If I know the lady like I think I do, she'll have media coverage of the event. When she's not the center of attention, she'll leave in short order. And we can use this in court as further proof of her unreliability. Do you think she'll bite?"

"I don't want that woman here. I plan to propose to Jackie tomorrow night over dinner. I can't do it with Cruella De Vil here."

"Trust me, this *will* work in our favor. I deal with the Catherines of the world every day. We'll make this work. I'll even blow

Ms. Wiggle off, and Cedes and I will appear an item. Catherine's a miserable woman, Terry. She does what she does to manipulate you and make you miserable, too. Trust me, Terry, please."

"What about Ari and Lisa? They'll be pawns in this little game. I'll not subject them to any unnecessary pain."

"Okay. I am confident my plan will work, and the worst that can happen is they'll see Catherine and get a nice gift or two. She'll be on her best behavior because of the pending court case and won't be able to stand a genuine family environment. She'll be there for less than an hour. I can almost guarantee it. Or better yet, if you call her back and invite her to dinner, she may not even come. She probably has plans with some young stud she bought for the week. The investigation is turning up some interesting stuff."

"I'm still hesitant, but you're the best at what you do. Just like you trusted me to design your house, I have to trust you on this. But, please, let me talk to Jackie first. I would do nothing to ruin Christmas for them. I can't believe her timing. She is a wretched woman. I can't believe I loved her at one time. Damn!"

"First thing you need to do is realize that this is not any fault of yours. You were young, and you're talking to a man who's still driven by his hormones. But we'll make this thing work for us. Believe me, her lawyer is putting her up to this. They want you to say no and deny her a visit to her poor children on Christmas."

They agreed that after he spoke with Jackie, he would contact Catherine through her office and leave an urgent message, even though Roland had her home number. He wanted it to be on record that Terry had called. And Catherine would take care of the rest for them.

Jackie was wonderfully understanding and said that if Roland felt this was best, then they would have to do it. She wanted nothing more than for this ugly mess to be over. If Catherine thought she was ruining any kind of celebration, she was sadly mistaken. With Momma C there, Catherine would quickly be put in her place if she got out of line.

The plan was set in motion. Within ten minutes of the initial call to Catherine's headquarters in Spain, she was on the phone again with Terry. "What is so urgent?" Catherine was hostile.

"I'm sorry I had to call your headquarters in Spain, but you left me no number here in the States to reach you. I assured the answering service that this was an urgent matter regarding your children, and she told me she would do her best to get you the message. That's some operation you guys have . . . the initial call was made less than fifteen minutes ago."

"Yeah. Yeah. Yeah. What is so urgent? Has there been an accident?"

"Well, Catherine, I may have been a little hasty earlier. I was being selfish regarding the girls at Christmas. We're having a family dinner tomorrow night at six o'clock. It would be a very nice surprise for them if you could join us."

"Why tomorrow night? Why not Christmas?"

Terry felt his blood pressure rising again. How was he going to get through this conversation calmly? Silently he began to pray in earnest. "We have other plans that will take us away from the house on Christmas. On such short notice this is the best I can offer. I do hope you can take me up on it."

"Well, I had planned to spend more time, but I guess I can just find other plans in Dallas. Perhaps I can visit them the day after Christmas, too. Maybe take them shopping?"

She had totally taken him by surprise with her last comment. The Great and Wonderful Oz of Texas family court had been wrong. Now what?

16

CHRISTMAS EVE DAY had dawned cold with cloudless azure skies. Jackie felt warm and secure as she rolled over to check the Bose alarm system Terry had given her for her last birthday. Terry made her life so full and wonderful. She made up her mind as she sat alone in front of the fire the evening before that she would no longer run from the inevitable. She loved Terry as much as any human being could love another. And she knew he would rather rip his own heart out than do anything to hurt her. If he did not ask her to marry him during the holidays, she would ask him! Jackie was startled back to reality with the early morning chime of the doorbell. "Who in the world—?"

As she tied the belt on her robe and checked the peephole, she was more than surprised to see a young man standing on her porch holding a huge poinsettia plant. Her smile broadened as she opened the door. "Good morning. I have a delivery for Mrs. Clara Rogers," the young man said enthusiastically, showing the handiwork of his orthodontist.

"Clara Rogers?" Jackie was disappointed, thinking it was from Terry. "I'll sign for it."

"Thank you, ma'am, and Merry Christmas!"

"Merry Christmas to you, too."

The plant was exquisite. She could not wait to see who sent it to her mother. Did Momma C have a suitor and fail to tell Jackie? Momma C had made an early start on the food preparations for Christmas dinner and was in the kitchen humming away.

"Mornin', baby. Ain't God good? It is just a perfect day for Chri'mas Eve. And don't you go worrin' none about this Catherine mess. Like I tol' y'all b'fo', I done prayed on that sistah and she betta watch what she do to Terry and dem dere babies." She gazed at the poinsettia. "Oh! Ain't that lovely. Terry's such a good man. You's a blessed woman, chile."

"Momma, I agree with everything you said, but this is not for me. It's for you."

"Fo' me?"

"Well, it's for Clara Rogers. Maybe there's another Clara Rogers."

"Don't be messin' wit yo' momma, chile, you know I be old. Who dey from?"

"Well, why don't you take the card, open it, and see for yourself?"

"Well, gimme here, chile."

"Who do you think it is from?"

"I ain't got no idea." Momma C opened the small envelope and read the card. Her face lit up almost as brightly as the sun shining through the windows on the east side of the house. "I think you needs to read dis one yo'self."

As Jackie looked down, she recognized the handwriting immediately.

A special thank-you for raising the most precious woman on this earth. I promise I will always take care of her. I love you, Momma C. Terry.

"Oh, Momma C, he *is* the most wonderful man." Jackie had a very faraway look in her eyes.

"Chile, you preachin' to da deacon board on dat one. Why you won't marry dat man?"

"Funny you should ask that question, Momma. I decided last night that if he doesn't ask me, I am going to ask him." Jackie's voice was just above a whisper.

"Now, ya know I don't have much good to say 'bout you modern-day womens, but baby, dat is the smartest thing you have said in a long time."

Cedes had spent hours on the phone with Charles. They talked way into the wee hours of Christmas Eve morning. Lately, they'd spent most of their free time talking on the phone or on the Internet to each other since his return to Seattle. She had not been so swept away with any man in her entire life. He was sweet, charming, intelligent, funny, and he insisted he was falling in love with her. But she had protested many times, telling him that she had done nothing to deserve his love, recalling a little something her mother had taught her about men when she was a teenager—"Talk is writing the check; action is cashing it."

But what had Charles said that had made her think she, too, was falling in love with him? Was it the dozen long-stemmed red roses that had arrived at her door two days after they had met? Was it apologizing for not being able to stay in town to get to know her better, or the promise to dedicate the entire month of January to making up for it? Was it the way he always made her laugh, no matter how bad she was feeling? Was it the passion he brought to life with a "Hello, my beautiful Nubian queen"?

She was tired and energized at the same time. She would get up, work out, and then check with everyone to see if they needed help to get prepared for the evening's festivities. As she threw the covers back, the phone rang. "Merry Christmas."

"My, my, aren't we filled with holiday cheer this morning!"

"Roland?"

"The one and only, my lovely Cedes. Did I wake you?"

"No, I was just about to go running. It is so beautiful out today.

I'm a little surprised to hear you at the other end of the phone though."

"Oh, see how you do a brotha?"

"Now seriously, Roland, when is the last time you dialed my number? And be honest. I know that's a stretch for you, but you can handle it."

"Oh, I'm crushed, attacking a man solely based on the bad reputation of his colleagues. I think I must hang up now. I am too distressed to continue."

"Oh, Negro, *paleeze*, save the drama." They both broke out into a chorus of laughter.

"I know, I know. I don't call and check on you like I should. Which is what I am doing right now. I just really want to make sure you're okay today. I know you're having a real rough time of it."

"Well, Ro, I am surprised, but I seem to be okay at the moment. I met a brotha a few days ago, and he has occupied a lot of my time—time I would have normally spent thinking about Momma. It's awfully sweet of you to check though. I am looking forward to tonight."

"You've met someone? Is it serious?"

"As serious as it can be with him in Seattle. He left the morning after we met, but we've spent a lot of time chatting on-line and on the phone getting to know each other. He seems really nice."

"Well, just be careful, Cedes. I care a lot about you, and I know you're really vulnerable at the moment."

"Roland, if I didn't know better, I would think you are jealous."

"And why is that so hard to imagine, Cedes?"

"I really don't understand what is so difficult for you to comprehend. I want a first-class seat to Dallas. I will not ride in coach. Are you telling me that there's not one first-class seat to Dallas today?" Catherine yelled as loudly as she possibly could at the travel agent.

"You obviously do not know who you are dealing with. Where

is your boss? I will have our account pulled from your agency and make sure that the owner knows you're the reason. Now, you find me a first-class seat and make sure I have all the things I requested upon my arrival at the Ritz-Carlton. Do you think you can handle that? I expect to hear from you within thirty minutes with everything I asked for."

Catherine slammed the phone down so hard that the picture of Ari and Lisa fell over. She couldn't believe how inefficient the stateside operation was. She would be sure to speak with headquarters when they returned from holiday in January. As she picked up the picture of the girls, she reflected on their striking resemblance to herself.

How dare Terry think that he can deny me custody of these darling girls? she thought. She had made a wonderful life for herself. She had a villa in the south of France and a condo in Spain and was looking seriously at a mansion in Jamaica. She could give them the world on a silver platter. Sure, she had not been there for them up until this point, but she was willing to make a few sacrifices now. *Terry seems to think he has the upper hand—the poor foolish man,* she thought. *He never has been able to compete with me—ever.*

Catherine would win the girls over. What young girl didn't like the things that money could buy? She needed the girls in her life now. Although it had not been clearly spoken, her behavior as a mother had come under question on more than one occasion with her employer. *The Spanish are so damned family oriented,* she thought. *Nothing is going to stand in the way of my presidency . . . especially not the sniveling Terry Winston.*

At Terry's, Christmas Eve day had dawned bright with crisp, clean air. But the clouds were rolling in, and the air was becoming polluted. The winds that brought this disparity blew straight from San Antonio.

Christmas Eve dinner promised to be quite interesting at the House of Winston.

1 7

IT WAS FINALLY here, Christmas Eve! Terry had waited a very long time for this day. Tonight he was going to propose marriage to Jacqueline Rogers. As he looked through his closet for the perfect suit to wear, he couldn't help but wonder if Catherine planned to ruin their perfect family celebration.

Roland had assured him that she would not accept the invitation to Christmas Eve dinner, but he had been wrong . . . very wrong. Now, not only was she coming for dinner, but she was staying in town for at least two days. *Oh my God, what damage could she do in that time?*

In the more than fifteen years he had known her, she had caused misery no matter where she happened to be. She never had a girlfriend for more than a few months, and he was the only man who had lasted more than six weeks. And it was no secret that he had been a fool. Why was she such an unhappy person? She was beautiful and brilliant. Well, at least she had physical beauty.

Nothing in his closet seemed right. *Oh no, I'm thinking like Jackie,* he thought, chuckling to himself. He finally settled on a black Brooks Brothers suit with an ultra-fine red pinstripe. Jackie's favorite. Veronica had given him a red silk Bachrach tie with black pinstripes and a matching pocket square for his birthday the year before, and the snow-white Destiny dress shirt brought the perfect I'm-gonna-ask-you-to-marry-me-tonight look all together. He was very pleased.

The house had been a beehive of activity all day. All the presents had been moved between the two houses, and a feast fit for royalty was prepared. All of the ladies were dressing. He could hear laughter from Veronica and his mother, and giggles from the girls' room.

The girls had protested that they were too old for the velvet and lace dresses he had picked out for them. They were also tired of dressing alike. They wanted totally different looks this year. After all, they were almost eleven, and they were each their own person.

With much debate and some embarrassment at the mall, he had given in to them. They each got a velvet skirt, one black, one burgundy, and matching lace blouses. Ari told him they needed training bras. Terry became light-headed, and he thought he was going to have to find a seat. There was no way his babies needed bras . . . training or otherwise. Besides, what did the bras train? And train to do what?

Jackie had called four times, each time saying that she had nothing to wear, and that she should have bought something new. He assured her that no matter what she wore, she would look stunning. She had asked the dreaded Do-I-look-like-I-have-gained-weight-to-you? question—the question to which any man will tell you there is *no* correct answer. But Terry simply replied, "Baby, if you have, I love every ounce of it, and damn, you wear it well."

She laughed and promised she would be there on time even if she were wearing a gunnysack. He laughed too and told her that if she wore the diamond heart pendant and earrings he had given her last Christmas, she would look like a Nubian queen in that sack.

He had not heard a word from Catherine since the phone call the day before. He really hoped she had changed her mind.

The day had been so perfect. The only contribution Catherine would make to this family celebration was tension. The doorbell chimed, and Terry's heart stopped.

"I'll get it," Ari sang out as she skipped to the door. Terry followed cautiously behind her. It would be like Catherine to arrive early.

"Hi, Miss Cedes! Are all of those presents for us?"

"Hello, my precious Ari. You are Ari, aren't you?"

"Yes, of course I am. You'll be able to tell us apart for sure tonight. We are dressing different, and our hair is different. And we got bras, Miss Cedes!"

Terry's eyes rolled in the back of his head.

"Well now, that *is* a cause for celebration. And not all of these are for you and Lisa, but a lot of them are and there are more in the car."

"Let me help you, Cedes. My goodness, you look like Ms. Kringle," Terry said, taking the packages and kissing her on the cheek.

"Thank you. There's a lot more in the car, and it's freezing out there this evening. It's going to be a cold night, perfect for Christmas Eve."

"I'll grab the rest of the stuff from the car. You come on in and make yourself comfortable. There's eggnog chilling in the punch bowl in the den. You look absolutely beautiful, Cedes. This vacation is working well for you. I'm so happy to see you smiling these days."

"Thank you, Terry. I am feeling better. The counseling is really helping, and with the love of my extended family I think I'm going to make it."

"As soon as I get these packages, I will finish dressing and join you," Terry added, going out for the rest of the gifts.

As Cedes stepped into the den, she felt like she was at home. Not because of the furnishings, but because of the ambiance. Everything was prepared with so much love and care. Her mother would have relished all this fuss for Christmas. She promised herself she was not going to cry, not even once, this evening.

She had promised Charles that if she felt like crying, she would call him. He was spending the evening with some friends. His big family celebration happened on Christmas day, during which they would listen to Christmas carols, watch *It's a Wonderful Life*, and get as drunk as possible. Terry joined her briefly to drop the presents under the tree. It took him four trips to get everything from the car.

"I'll place your bag in my room since you and Veronica are sleeping there tonight."

"Thanks, Terry. You know who called me today?"

"Roland."

"How did you know? Oh, what am I saying? I know you two tell each other when you spit."

"Not as much as you might think, but he did call me after he spoke to you."

"Is he staying over for the slumber part of the party?"

"Yes, he is. He wasn't sure at first, but apparently his plans for later fell through."

"Oh, and were his plans named Bambi?"

"Dang, gurl, draw in those claws." They both laughed, then Terry went to change. While he was gone Jackie, Momma C, and the twins arrived. Everyone looked beautiful.

While they waited in the den for Terry to return, the laughter was plentiful.

Meanwhile, Terry checked his reflection one last time. Then he pulled the velvet box from the top drawer, opened it, stared at it, took a deep breath and closed it, opened it again, then closed it, put it back in the drawer, and headed for the door.

He lost his nerve. As he stepped into the den, his entire family was there, except Roland. Some were drinking eggnog, others soft drinks or wine. It was a Norman Rockwell painting.

There before him stood Jackie, holding a glass of wine. She wore his favorite, a black dress that clung to her every voluptuous curve, and she wasn't wearing a jacket. *My God, she is breathtaking, and she is mine . . . All that woman is mine to love for all eternity.* Just as he was about to speak, the doorbell rang. Fear gripped Terry's very soul. It had to be Catherine. It was seven on the nose.

"I'll get it," he said, but Terry's voice was weaker than he had intended.

Much to his surprise, a chauffeur stood before him heavily laden with packages. "Good evening sir. Where may I place these packages?" the tall black man with the perfect posture asked in his British accent.

"In there, my good man," Terry jibed, smiling to himself, thinking how pretentious Roland could be. But this was not his usual chauffeur. Perhaps he was on vacation. He stood at the door and waited for Roland to appear, but saw no one.

As the chauffeur disappeared into the den, another limousine pulled in front of the house. *What is going on here?* he thought. It was beginning to look a lot like prom night. This time Roland stepped out of the chariot accompanied by his usual chauffeur, Paul.

The British chauffeur returned, removed his cap, and began to speak without looking directly at Terry. "Sir, Ms. Hawkins sends her regrets. She was unable to get a first-class seat on a flight this evening before midnight and will not be able to join you for dinner. She will call you on the twenty-sixth to make the necessary arrangements for a visit on that day. She will be checking into a suite at the Ritz-Carlton tomorrow." He had not looked at Terry once while speaking.

"Someone would think you livin' large when they pass this house, my brotha." Roland spoke taking the steps two at a time, then stopping in the doorway next to Catherine's chauffeur.

"Thank you and tell Ms. Hawkins she'll be missed this evening," Terry said, pressing a twenty-dollar bill in the chauffeur's hand.

"Roland!" Terry grabbed him and hugged him.

"Paul, place the gifts in the den and drop my bag here in the foyer. That will be all for this evening. No need to worry about picking me up tomorrow; I'm sure my boy here will get me home. And Merry Christmas, Paul."

"Very good, Mr. Carpenter, and Merry Christmas to you, too," Paul said and excused himself as he took the packages inside.

Catherine's chauffeur was out of earshot when Roland said, "What did I tell you? I knew she would not be here. What a crock. She couldn't get a first-class seat."

"I don't know or care why she isn't here. I'm just glad she ain't." Terry high-fived Roland and hugged him again.

"Everyone is in the den. Let's go celebrate some Christmas," Terry said patting Roland on the back; he was dressed in an Armani tuxedo with a red silk vest. *The brotha does know how to throw on his clothes,* Terry thought. When Roland stepped into the den and caught a glimpse of Cedes, he could not believe what he saw or felt. It was as if he were seeing her for the first time. She looked magnificent in a black, raw silk, floor-length dress. Perfectly accented by a single strand of matching pearls and earrings. What had he missed all the other times he had seen her? He truly planned to find out before dawn on Christmas morning.

"Excuse me for a moment. I forgot something in the bedroom," Terry said, almost skipping as he went back to his room.

He opened the drawer and without another thought, he slipped the black velvet box into his breast pocket. His nerve returned with him this time.

THERE COULD NOT have been a better celebration for Terry. As everyone laughed and partook of their favorite holiday beverage, the scene seemed like something from a movie. Jackie was far too beautiful to belong to him. He was not the one who got the decent and kind girls. Ari and Lisa, for the first time, no longer looked like his little girls. He now saw what they had been telling him all along. They were becoming young women.

His mother and his sister were very loving and supportive. Teresa and Veronica had been there for him and the girls from day one. Veronica would juggle baby-sitting, graduate school, and work while he got his degree. Teresa was there whenever Veronica couldn't be. She never let him forget how proud she was of him for taking his responsibility as a father so seriously.

Roland appeared to have it all—money, looks, prestige—but Terry knew that there was one very important thing missing . . . someone special to share it all with. Only Terry knew the true Roland and all the pain he had lived through.

Cedes, that was his gurl . . . She was funny, kind, Jackie's best friend and confidante, and she knew everything about everything that had to do with football.

Momma C was a kind and wonderful woman. Her down-home

personality made everyone love her. She never pretended to be anything she wasn't . . . she was Momma C. No one would ever guess that she was a very successful real estate mogul. She owned more than thirty pieces of property in the greater Dallas area. Terry wasn't sure how she negotiated such lucrative deals, but she had a skill that was envied by many in real estate.

Mikey and Ikey defied description. Their high energy and good nature always made being with them an adventure. It was no wonder they could fall asleep standing up—they literally ran everywhere they went. Although they were fraternal twins, their personalities were more identical than Ari's and Lisa's. Michelle was a carbon copy of Michael with long hair and earrings.

A gentle touch on his back brought a warm smile to his face. There was only one person who could warm him from the inside out.

"A dime for your thoughts," Jackie whispered in that voice that always made his manhood stir.

"A whole dime?"

"It's the holidays. I am feeling generous."

"Mmmm. Come here, you." Terry pulled her gently in front of him, holding her so close he could feel her breath on his face.

"You are so bad, Terry Winston, and I love it!" Jackie whispered as she gently kissed his lips.

"Just wait until I have you under that mistletoe."

"Enough of that, you two. Gonna make people think y'all in love or something," Roland chimed, walking toward them with a drink in his hand for Terry.

"Think he's a keeper, Roland?" Jackie's eyes never left Terry's.

"Yeah, I think he'll do in a pinch," Roland quipped. Turning his gaze toward Cedes he continued, "Damn, Cedes is beautiful tonight!"

"She *is* very striking in that dress." Jackie turned her attention to Roland as she continued, "Have you told her that?"

Looking a little perplexed, he hesitated momentarily. "You think I should?"

"Sometimes I swear you're too smooth for your own good.

Of course, you should tell her! There isn't a woman alive who doesn't want to hear a compliment, especially from a brotha with skills *and* benefits." The three of them began laughing just as Cedes joined the conversation.

"And just what is so funny?" Cedes's eyes always lit up when she smiled.

"Well, your sistah here was telling me how remiss I had been because I neglected to tell you how stunning you look this evening, Cedes."

"Why, Roland, thank you. You're looking pretty smashing yourself. I understand that part of the plan for this evening was for us to look like an item for Catherine's sake. Now that she's not coming, I guess that won't be necessary."

"Perhaps we can practice for the next opportunity?" Roland struck an Eddie-Murphy-in-*Boomerang* pose.

"Boy, Roland, that's twice today." Cedes blushed.

"Twice, what?" Terry shot a quick glance to Jackie with a Do-you-know-about-this? look.

"Well, there seems to be some competition in the camp. Cedes here appears to have a suitor." Roland stared into Cedes's eyes as he spoke.

"And?" Cedes now had that defensive sistah-gurl stance.

"Well, let's just say I may be seeing you in a new light, Cedes." Roland flashed her a million-dollar smile.

"What time are we going to eat, Mommy?" Michael asked as he patted Jackie's hip several times.

"In a few minutes, baby. Uncle Roland is about to make a very interesting revelation."

"Oh, I think it can wait until later. After all, we don't want to keep the little ones waiting for dinner," Roland interjected.

"Mikey, you and your sister wash your hands. We're going to eat in about ten minutes. Do you think you can wait that long?" Terry said, not about to let Roland off the hook that easily.

"Yeah, I think so. I'll just eat some more carrots," Michael said as he ran to tell Michelle that dinner was coming very soon.

"So now, Roland, you were saying?" Terry returned his attention to the adult conversation.

"This can wait."

"I don't think it should. Come on, Roland, we're all family. Let's hear it." Jackie spoke up this time.

"It's just that ever since Cedes and I had that misunderstanding and I helped her through her crisis, I've seen her differently. She's not as tough as I once believed, and she is by far one of the most beautiful women I have ever encountered." Roland looked away from Terry to Cedes as he continued. "She's warm and caring and could give a rat's ass about my success. She likes Roland for Roland. I've taken that for granted . . . and I shouldn't have. Now that she is interested in someone else, I guess I've had a wake-up call. I've been looking for someone special, when someone very special is right under my nose."

Everyone was silent.

Terry looked at Roland with pride for taking responsibility for his ineptitude and oversight in matters of the heart. Jackie stared at Terry as if to ask, Did you know anything about all of this? Cedes dropped her head as though she was embarrassed. Roland looked relieved.

"Dinner is served," Terry's housekeeper Carlotta announced, having generously volunteered to serve dinner for the annual event, a service for which she was being paid handsomely.

"Saved by the dinner bell." Cedes laughed nervously.

"But dinner will not last all night," Roland whispered.

The dining room was picturesque. The room was lit solely by candles. The fine china and crystal glistened. The food . . . oh, the food—roasted duck stuffed with mushrooms, turkey roasted to a perfect golden brown, ham, greens, candied yams, potato salad, macaroni and cheese, dressing, homemade rolls, and cranberry sauce—dressed the banquet table.

Everyone began taking their seats as though there was assigned seating. As Jackie headed for the seat next to the head of the table, where she assumed Terry would be seated, he took her by the arm. "I think you should sit at the other end of the table, opposite me."

Jackie gazed at him with a knowing smile and kissed him lightly.

Roland pulled out Cedes's chair, then Veronica's, and seated himself between them. Ari and Lisa sat on either side of their dad. Teresa sat next to Ariana. Momma C sat on Jackie's right. Mikey and Ikey sat to the right of their grandmother. The chair next to Alisa was empty. It had been reserved for Catherine.

Terry explained to everyone that Catherine couldn't make it and would be in touch the day after Christmas. Lisa looked disappointed, and Ari had no reaction at all. He had forgotten to tell Carlotta. "Momma C, would you bless the table?" Terry asked as he took Ari's and Alisa's hands. Lisa couldn't reach Michelle's hand. Seeing this, Momma C stood and everyone followed suit.

"Dear Fatha, owah Lord, owah God. We thanks you as we come togetha to celebrate dat you gave yo' only Son to dis here wicked world so dat we can spen' all eternity wit chu. Fatha, we ax dat you bless everyone here, especially dese babies. Bless da food fo' the nourushmen' of owah bodies. Amen."

And they all sang in unison, "Amen."

THE CHATTER WAS as plentiful as the food. Every dish expressed the love that went into preparing it. As Carlotta cleared the dishes away from the table, everyone commented on how full they were and how there was no possible way they could have dessert.

"Well, b'fo' we move this party back to da den, I wants to go 'round dis here table and I wants everyone to say just one thing they is grateful fo'," Momma C said with authority. "And since it was mah idear, I will start.

"I'm grateful that mah fam'ly has grown and now includes da Winstons. Y'all is good people and I just wants to thank Terry and mah Jackie here for bringing us togetha'. Ari and Lisa, babies, I know y'all hurt and disappointed 'bout yo' momma not comin', but we is yo' fam'ly and I couldn't love you any mo' than I loves mah own grandchirren."

"I'll go next," Jackie declared. "I am grateful for so much—two healthy and happy children, and for a mother that wins my vote for mother of the year, every year! For giving me a sister that loves and supports me in everything I do. I'm truly thankful I've found a man who loves me as much as I love him. One who wants me to grow and to succeed and be everything I can be. One that fills my needs on all levels. A man that is 'all that' and a Craftsman tool set!" Jackie blew him a kiss.

"I want to do it, I want to do it!" Michael surprised everyone by raising his hand. "I thank Jesus because Terry takes me to my Cub Scouts meetings, and I'm not like the other little boys who don't have a dad." Terry smiled broadly.

Michelle spoke up this time. "My turn. I am thankful for two big sisters and that I am the only one who can really tell them apart. I am glad we are having Christmas all together this year."

"Me too, baby, me too," Momma C whispered more to herself than to anyone else.

Roland sighed, then took time to speak. "When I met Terry in college, we hit it off immediately. He was a true friend, one who helped me through a lot of emotional baggage from my child-hood. Now that I know Mrs. Winston and Veronica, I know why he's such a good brotha. I want to thank all of you for em-bracing me since the first Thanksgiving I came home with Terry because anything was better than being with those dysfunctional people who called themselves my family. I have to agree with Momma C. Thank you, Terry and Jackie, for bringing two wonderful families together." Roland's voice cracked as he trailed off.

Cedes touched Roland's hand gently as she began to speak. "Where do I begin? I am grateful for so much. My gurl, Jackie, whom I have known all my life and I truly consider my sis-ter. Momma C for all of her love and support. I know you've been hurting as badly as I have since Mother died, but you have been there for me every step of the way, going so far as to insist I get some professional help. Terry is a wonderful man, I want one just like him of my very own. All these precious children—if I never have any of my own, I am truly blessed to have them in my life. I thank God for the talent he has given me and the opportu-nity to do what I truly love. I also thank Him that I am gathered here with the people I love most in this world." Cedes couldn't continue. Roland placed his arm around her and pulled her close.

"I want to go next." Alisa spoke softer than she normally did. "I'm thankful for my dad. He loves us, and we never have to guess about it. He always puts us first. Until he met Miss Jackie, he never even dated because of us. I never want to leave him, not ever, and no one can make me."

"I agree with her, Daddy. No one is going to make us live somewhere else, not even sometimes. I wish Catherine was here so I could tell her that I am thankful for my dad, not her. I am thankful for Miss Jackie and Momma C. But I will. I promise I will," Ari said with defiance.

Ari and Lisa hugged each other and held hands as Veronica started to speak. "Lord, I am thankful for so much. For my mother, who raised us to strive for what we want and never stop short of it. For a brother who would give anyone the shirt off his back. For the good friends that have come into my life. For a wonderful career, and that I don't owe American Express a dime as a result of this Christmas!" For the first time since the "I am thankful for" session had started, all of the adults laughed full-heartedly.

"Well, you all have said so much of what I am feeling," Teresa began. "Like Clara, I couldn't love Mikey and Ikey any more if they were *my* grandchildren. I am thankful that Terry has chosen a good woman, one who will not use and abuse him. For my daughter and her adventuresome spirit, I am grateful for how God protects her when she is who-knows-where in this world, taking pictures. He always brings her back to Dallas unharmed. I thank God for the love that is in this room. For all of our children being good, responsible adults with morals. I thank God for how He has blessed this ole almost-sixty-year-old body to still do what I want it to do on most occasions. I love you all."

"I guess that leaves me." Terry rose as he began to speak.

Carlotta appeared—almost magically—with two champagne buckets.

"You all have said so many wonderful and meaningful things here tonight. Momma, I want to thank you for raising me right. You taught me how to be a man, how to love and respect a woman," Terry said. "And Veronica, you have *always* been there. You even taught me how to comb the girls' hair. Baby-sitting for free while I got my degree. I could never thank you enough for giving up so much of your life for my children." He looked at Momma C with loving eyes, then said, "Momma C, you are a special woman. You have raised an extraordinary daughter, one who I am proud to say I love. You have been like a second mother to me since that first day in the kitchen four years ago. I thank you." Then his gaze went to Cedes and with a warm smile he began. "Cedes, you have come to be like a sister. Just as happy, helpful, cranky, loving, pushy, and special as Veronica." He turned to Jackie's twins: "Michael, I am proud to call you my son. You are so special and for as long as you want me to be your dad, I will be. And Michelle, you are the baby girl. Just as beautiful and precious as your mother. I love both of you." For a long moment, his gaze stayed with Roland. Easily, he stated, "Roland, brother, and I mean that in every since of the word, I could never give you all that you have given me. When I look up 'friend' in the dictionary I see your picture. I was truly blessed that day in the registration hall." Then to his lovely daughters, he spoke words that lay deep in his heart. "Ari and Lisa, I am the one who feels blessed to have two such beautiful young ladies in my life. You have never ceased to amaze me throughout the years. Since the day you came home from the hospital, you have filled my life with joy and happiness." Terry paused, "And now to the love of my life."

Terry moved to the opposite end of the table to Jackie. "I have no idea what I did to deserve a loving, intelligent, generous, warm, beautiful, sexy woman like you. All I know is that God has seen fit to shine His glory through you into my life. I would have never guessed a man could be this happy."

Then he knelt before Jackie and took her hands into his. "My life with you is wonderful. You complete me. You are the whipped cream to my strawberries, the popcorn to my movies, the peanut butter to my jelly, the Tom to my Jerry, modem to my computer."

Jackie laughed through her impending tears. "Modem to your computer?"

"Okay, the activator to my Jheri Curl."

Now everyone laughed. "But I think you get the point of what I am saying. My life is almost complete, but there's only one thing missing, and that is . . . you . . . as my wife. Make me the happiest man on planet Earth and tell me you'll spend the rest of your life with me."

The air was thick with quiet anticipation, and then Momma C piped up with the words everyone was thinking: "Oh mah God, chile, say *yes!*" then placed her hand over her mouth.

Without any further hesitation Jackie answered quietly, "Yes, Terry, I'll spend the rest of my life with you . . . as your wife."

Jackie leaned into Terry's arms as everyone laughed and applauded. He pulled her up as he stood and reached into his breast pocket. "Since you have consented to be my wife, I would like to present you with the first of many gifts to be bestowed upon you this Christmas." Terry opened the black velvet box.

Jackie gasped audibly. "Oh my God . . . Terry, this is magnificent."

"I love you, Jackie," he said as he slipped the ring on her hand.

Roland popped the cork on the Dom Pérignon.

GURLLLLLLLLLLLLL! GO ON, Ms. Prudential!" Ve-
ronica high-fived Cedes, and then they both hugged Jackie at the
same time.

Jackie, still with tears in her eyes, looked at Terry as she began
speaking. "Oh my God, I cannot believe the size of this ring."

"Ladies . . ." Roland offered Veronica and Cedes a glass of
champagne. "My man did aiight, didn't he?"

"I'll say!" Cedes said, flashing her stellar smile. "I knew he
loved my sister, but dayummmm!"

"Let me see it on your lovely hand, Jackie." Roland stared at
her hand before he leaned over to kiss it. "I've known Terry for a
lot of years, and I assure you, you've changed his life for the better. There's no diamond big enough to express how that man feels
about you."

"But it is a hell of a start!" Veronica interjected, and they all
laughed.

"Does this mean you're going to be our mother, Miss Jackie?"
Ari had entered their circle unnoticed.

"Oh, Ari, I'll do everything within my power to be all a mother
can be to you. I love you and Lisa so much."

"We love you, too, Miss Jackie." Ari stepped to Jackie and hugged her very tightly.

Roland, Veronica, and Cedes left them alone for what would be the first of many mother-daughter moments. "You know I'll never try to replace Catherine," Jackie began, "but I will love and respect you and Lisa. I will always be there to listen, encourage, and sometimes discipline. Just as I am for Mikey and Ikey. Your acceptance of me as your dad's wife is very important."

Ari threw her arms around Jackie and simply said, "I love you, Mom."

"Lawdhamurcy, mah baby gots herself a rock. I knows Terry loves mah chile. Umph, umph, umph, I wish mah Willie was here. He would be mighty content to see owah baby dis happy. Terry is a good man. Teresa, you done raised him the right way. Mah God is good all the time. He done blessed me here on the eve of His Son's birthday." Momma C and Teresa Winston embraced as the joint matriarchs of this clan.

"I say we take this party back to the den. We got some carols to sing!" Terry almost sang as he talked. There was no doubt he was the happiest man on Earth, perhaps in the universe.

"I think that is a wonderful idea. That's where the mistletoe is hanging, isn't it?" Roland stared at Cedes. She lowered her head in embarrassment to break eye contact.

"Gurl, don't be acting all shy with Roland! You've wanted him to notice you since Skippy was a pup, and now he is. You betta recognize!" Jackie whispered through her laughter.

"Shhhhh, he may hear you, gurl!"

"And your point? Somebody gotta get you two buppies together 'cause Lord knows y'all ain't gonna make a move on your own. Though I gotta give it to the brotha. He's on his game tonight. Is he wearing that tuxedo or what?"

"Yeah, Lawd!" They high-fived as they laughed.

For more than three hours they all sang along with all their favorite Christmas songs. Champagne flowed endlessly, but the euphoria was not alcohol induced.

"Well, I think it's time for you kids to get ready for bed," Terry announced as Mikey and Ikey settled down.

"I thought we were going to open a gift before we went to bed, Daddy?" Lisa was working her best Daddy's-little-girl routine.

"Of course you can, princess, but let's get into your PJs. We'll sing 'Silent Night,' and then we each can pick one gift."

"Can I call you Daddy, too?" Michael looked up at Terry with Jackie's warm brown eyes.

Terry picked Michael up into his arms. "You can call me whatever you like Michael, but I would really like Daddy the most."

"Good!" Michael leapt out of his arms and ran to change into his pajamas.

Terry felt there was no present under the tree that could possibly come close to all that been given to him tonight. God had truly been good to him. He knew without a shadow of a doubt he was doing the right thing. He had prayed in earnest and had waited on the Lord to answer him. The Lord had given him far more than he would have ever asked for.

"I'm really glad you talked me into doing this, man. I wouldn't have missed this evening for anything. I gotta tell you one more time, you are one lucky hombre. Jackie is *all that*! You know, Cedes is really something else. She's wearing that dress—or better yet that dress is wearing her." Roland looked at Cedes as the ladies sipped champagne and talked about Jackie's ring for the nine-hundredth time that evening.

"I am glad you decided to stay, too. It's been a wonderful evening, hasn't it? And it is only going to get better. Wait until the kids go to bed. I think that Mom and Momma C will be close behind them. It will be time to get some Christmas romance jumping off."

"Brotha, don't you know romance has no clock? It's been romantic since the moment I walked in here and saw Cedes. Where is Veronica's flame du jour?"

"Look where you standing with yo' foine self. Come here and kiss me." Veronica was definitely feeling the effects of the champagne she had been drinking like it was 7UP. "And he will be here when he gets off work. He's out there making the streets of Dallas safe."

"Come here, sis, and let me plant one on ya." Terry opened his arms to Veronica.

"Not you, fool. I meant Roland." Veronica took another sip of champagne.

"Oh, that is so cold, sis."

"Now I ask you . . . You under the mistletoe with me and some foine sistah, who you gonna wanna kiss?" Veronica's speech was slurred.

Roland was very amused. He knew that Veronica thought of him as her brother and that it was definitely the Dom doing the talking. "Come here and let me lay one on ya, Veronica. Now, you think you can handle *all this?*" Roland quipped.

"Are chitlins high in cholesterol? Does Don King need a mirror? Does O.J. need to find hisself a good sistah?"

"Come here, gurl, you are a mess." Roland hugged and kissed her, as his eyes fell on Cedes once again.

The children returned with much noise and activity, and the family gathered around the tree. There were so many gifts, they couldn't get within four feet of it. Everyone chose one gift and opened it.

"Can we sing 'Silent Night' now?" Michelle rubbed her hazel eyes, one of the few features she hadn't inherited from Jackie.

"Of course we can. Come here, sweetheart," Terry said as she climbed onto his lap and laid her head on his chest.

Everyone gathered in close. Terry slipped his free arm around Jackie's waist. Momma C picked up Michael. Teresa put her arm around Ari. Lisa hugged Veronica around her waist. Roland embraced Cedes from behind, and she let herself relax against his strong body.

"Silent Night" filled the air.

2 1

W ITH ALMOST NO encouragement, the children went off to bed. Ikey and Mikey were afraid that Santa would be confused and not know that they were at someone else's home. Lisa took on the role of comforter as she assured them that Santa could be everywhere and of course he knew everything. This eased their anxiety.

"I was really sincere when I told you how lovely you look this evening. Will you forgive an otherwise intelligent man for his lack of social skills?" Roland stood very close to Cedes as he spoke.

"Now, Roland, you and I both know that you lack no social skills, but thank you very much for the compliment. I must tell you, you're sharper than Uncle Harvey was when Momma died yo' damn self. There's no wonder a sistah has to take a number to get on your dance card."

"Are you asking me to dance?"

After a long pause, Cedes admitted quietly, "Yes."

"Maestro, if you please . . ." They both smiled.

"Well, I'm glad you two have finally come out of your respective corners. Y'all was wearing me out. A woman is not supposed to have to work this hard on the night she gets engaged," Jackie teased.

"How about another round of champagne?" Terry said as he uncorked another bottle of the bubbly stuff.

Veronica already had her glass in the air when she slurred. "I wanna propose a toast." "Toast" had three syllables.

"Go right ahead, Ms. Toastmaster," Terry said as he filled her glass.

"To my new sistah-in-law. Welcome to da Winston fam'ly. We be so proud to have ya."

"Here, here!" Roland added. He made a mental note to talk to Terry about how much Veronica had been drinking since she returned home.

"Now, sistah-gurl, can I borrow them twins and go out in a rainstorm to catch me a brotha as wonderful as Terry?"

"I know that is *correct*, Vee!" Cedes, too, was beginning to feel the effects of the champagne.

"Cedes, you don't have to look too far, ya know." Roland's smile was quite warm and even more sincere.

"We'll be back in a few minutes." No one was listening when Terry grabbed Jackie by the hand and disappeared.

"Roland, are you trying to mack me?"

"No, Cedes, for the first time in longer than I care to admit, I am being sincere."

"Well, I'm sure Mr. Pérignon is helping you with that sincerity."

"I guess I'll just have to prove it to you now, won't I?"

"And just how do you propose to do that?"

"I have a side you have never seen. Hell, I ain't seen it in a long time mah self. But I assure you it *is* there."

"And to what do I owe this unveiling?"

"Let's just say the espresso is brewing and my senses are finally alive."

"You know I just started seeing someone in the past couple of weeks?"

"With all due respect to the brotha . . . and please tell me it *is* a brotha . . . he betta come correct or stay at home."

"Ahhhh, suki, suki now! That sounds like a love challenge to me!" Veronica poured her own champagne this time.

"Did I hear 'love challenge'?" Jackie held Terry's hand as they returned to the room.

"Where y'all been? Trying to get an 'engagement slash Christmas Eve slash they too drunk to miss us' piece in the pantry?" Veronica was on a roll.

Everyone laughed hysterically.

"Gurl, let me see if your dress is on like it was earlier." Cedes laughed as she inspected her best friend's appearance.

"Y'all need to quit. We were just in saying good night to our children . . . something y'all single-may-never-have-a-child-if-you-don't-date-someone-more-than-three-days buppies wouldn't understand."

"Now honey, that's not true. Roland once dated a woman for a whole week."

"Damn, bruh, that's cold."

"But true."

As the clock struck midnight, the five of them laughed their way into Christmas. The chorus played by this quintet of friends was far more melodic than anything that came from the state-of-the-art sound system. "What are you doing over there, Veronica?"

"Mind ya bidness, Terry, I got this!" "Electric Boogie" filled the air.

"Oh *wow*!"

With that the women simultaneously kicked off their shoes and formed a line. Roland and Terry shrugged their shoulders in an oh-what-the-hell manner and fell into step. Mr. Pérignon had stolen most of their coordination, and no one was in step, which made the sight quite comedic.

The dancing went on for more than an hour before Veronica said that was all she could handle. She was going to bed since, obviously, Mr. Policeman was not going to show up *again*. She grabbed a half bottle of champagne in one hand and her Stuart

Weitzman shoes in the other, and kissed them each good night, lingering a long time with Jackie. "I do love you, sis, but most of all I love how happy you've made my favorite brother."

"I am your *only* brother!"

"So then you gots to be mah favorite, now don't cha!"

"Good night, Veronica." Terry kissed her once again.

The men had lost their jackets halfway through the first rendition of "Electric Boogie," and the shoes had come off somewhere between "Down Home Blues" and "Sexual Healing." The effects of the champagne and the flavor of the season had descended on the four of them like a homemade quilt on a cold night as they gathered in front of the fireplace. Soft Christmas music had replaced the dance tunes that had had them breaking a sweat earlier.

Jackie and Terry settled on the love seat. She leaned in and kissed him softly on the lips, mouthing the words "I love you." He responded with a long and passionate kiss.

Roland positioned himself in the corner of the plush sofa. Cedes slipped under his arm as though it was where she belonged. "I have no way of knowing what dawn will bring, but as for me and mine . . . we are truly blessed," he said, cuddling even closer.

"Amen, mah brotha, amen," Cedes echoed, and Roland lightly kissed Cedes on her forehead.

Merry Christmas and good night.

Mommy, mommy, santa came, Santa came!" Mikey and Ikey screamed into the den with the intensity of a fire engine on a 911 call.

"Merry Christmas, my babies! Yes, he did! Did you wake Ari and Lisa and Auntie Veronica?" Jackie felt as if she had just fallen asleep.

"Oh my God, it can't be morning." Cedes wasn't sure where she was until she felt Roland's warmth next to her. Despite herself, a smile crept across her face.

"Dis is da day dat da Lord has made. Let's rejoice and be glad in it!" Momma C came in fully clothed with Teresa following close behind.

"Merry Christmas. Y'all didn't go to bed?" Teresa greeted them each with a kiss. "And where is your sister?"

"She went up about three, but she took a bottle of champagne with her, so we may need to get a crane to get her out of bed." Terry was stretching awake.

"Wake up, man. If I'm up, every able body in the house gotta be up." Terry threw a pillow at Roland's head.

"Don't wake me now! I'm dreaming I have the lovely Cedes in my arms." Roland sighed with his eyes shut.

Both sets of twins returned, and all attention was focused on the major commotion. Even the normally reserved Ari was excited by the prospect of what the array of packages held for her.

"Merry Christmas!" Ari and Lisa sang together as they kissed Terry on both cheeks.

"May I have the honor of playing Santa's helper this year?" Cedes was the only one that was up and moving.

"Miss Cedes, you can't be Santa's helper! Santa's helpers are little men in tights and funny shoes with turned-up toes," Michelle admonished while jumping up and down.

"Is it okay if I pretend?" Cedes smiled to herself.

Michael and Michelle looked to Alisa for guidance before answering. Alisa smiled and nodded in approval.

"Okay! Can Uncle Roland be Santa's helper, too? There are so many presents it will take too long with only one helper," Michael said, practically yelling.

"Now he sounds like a man with a plan," Roland said looking at his diamond-studded Swiss watch. "Oh my God, it is four-forty-three. Please tell me we have slept into the afternoon."

"Welcome to my world, man. Welcome to my world," Terry said, finally wide awake.

Roland and Cedes distributed brightly colored packages in all shapes and sizes until there was not a spot left uncovered by ribbons and paper and packages on the rich milk-chocolate brown carpet.

Momma C's eyes filled with tears as she opened the gift from Cedes. She did so miss her best friend. It was a leather, hand-bound Bible with a gold inscription: "To Momma C with love." When she pulled out the Bible, an envelope fell to the floor. Inside was a round-trip, first-class airline ticket to the Holy Land.

"Mah God, baby, this is a won'ful gif'!" Momma C was so stunned, she didn't realize Cedes had not heard her.

"Let me see, Clara." Teresa took the Bible from her with the envelope.

"Oh my God!" Teresa gasped. The outburst got the attention of even Mikey and Ikey.

"What's wrong, Momma?" Terry said, moving toward her quickly.

"Look at what Cedes got for Clara. A tour to the Holy Land." Teresa's eyes, too, had filled with tears.

"What a wonderful gift, Cedes!" Jackie gushed, genuinely thrilled for her mother.

"Oh, please don't make all this fuss. It's just something I knew Momma C would enjoy. Momma wanted to go next year and take Momma C with her. I really hope you go and take Momma in spirit." Cedes's voice began to crack.

"What you say we start to clean up this mess, Ms. Santa's helper." Roland stepped in to short-circuit the inevitable shower of tears.

"Clean up?" Cedes was half laughing through her tears.

"Yes, Ms. NFL, you know, picking up of said trash, putting it into said trash bags. I am sure you have heard of it at some time in your not-so-distant past." Roland had moved very close to her and was staring down at her beautiful deep brown face.

"Oh, what a smart a— butt you are. Mister got a chauffeur, housekeeper, cook, and Lord only knows who else working at Chez Carpenter." Cedes laughed wholeheartedly now and pretended to hit Roland.

"But I still know what the phrase 'clean up' means, my woman of the new millennium." Roland picked her several inches off the floor by her waist. Their faces were inches apart. Cedes, for the first time, really wanted to kiss him. She wanted to lose herself in his embrace.

"Y'all can't be doing that if you not under the mistletoes!" Mikey rolled his fire truck across the floor as he chastised them.

"Yes sir," Roland said as he let Cedes slip from his grasp, never taking his eyes from hers.

"Well, let's all get busy and clean up this mess and maybe we can get Grandma C and Grandma Teresa to make us a traditional Christmas breakfast," Jackie encouraged the twins.

"What is 'traditssal'?" Michelle said in her sweet but high-pitched voice.

"It's 'traditional,' honey. And it means that we have done it many times before," Jackie explained.

"So, Momma, what do you say? We have all the fixings in there for that killer breakfast." Terry turned on that boyish charm that used to get him his way when he was younger.

"How can a mother resist these big baby browns?" Teresa laughed now. "Clara, would you do me the honor of joining me in the kitchen, and we can talk about how shamelessly these children of ours spend money."

"Now dat's da truf. But they sho' mus' love us a whole lot, chile." Momma C was looking at the mother's ring Jackie had given her, which had the birthstones of her, Jackie, both sets of twins, and Terry surrounded by diamonds.

"Gurl, I know what you mean." The two matriarchs laughed as they hugged each other and compared rings. Teresa, too, had received the same ring, except her garnet birthstone replaced Momma C's aquamarine.

"Let's go make these babies some breakfast. Lord knows they're probably tired of oatmeal and bagels." Teresa grabbed Momma C's arm and marched her into the kitchen, both women laughing hysterically.

"Mommy, can we go outside and ride our bikes?" Mikey was jumping as though he was on a pogo stick.

"Michael, it is six-thirty in the morning. No, you may not ride your bike."

"Mommy said we can't." His comment was directed more at himself than at Michelle.

"How about we play a game until it is time to go outside, Mikey?" Ari was always the big sister.

This was the Christmas for jewelry it seemed—rings for all the moms and watches for Veronica and Cedes. Terry had given Veronica a Movado watch, and Roland had given Cedes the exact same one. Neither man had known about the other's purchase. They were indeed brothers.

Lisa and Ari had both been excited by their in-line skates, their Air Jordans, their own personal—but distinctively different—

fragrances, tons of sweaters, jeans, jackets, coats, hats, gloves, scarves. But the gift that made them happiest was their own phone line, which had been installed two weeks before, while they were in school. They already began to argue about who would talk when.

The boxes that had been deposited under the tree by Catherine's chauffeur were filled with designer items from Coach, backpacks to matching Donna Karan business suits, which were in the wrong size. The items had impressed Jackie, Cedes, and Veronica far more than Ari and Lisa.

Terry was stunned by Catherine's feeble effort to impress Ari and Lisa. But, then again, perhaps this vulgar display of fiscal frivolity was directed at him. Why would someone spend nearly nine hundred dollars on a backpack for a ten-year-old, no, make that two ten-year-olds? Better yet, why would someone spend that kind of money for a purse that you wear on your back regardless of their age?

Jackie had witnessed the pain she saw on Terry's face before. She moved to his side and rubbed his back between his shoulder blades. Her touch helped to relax him.

"You have been so generous, Roland. Thank you," Cedes said as she admired her wrist.

"It was a pleasure to purchase such a fine piece of man's workmanship for one of God's most magnificent creations."

"Oh, *paleeze*. You can take the player out of the club, but you can't take the club out of the player."

"I swear, Cedes, it is not a line. Many times we sail oceans looking for treasure that's already in our own backyard. I sincerely care a lot about you and not like the buddy you think I am. But I don't want to tell you how I plan to win you over; I want to show you. I think you women call it walkin' the walk versus talkin' the talk."

"But Roland," she began, "I am not for sale. I love this watch. It's gorgeous, but I can buy it myself. A watch is not what I need from you."

"Why are you sistahs so defensive? All I want to do is prove to you that I'm not playing you. I adore you and always have. I just never knew how much until I saw you in pain that day."

"What do you mean 'you sistahs'? This is Mercedes, not a sisterhood, talking. I really don't know what you mean by defensive. I just know what I need, and an expensive watch is *not* it."

"So then tell me, Mercedes. What do you need?"

"Someone who will understand when I say I need to be alone because I have some things to work out and not freak out thinking it is a football player I'm working out. Someone who is not intimidated by my strength and my ability to make things happen. Someone who can hug me and make me forget what I buried when I buried my mother. Someone who can look at me and make me know if he can't make it alright, he will die trying."

"That sounds like what I want to offer you, but again, I can *say* anything. After all, I'm the best lawyer in these here parts. But I am asking that you just give me half a chance, Cedes, to show you."

All of her anger faded and she smiled. "You are too much, Roland."

"Too much for one woman, but not enough for two?"

"Johnny Taylor?"

"I am not sure, but it's from one of those songs we danced to last night . . . so I guess I'm busted. But nonetheless sincere." With that, Roland took Cedes in his arms and kissed her the way he had wanted to do since the moment he saw her standing near the Christmas tree when he arrived. But this was so much better. She wore no makeup, her hair was less than perfect, but she never looked better to him.

"Whoa. Is there mistletoe over your heads? Or is being in the general vicinity enough?" Veronica teased them. Everyone laughed.

The smells coming from the kitchen were divine. Christmas music played softly in the background but was hardly audible over Mikey and Ikey. The sun had risen brightly and powerfully to echo that the Lord God had truly made this day.

The door chime startled everyone. Who could be making a

visit at seven-thirty on Christmas morning? *Perhaps Catherine was sending ponies this time,* Terry thought as he headed for the door. With Mikey and Ikey in tow, he opened the door without checking to see who it was. His warm smile vanished when he was greeted by a fully minked Catherine. "Merry Christmas, Terry," she barked. "And who are these urchins?"

All of a sudden Christmas Day seemed like Halloween.

WELL, ARE YOU going to ask me in, or do I have to stand out here in the cold?" Catherine's words pierced Terry's shock-induced wide-eyed coma.

"What are you doing here at this hour of the morning?" Terry managed.

"Is that any kind of a greeting for the mother of your children? Speaking of which, who are these two? Doing a little charity work this year?" Catherine pointed her leather-gloved finger in the direction of Michael and Michelle.

"Why are you here, Catherine, with your mean-spirited self? This is our Christmas morning. Your messenger told us that you would be here tomorrow because you couldn't get a flight last night."

"Well, I got the earliest available first-class seat this morning, and you know that Dallas is just a hop, skip, and jump from San Antonio. So here I am. Again, do I have to conduct this entire conversation on the porch?"

"Come on in, I guess." Terry stepped aside reluctantly.

"Oh, how quaint. I like what you have done with the place. You must have had one of your gay decorator friends come in and give you some tips," Catherine said as she removed her gloves and eyed the house.

"Catherine, I don't understand why you are intruding on our Christmas morning celebration. We are not moving one step until you explain your actions. Why are you here?" Terry's stance was defensive.

"Well, I really wanted to see my babies on Christmas. I have been missing them so. I was hoping to get here before they opened the gifts I sent them. They are so precious to me."

"So precious that you couldn't fly coach to get here as promised?" Terry spewed.

"You obviously haven't flown first class. But on your meager salary, how could you?" she chided.

"So are these the children of that Jackie woman? Alisa told me all about Jackie and her crumb snatchers. How nice, you all together on Christmas morning. I'm sure her children appreciate having a father figure around."

"My children certainly appreciate having Jackie as a mother figure. Yes, this is Michael and Michelle. Say hello to the *nice* lady."

"Hi, nice lady. Terry is going to be my daddy!" Michael was his normal animated self.

"Oh really?" Catherine was not so shocked as amused. "That *is* very nice."

Michelle stared at the very tall woman who wore a hat and coat that reminded her of Lady, their cocker spaniel. "Hi, nice lady. My mommy says that people shouldn't wear clothes that animals had to die for."

"Well, little one, people who say that normally can't afford to buy anything that an animal was willing to lay down its life for." Catherine bent down so that she could whisper.

As Jackie rounded the corner from the guest bathroom, she stopped abruptly. The sight of Catherine caused the blood to rush to her face.

"Mommy, say hi to the nice lady," Michelle said innocently.

"Honey, this is Catherine." Terry could read Jackie's expression as if it were the headline of the Dallas *Herald.*

"You must be Jacqueline. Alisa has told me so much about you. It is a pleasure to meet you finally. You know I had a weight problem until I hired a personal trainer and a nutritionist. It is quite expensive, but there is no price that can be put on one's appearance." Catherine extended her hand to Jackie.

Jackie couldn't believe that Catherine could be so insensitive. Who did she think she was, coming into her man's house and insulting his woman? "Hello, Catherine. At last we meet."

"Catherine, Jackie is absolutely gorgeous just the way she is. I would not want her to change a thing." Terry made his annoyance obvious.

"I was only trying to share a tip with her, Terrence. No need to get hostile with me."

"Come and see all of the stuff Santa gave us." Michelle grabbed her hand and tugged Catherine in the direction of the den before Terry could stop her.

The den was filled with laughter and chatter. Silence descended on the room like a rainstorm on a parade. Michelle dragged the stranger to the center of the room as each adult turned their attention one by one to Catherine. David Copperfield couldn't have made their smiles disappear any faster.

"Well, well, well, this is even more picturesque than I imagined. Merry Christmas to you all. I'm sorry to intrude on this wonderful celebration. But I just had to stop by to wish my wonderful daughters a Merry Christmas. It has been so long since I saw them, I am just heartsick about it." Catherine acted as though she was genuinely choked up. *Who is this woman, and what did she do with Catherine between the front door and the den?* Terry wondered.

The adults looked from one to the other. "Terry, don't be rude. Please introduce me to all of these people celebrating with my children." Before Terry could open his mouth, Catherine extended her hand to Cedes.

"I am Ariana and Alisa's mother, Catherine—Catherine Marie Hawkins." It seemed as though she was waiting for applause or some sort of other accolade.

Her eyes fell on Roland. "As always, it is good to see you, Roland. Is this the flavor of the day?" Catherine gestured toward Cedes.

Cedes opened her mouth to accost Catherine, but Roland jerked her arm and smiled. Cedes recognized his authoritative manner and backed down, much to her own displeasure.

"Catherine, nice to see you again." Roland nodded slightly at Catherine and quickly glanced at Cedes. She had caught his inference immediately. He was very pleased.

"I know you did not stay out all night and leave my precious babies here alone on Christmas Eve, Terry. You're all still dressed from the party you attended last night?" Catherine's tone dripped in sarcasm.

"Catherine, I refuse to allow you to upset me this morning. You know that is absurd. This is my fiancée's mother, Momma C. That is Cedes, Jackie's sister. Of course you know my mother, Veronica, and Roland." Terry struggled to maintain his composure.

"Oh how charming. Just one big happy family. I am not comfortable calling anyone Momma except my own . . . What shall I call you?"

"You don't haf to call me nuthin' at all. And I does piddy da woman you calls Momma. I'mma pray for dat poor thang . . . She just don't know what it be like to have a decent chile."

"I'm sorry. Did I do something to offend you, Mrs.—I'm sorry, what did you say your name is?"

"Mah name is Clara." Momma C could feel her blood pressure rising.

"Well, Miss Clara, very nice to meet you. You must be from the rural South?"

"My mother is from right here in Dallas, Catherine." Jackie wasn't sure how much longer she could remain calm.

"Cedes, no family resemblance. Different fathers?"

"You bitch!" Roland had to leap forward to restrain Cedes as she moved toward Catherine.

"Oh my, you must be from West Dallas!" Catherine grabbed her throat in her best soap opera princess pose.

"Teresa, how have you been? Found a new husband? Poor Terry grew up without his father. He left you for a neighbor, if I remember correctly. Such a shame you couldn't find a man who wanted a ready-made family the way Jackie here did. Let's just hope you will find someone in your old age."

"Actually, Catherine, I am quite happy with the way my life turned out. And I couldn't ask for a better son than Terry. I understand you're still single," Teresa said, as she thought, *No one wants your evil ass and you will die a lonely old woman.*

"Veronica, I see you still enjoy the spirits a little more than you should, just like back in college. A little hung over, are we?" Catherine was relentless.

Teresa and Veronica stared in disbelief. Veronica had disliked Catherine since the first time she met her when Terry was in college. She had despised her since the birth of the twins.

"Catherine, again, why are you here? Our understanding was an hour or so last night or tomorrow. Not today, especially at this hour of the morning." It took all of Terry's strength to remain civil.

"I assure you that I will not impose on your little Norman Rockwell Christmas much longer, but I just want to wish my babies a Merry Christmas *on* Christmas and give them the love only a mother can give. No one would deny a mother the right to see her children on Christmas, now would they? Where are they anyway?"

"Going into labor does not a mother make," Teresa mumbled loud enough for all to hear.

Mikey and Ikey reentered the den with their usual flurry, dragging Lisa by the hand.

"Daddy, Mikey said you have a sur— Catherine!" Lisa was

genuinely happy to see her mother. Lisa hugged Catherine and kissed her lightly on the cheek. "Merry Christmas, Catherine. Thank you for the gifts. They are very nice."

"Oh darling, you are so welcome—only the very best that money can buy for my precious ones. I can't wait to see you in those Donna Karan suits. You may not know this, but she is one of the top designers in the world, and every young woman should have at least one designer suit in her closet."

"They don't fit." Ari spoke with a stone face. She had stopped cold in her tracks when she saw Catherine.

"Merry Christmas, my darling Alisa, come to your mother and give her a big hug and kiss. I can't believe how much you have grown. You are absolutely gorgeous. You look more and more like me every day." Catherine approached Ariana with outstretched arms.

"I am *not* Alisa!" Ariana stepped back in disgust.

"Oh honey, I am sorry. I guess you look so grown-up, I got confused." Catherine was almost embarrassed by her mistake. She didn't notice the devastation on Ari's face.

"Ain't that nothing! She doesn't even know her own child. She gets my vote for mother of the year." Veronica really needed a drink.

"As the barren dateless wonder who I assume you are, how would you know anything about motherhood, Veronica? Anyone could have made that mistake. After all, they *are* identical." Catherine had no sense of shame.

"You're right, most strangers do confuse them!" Terry's comment stung as much as an open-handed slap.

Turning her attention back to Ari, Catherine continued. "Well, we will just take them back to Saks tomorrow, my precious. Now come over here and hug your mother and thank her for the lovely, and quite expensive, gifts."

"You can take the gifts back for all I care, and I don't want to hug or kiss you. Besides, Miss Jackie is my new mother, and Momma C is my new grandmother." Ari clenched her fists as tears formed. Defying gravity, the tears hung heavily.

"The only reason I don't tell you everything I am really thinking is because Daddy would get mad at me for being disrespectful. Lisa can be a suck-up and hug and kiss you, but not me, not on Christmas, not on our birthday, not never. I won't live with you either. I'll run away first."

"What sort of poison have you been feeding this child against her own mother?" Catherine appeared hurt.

"Terry here is a good man," Momma C piped in. "He done raised dese babies to da best his ability and I won't let you accuse him of poisonin' dese chirren 'gainst you. You need to check dat mirror to see who done turned this chile 'gainst you. You need to come ovah here and let me check your scalp for them three sixes 'cause I is sure you be Satan's offspring."

"I guess I am not welcome here. I will leave you all to your celebration. Please don't begrudge a mother her special time with her children." Tears formed in Catherine's eyes this time. No one was sure if it was hurt, anger, or pretense.

As Terry approached her with the perfectly matched fur coat, she snatched it and stared coldly into his eyes before she turned to leave. This woman had descended on the joy of Christmas the way the bomb had descended on Hiroshima . . . destroying everything it came in contact with.

The stunned group stood silent for several moments after Catherine stormed out of the door. Ari collapsed on the sofa in a heap, sobbing. Pain filled Lisa's eyes as she stood in the middle of the den. Roland released his vicelike grip on Cedes and moved to comfort his goddaughter. Jackie went to comfort Ari. Terry stared blankly at his mother and sister. The devastation from Hurricane Catherine was catastrophic.

2 4

As the door slammed behind Catherine, she stopped to catch her breath. The cold air stung her face, and tears began to crystalize. She had had no idea seeing the twins would affect her this way. She had not seen them for nearly two years. They were no longer little girls, and they were her mirror image. She had never missed having a family until this morning.

She could see the chauffeur moving toward her in what seemed like slow motion. "Are you alright, Ms. Hawkins? You look like you might faint, ma'am." The chauffeur was at her side on the porch.

"I'm fine, Jonathan. Just get me the hell out of here." Catherine's breathing was labored as he assisted her down the steps.

Despite the bitter cold air, Catherine was sweating. What was happening to her? She had never expected that the visit would affect her this way. Was it Ariana's lack of affection and defiance? Was it Alisa's display of affection? Surely not. Affection had never found its way into her life. Was it that Terry was marrying Jackie? That was impossible. She had never loved his passive, do-gooder ass. Then what was it?

As she settled in the back of the limousine, her breathing became more normal. She heard Jonathan slam his door as the intercom buzzed. "Where to, ma'am?"

"Just drive, Jonathan . . . drive until the pain leaves my chest." Catherine's voice trailed off as she stared at Terry's house, Terry's home.

The car pulled from the curb, and Catherine watched the house until it disappeared behind her. She had to get ahold of herself. What was this emotional vulnerability crap? She could let nothing stand in the way of her presidency of the company. She had worked too long and too hard. There were many dead bodies along the trail to her success. Terry would just be another casualty. But what about those children? How would all this affect them? She had never considered that they were growing up and had such strong opinions. Well, they would just have to adjust and come along for the ride. She had more than enough money to ensure them the life of twin princesses.

➤ She would just have to show them all, especially that Roland. Her love for him had been eternal. Foolish man. He could have had it all. They could have ruled the world.

But his stupid loyalty to Terry had stood between her and the only man she ever loved. *Well, Mr. Carpenter, you've chosen your sides, but you're not armed for this battle. Who would have ever guessed I would get two pigeons with one shotgun blast?* Catherine laughed bone-chillingly to herself, and for the first time since she left Terry's house, she felt warm inside.

"What a wretched woman!" Cedes said through clenched teeth, trying not to be overheard by the children.

"If we let this ruin our beautiful Christmas morning, she'll win—that's what she wanted to do. She is a very unhappy woman and wants everyone else to be as miserable as she is." Terry tried his best to bring peace back to the room that had been so filled with joy such a short time before.

"Terry, you is truly amazin', son. Even I could lose mah

religion wit dat woman. She need prayer. She be needin' Jesus. I done met some mis'rable people in mah time, but none like dat." Momma C shook her head.

"Okay, okay. Don't we have some breakfast to eat? I didn't do all of this cooking to have some forgot-where-she-came-from Negress come in here and ruin my family's happiness. Jackie and Cedes, come help Clara and me in the kitchen," Teresa said, trying her best to lighten the mood.

Ariana and Alisa sat side by side—so close you couldn't tell where one stopped and the other started. Alisa's face showed pain, while Ariana's showed nothing.

"Come on, you guys. Let Uncle Roland show you how to clean up a Christmas mess in record time. Michael, after breakfast, how about Uncle Roland and Aunt Cedes take you for a little spin around the block on that new bike? I bet I can convince your mom to let you go outside early this morning." Roland smiled at Cedes as she followed the other ladies into the kitchen.

"Really? Uncle Roland, why was the nice lady so mean to my new daddy?" Michael looked up at Roland with wide-eyed innocence.

"Well, champ, sometimes people who seem nice at first are really not. It's my job to spot the bad people and not let them hurt the good people. Do you understand what I'm saying?" Roland stooped down so that he was at eye level with Michael.

"Are you like a Ninja Turtle, Uncle Roland?" Michelle asked moving in closer.

"I guess you could say I sorta am. I never thought about it in those terms. I fight the bad people with words instead of with my fists."

"Oh, I understand now, Uncle Roland!" Michael hugged his neck.

Roland hugged him and Michelle together and looked up at Terry, who smiled.

Terry knew why he loved this brother so much. With much animation, Roland convinced all four of the children to help him clean up the den. He slam-dunked balls of wrapping paper into trash bags, flew Michael and Michelle around like fighter planes, and danced with Ari and Lisa. By the time he had finished cleaning the den, everyone was laughing and having a good time once again. Even in Terry's eyes, Roland was a Ninja Turtle.

The smells from the kitchen had filled the house with a warm holiday feeling of love and family. Veronica reluctantly joined the other women in the kitchen, but mainly to plead for coffee. She had drunk her own (and about three other people's) share of champagne. Her head pounded as if the Little Drummer Boy had taken up residence in her skull.

"This woman is going to make our lives miserable," Jackie said, more to herself than to the other women.

"Gurl, only if you let the bitch." Cedes was still fuming.

"She has as much money as God, and she'll spend it all to get what she wants. Why can't she just leave *my* family alone? I've found happiness with the most kind and loving man I have ever met, and she wants to ruin our family. It kills me to see what she does to the girls, especially Ari. She has very deep feelings about all of this and unless she gets them out, she'll have some real problems." Jackie had tears in her eyes.

"You know what really burns my grits? She doesn't want those girls," Teresa added. "They would cramp her style. She just doesn't want Terry to have them and be happy. She is just selfish. I've known her a long time. When I came to help Terry after he and Roland picked them up from the hospital, I could not believe any mother could not want those beautiful babies. They were perfect." Teresa shook her head.

"Well, I got a monster hangover and PMS; I say we just take her ass out." Veronica was trying to sip the hot coffee.

"Chile, I would agree wit cha, but I say we let da Lord handle dis. And believe me when God handles you, you been handled." Momma C smiled.

All of the women laughed. They chatted more about the impending litigation and moved on to discuss the beautiful gifts they had each received. Veronica and Cedes set the table and the other ladies began to serve. Then everyone began to gather around the table and take seats.

Michelle spoke up first. "Can we hold hands and pray?"

Jackie was a little perplexed since Michelle had never made such a request before. "Of course, Ikey."

"I want to pray first." She bowed her head. "Jesus, this is Michelle. I want you to make the mean nice lady go away. I don't want Uncle Roland to have to be a Ninja Turtle on her. I don't want my sisters to go away either, even sometimes. Bless this food, amen."

The adults looked at each other and simply said, "Amen."

CATHERINE HAD CAST a dark cloud over the morning, although everyone, except Ariana, seemed to be enjoying the feast that had been spread before them. Ari was quiet and only picked at her food, even her nana's cheesy grits, her absolute favorite.

"May I be excused?" Ariana whispered as she looked at her dad.

"Honey, I know you're upset, but could you try to eat a little something and stay here with us?" The pain on Ari's face broke Terry's heart.

"Daddy, I'm so sad, I think I am having a heart attack."

"What makes you think that, Ari?" Terry tried not to panic.

"Well, my chest hurts, and I can feel my heart beating. I remember Momma C said that grieving attacks the part of your heart that makes the love flow. So I think my heart is being attacked."

"Oh, honey, that's a heartache, and if you feel you just can't sit here any longer, then yes you may be excused." Terry could not stand the pain Catherine caused his girls, especially Ari.

"Ari, please don't go to our room," pleaded Lisa. "That'll only make it worse. Stay in here with us. All the people in this room love us. They only want what's best for us. They are not going to let our mother win. Uncle Roland has promised us."

"That woman may be your mother, but she ain't mine—isn't mine, I mean." She shot a quick look at her dad.

"Jackie is my mother and Momma C is my grandmother. I don't ever want to see Catherine again, ever." Tears fell into her grits as she spit the words at everyone. Before Terry could reach her, Alisa hugged her sister and they both cried, rocking back and forth. Their movement was so synchronized it was almost artistic.

"Ari, please don't leave the table. Please don't let her ruin Christmas any more than she already has." Jackie was pleading.

"Please stay, Ari. I'll try to blow milk out of my nose to make you laugh." Michael was his normal self and saw nothing wrong with his offer.

"Okay, I'll stay. And Michael, that is so gross, *eewww*." A smile found its way to Ariana's beautiful face. But her eyes were still filled with pain.

"Chile, let me git you some mo' grits. Dese got tears in 'em." Momma C disappeared in the kitchen humming "O Come, All Ye Faithful."

"Thank you for not leaving, Ari. I wouldn't be able to enjoy breakfast without you. We'll be fine. Daddy and Uncle Roland promised us." Alisa hugged her sister tightly and wiped the tears from Ariana's eyes first, then her own.

The conversation for the remainder of the meal steered clear of the holocaust known as Catherine. Michael and Michelle dominated much of the dialog with their plans for the day, which included much outdoor time. Terry pretended to be interested in the idle chitchat around the table and tried not to show the anxiety that was tearing his gut apart.

"Why don't Terry and I clean up the kitchen?" Roland surprised everyone, especially Terry, with his suggestion.

"You ladies did so much last night and today preparing these magnificent meals, it's the least my brotha and I can do. Right, Terry?" Roland showed twenty-eight of his thirty-two teeth.

"I think that's an offer I dare not refuse." Terry shot an amusing look to Roland.

"What a nice gesture. We'll clear the table and leave you men to the rest. At least we cleaned as we cooked, so it is not so terrible in there." Teresa looked at her son with concern. She could tell that this whole Catherine mess was tearing him up inside.

Everyone pitched in to clear the table. Jackie and Cedes stored the leftovers. Roland and Terry debated who was qualified to fill the dishwasher most efficiently based on education and technical skill. The women just looked at each other, laughed, and shook their heads. Only men would have to discuss the "technical" aspects of loading a dishwasher.

"We've got this, ladies, thank you for your help, but let us do our man's work." Roland knew he was not fooling anyone with this façade. The women knew he wanted to have a private conversation with Terry.

"Brother, Catherine is even more vicious than I could imagine. I'm not saying I'm not up to the challenge, but it's going to be a hell of a blowout at the Alamo. It's obvious she's being vindictive. There's nothing she wants less than these girls," Roland said as he rinsed dishes.

"Man, she doesn't even know who is who," Terry said. "Can you believe that crap? She can't even tell her own daughters apart! The man at the dry cleaners knows Ariana from Alisa. You're right that she doesn't want them. She just doesn't want me to have them. But why? I cannot figure this one out. All this time she's wanted nothing to do with raising them. You know that. Now all of a sudden, it's like her life depends on it. What is up with that?"

Roland turned and looked at his best friend as though he had just given him a winning lottery ticket. "Terry, you are a genius. Why didn't I think of this? Damn, I must be slipping. Her life may not depend on it, but something that means everything in her life may!"

"What are you talking about, Roland?"

"You know Catherine works for a Spanish-based company, right?"

"So what?"

"She's worked her way up to senior vice president in record time. With her being black and female, that's a phenomenon on its own. But perhaps she's set her sights even higher, and they're questioning her marital and dependent status. These are the Spanish after all. Family is everything to them." Roland stopped rinsing dishes.

"So you're saying her company wants to know where her children are? How do they even know she has any?"

"Trust me, Terry, they know."

"Okay, so they know. What does that mean?"

"I'm not certain, but they probably want to know if working in Spain is interfering with her duties as a mother. Think about it. All of a sudden she is back here in Texas. And believe me, there has to be something in it for Catherine. She did not wake up one Sunday morning with a case of maternal longing."

"How can we find out? Is this something the investigator can look into? How can we stop the b— woman?"

"Man, you've really got to let some of this emotion go. Call her names, get mad about it. It's your right. She's messing with what belongs to you. Giving birth alone does not a mother make. As far as finding out, we will do some checking. She has to have pissed off a secretary somewhere willing to tell us what we want to know. Believe me, no one sings like a bird who has had her feathers ruffled by a vulture." Roland's entire persona had changed. He paced the floor as if it were a courtroom and he was delivering a closing argument.

"You know I trust you with my life, man. Do you really think this is what is going on? It sounds far-fetched to me. You're telling me that her not having her kids can affect her chances for promotion. Isn't that sexual discrimination or something?"

"First of all, these people are not Americans. The rules are different in other countries. And if my thinking is correct, the Spanish don't take too kindly to men who don't take their paternal responsibilities seriously. So imagine how much stronger they would feel about a woman. If she cannot manage her family life, she can't be trusted to manage billions of dollars."

"What is the next step? Contact the investigator, confirm what we believe, then what? How will this information help us? I don't understand any of this. Damn!"

"We'll convince a judge that Catherine is only using them and has no genuine concern about their well-being. It's a long shot, but if it pays off, it will be like winning the Triple Crown." Roland slam-dunked the towel into the sink.

"And the home team scores!" Terry smiled weakly. "Like I said before, I trust you with my life. But this is not my life; it is the life of my children. Ari does not want to be moved. She has said it time and time again. We have to win this, man, we have to." Terry dropped his head to his chest and breathed deep.

"So you guys need any help in—*wow*! You're finished! It looks great. I'm impressed." Jackie peeked in the door.

"Come in here with your sexy self. Have I told you how much I love you today?"

"In the words of a great balladeer, 'Never Too Much.' I can never hear that you love me too much." Jackie walked slowly and deliberately toward Terry.

"Oh Lawd, it's my time to go check on the stock market or something. Now let this be a lesson to you womenfolk; us menfolk do know a little sum'n sum'n about cleaning a kitchen. I think I'll grab a shower and change so I can take Mikey and Ikey out like I promised. Don't y'all be startin' nuthin' up in here," Roland teased his brother and his soon-to-be sister-in-law.

"If I make no promises, I will tell no lies." Jackie had come to love him almost as much as Terry did. He was so wonderful with the kids, and they too loved him. He was so genuinely good. She was lucky to have such good, strong, *positive* black men in her life. And now, maybe, just maybe, he and Cedes would get a little something started.

"I promised the kids if they cleaned up the den, I would take them for a run around the block to test-drive the new bikes. I hope that's okay with you. I probably should have asked you first, huh?"

"Yes, you should have, Mr. Man. But it's perfectly alright. Thanks Roland . . . for everything." Jackie smiled a knowing smile.

"You know, Jackie, I should be the one to thank you for making my boy here the happiest man on Earth and for having a wonderful best friend like Cedes. I'm hoping that she'll give me half a chance to prove I am sincere about this thing, you know."

"Roland, I'm glad one of you two woke up and smelled the outhouse."

"Smelled the outhouse? Man, I don't know, Jackie. Not sure if I like that analogy." The three of them laughed.

"When the coffee was brewing, you two had no clue it was burning in the pot."

"I am expecting this New Year's Eve to be totally different for us, Jackie. Totally different." Roland had a very distant look in his eyes. The look he had when he was planning something big, very big.

CHRISTMAS DAY, DESPITE a very rocky start, had turned out to be wonderful. Mikey and Ikey had been an endless source of energy since before dawn, with no signs of slowing down in the near future. Ari and Lisa, though nowhere near as animated as the other two, were pretty excited about the prospect of being one big happy family.

The adults busied themselves with preparations for the big dinner. The grandmas had the kitchen under control, from which heavenly aromas came. The den had been returned to its usual organized chaos. The party people had showered and changed, but still moved around like zombies for hours until Roland recommended a friendly game of bid whist. Veronica didn't play; she made herself a pitcher of Bloody Marys and called the police officer who had stood her up for the last time. She spewed venom as she left a farewell message.

Roland and Terry partnered against Cedes and Jackie. The women sent them packing off to Boston so many times it became embarrassing. Each man blamed the other, claiming their skills had been hampered by the sheer beauty of their opponents. The women laughed in their faces and continued to stomp them into the ground.

The move to Jackie's had taken only three trips in two cars. Thank God she lived nearby. With everyone dressed in their Sunday-go-to-meetin' best, they piled into the cars and headed to Jackie's to finish off the Christmas celebration. The evening was filled with good food, loving family, and great fun. As every rendition of "This Christmas" ever recorded played, the decision was unanimous: this Christmas was truly the best ever.

As the events of the previous two days drew to a close, a mild sadness fell on the group as everyone prepared to return to their own homes. "You know, this has been the best Christmas I have ever had." Roland addressed the group, but looked at Cedes.

"I have to agree with Roland. I didn't know how I would get through today. You all made today wonderful. *All* of you." Cedes stared at Roland with tears beginning to fill her eyes.

"Oh dayummm! Don't start that crying now; we almost made it through the day without a tear." Veronica fought back tears of her own.

"Gurl, look at you, starting your own snot fest and telling somebody else not to cry." Terry was laughing as he pulled his sister close to hug her. "This has been a very special day. My baby has made me the happiest man alive. Despite the wicked witch of San Antonio, all is well in the universe and my boy here promises me that the natural order of things will be returned."

"Truer words were never spoken, my brotha." Roland gave him some dap.

"I don't think I have ever met anyone as evil as Catherine. And I have met some real bitches in my job—some of those players' wives are contemptible. But none of them can touch that woman." Cedes shook her head in disbelief as she spoke.

"Well, you know what, miss lady?" Roland walked over to Cedes and looked into her eyes. "I have never met any woman quite as special as you. And I plan to spend a lot of time showing you just how special I think you are."

"Oh, maybe we should leave them alone, what y'all think?" Veronica made faces at them. "We betta hide the mistletoe!"

"You just playa hatin', Vee." Jackie laughed as she high-fived Cedes. Everyone laughed.

"So I guess we will all be together New Year's Eve for that fancy lawyer shindig. My dress is fierce. I looked so good I turned myself on." Veronica posed for effect.

"Cedes, do I have to wait almost a week to see you again, or can I convince you to have dinner with me tomorrow night?" Roland's arms seemed to envelop Cedes's entire body. The feeling of warmth and protection had been absent way too long.

"Roland, that could be arranged. Call me later, and we'll set something up. This feels so weird. It's a good thing, but still weird. We've been like brother and sister for four years, and now we are talking about dating."

"Well, Mercedes, you are not my sister and, correction, we are going to date, not talk about it. We've wasted four years talking."

"You go, boy!" Veronica shouted, amused as she watched this exchange.

"May I drive you home, Roland?" Cedes's words surprised even her.

"I'm supposed to say, oh no, that is too far out of your way, but that's an offer I cannot refuse. And because I want this as much as the air I breathe, I'll say, oh hell yes, you can drive me home." Roland beamed.

Everyone piled into their respective cars and headed home. Christmas carols played on the radio in each car, and everyone reflected on the blessings of the season.

As Jackie closed the door behind Terry, she realized for the first time since the Christmas Eve dinner that she was going to be Mrs. Terrence Winston. Soon she would not have to watch Terry back his car from her driveway to go home. She never knew love could be this good. Whoever said love is not supposed to hurt was really onto something.

December 26 dawned cold and cloudy with the threat of rain. Catherine sipped tea as she enjoyed the penthouse view of Dallas. It was really unfortunate that her office was not here. She did so love the finer things in life. Dallas was Texas at its best. Everything was truly bigger in Texas, and she really believed bigger was better.

She pulled the plush terry-cloth robe with the hotel insignia tight around her body to warm her as she planned her day with the twins. But the chill she felt came from within. The suite was warmed not only by a central heating system, but by the roaring fire in the massive fireplace. As she thought about the icy look in Ariana's eyes when Ari had looked at her Christmas morning, she shuddered.

She was confident she could sway Alisa over to her side. Ariana was another story. She had to find out what made her tick, what she wanted. Once Ariana knew she could buy her anything she could imagine, she would not think her mother was so bad. She had to convince them they would enjoy living with her some of the time. She would buy them the world. After all, it was an investment in her future.

The phone rang and abruptly interrupted her thoughts. A quick glance at the grandfather clock indicated that it must be the driver. She had lost track of time, truly a rare occurrence. "Good morning, Catherine Hawkins here . . . Yes, I'll be ready in an hour. Please be waiting." She wasn't sure if it was apprehension or raw fear she felt. She had brought Japanese businessmen to their knees in her dealings. How could two ten-year-old girls instill fear in her?

"But Daddy, I don't feel good," Ariana whined.

"So tell me exactly what it is that is wrong with you, other than that you don't want to go with Catherine today?" Terry spoke softly as he looked into her eyes.

"I think I have a temperature." Ariana dropped her head, embarrassed that her dad caught her in a lie.

"Let's hope you have a temperature of ninety-eight point six."

It tore Terry up to have to force her to be with Catherine, but he managed a smile.

"Daddy, you know what I mean. I think I am going to have a headache and a stomachache."

"Look, princess. I know you don't want to go with Catherine. But if you don't, there may be trouble when we go to court. She may tell the judge that I refused to let you spend time with her. She'll use whatever she can to get her way."

"But I don't want to go. I hate her."

"You don't really hate her. You don't like how she has treated you, but hate is pretty strong."

"I do hate her. Lisa doesn't hate her, but I do." She began to cry.

"Well, do this for me. Give her a chance today. Try to enjoy the trip. She'll probably pick you up in a limousine. You'll go shopping and have lunch and dinner at some pretty nice restaurants. Then she'll buy you whatever you want. Doesn't that sound like a fun day?" Terry couldn't even convince himself.

"Daddy, you just don't get it. I don't care about a limo or shopping or fancy restaurants. I want to be with you and Miss Jackie. I would rather go to McDonald's anyway. I'll go, but I don't want her to buy me nothing, and I won't eat and I won't talk, and I won't even look at her!" Ariana yelled through her tears.

"Honey, I do understand, but it has to be this way for now. It just has to be. I'm sorry you have to go through this. How is Lisa, and where is she?"

"She's in the shower. She's all excited. I'm mad at her. Why is she so happy to be going with Catherine?"

"She has a right to be happy, Ari." The words hung in the air like the stench from a cattle ranch. Terry would have never guessed that Lisa would be excited to be with Catherine. What did this mean?

"Well, don't be mad at her. Just let her enjoy this time. Catherine *is* her mother, just like she is yours."

"She has never been my mother. And you know what, Daddy?"

"What, princess?"

"She never will be, *never!*"

Terry had no response.

2 7

MINUTES TICKED BY like hours. It had only been forty-five minutes since the limousine had pulled from the curb carrying Lisa and Ari into the unknown world of Catherine the Terrible. Terry promised himself that he would keep busy with the traditional post-Christmas cleanup. He loved all the Christmas hype and decorations, but once Christmas was over, that tree had to come down.

He thought back to how Christmas Eve and Christmas day had been miraculously wonderful. Jackie said yes. She had agreed to be his wife, his partner for life. There was a wedding to plan, a future to plot; but once again, Catherine was casting her dark shadow over him. Instead of clicking his heels with glee, he worried what was happening with the twins and Catherine. Were they comfortable? Was she her normal, evil, contentious self? Was she talking down to them, treating them like babies? Ari so hated to be treated like an infant. The phone rang and broke his concentration, a very welcome diversion.

"Hello."

"Terry, my brotha. How ya livin' this glorious morning after Christmas? The sun shines bright for me, man." Roland was so animated, Terry hardly recognized his voice.

"In case you haven't checked, it is cloudy and cold. Man, are you happy or what? You would think you are the one who got engaged. So tell me, does Cedes have anything to do with this bliss?"

"Tell the brotha what he has won. Terry, I haven't been to bed. She just left. I invited her in for a nightcap. She protested. I made her a counterproposal and let's just say the rest is history. Man, I think I'm in love. I guess I've been all along, but was too blind to see it."

"Whoa! Cool your jets. What do you mean she just left? She spent the night with you? Man, you know how vulnerable she has been. Do you think that was a good idea?"

"Man, give me a little more credit than that! We talked and drank champagne until dawn, and then she fell asleep in my arms. I am still dressed from dinner last night. Damn, I spent the night in my clothes two nights in a row. It was wonderful. This woman could become my best friend. Now don't take that wrong, my brotha."

"Roland, man, you know I understand probably better than anyone else on this earth what you mean by that. So y'all just talked all night in that love nest called Chez Carpenter? Is that a first?"

"Okay, okay, you can lighten up on a brotha. But you might be right about that. Man, she doesn't give a rat's ass about what I have. We have known each other for so long and yet don't know each other at all."

"So maybe it will be a double wedding?"

"Don't joke. It very well could be. Best friends marrying best friends. Is that like twins marrying twins?"

"You're nuts, but I guess it is similar."

"So enough about me and Cedes. Did Catherine pick up the girls this morning? Did they want to go?"

"Ari definitely didn't want to go. She was faking illness, but much to my surprise, Lisa was very excited about the prospect of a day with Catherine."

"Do I hear something in your voice other than the normal concern over the situation?"

"Well, I *am* disappointed by her willingness to go with Catherine. It seems like she wants to be with her. This woman has done virtually nothing for her. That is a little tough to take. Although I told Ari that she had to do this and to try to make the best of it, I liked the idea that she wanted nothing to do with her mother. Catherine could end up convincing Lisa that joint custody is alright."

"Don't read more into it than is there. Lisa is excited about riding in a limousine and shopping with a bottomless source of money. This is all new to her."

"You must be forgetting the shopping trips you have taken them on. This is nothing new to them. Are you just trying to make me feel better?"

"I see it isn't working."

"No, it isn't. Roland, this cannot happen. It just can't. I'm too happy right now. Promise me it will not happen."

"Terry, just calm down. Let's see what happens when they get home tonight. When are they due back?"

"Around seven. They are going to dinner before they come home."

"Well, I'm having dinner with Cedes at eight-thirty. Maybe we will come by there afterwards so we can scope it all out."

"Roland, just enjoy your evening. Jackie will be here. She's always objective. She says she needs to be here to keep her future husband out of jail." Terry laughed.

"Smart woman. Well, I'm going to get some sleep. I'll call you when I get up. And Terry?"

"Yes, Roland. How do I know this is going to be profound?"

"This is going to work out. Trust me."

"I do trust you, man, I really do. Get some sleep and congratulations."

"Congratulations?"

"Yeah, for finally waking up."

"Okay, my brotha. I am smelling that coffee. Lata."

Roland did have a way of calming him down. The only other person who was better at it was Jackie. She had promised to spend the evening with him. Her mother would watch the twins, and they could have some time alone before Ari and Lisa returned. She said they could start to make wedding plans, including setting the date. She had rambled on for what seemed like hours about all that had to be done and that there was virtually no time left if they wanted a garden wedding this summer. My God, July was seven months away. God created the universe in six days.

I guess this is one of those fundamental differences between women and men I have heard and read so much about, Terry thought. As far as he was concerned, if the children, their parents, Veronica, Roland, and Cedes were there, what else was needed? *She's talking about caterers and musicians and tents. Lawdhamurcy, this sounds like a major production. Roland attended the Clinton inauguration and told her about it. Now she thinks she has to compete.*

But as long as she was happy, nothing else mattered at all. Well, almost nothing.

"So tell me, Ariana, what would you like to shop for after we exchange the suits?" Catherine tried to make polite conversation.

"I don't want anything from you. You can just return the suit. I'll never wear it." Ariana was defiant and rude.

"I'm going to tell Daddy you're being rude to Catherine, Ari. He's going to be mad at you." Lisa tried to keep Ari from hurting Catherine's feelings.

"He won't care. He doesn't like her either." Ari stared at Catherine with contempt.

"Well, I'm sure Ari doesn't mean to be rude," Catherine purred in her best maternal voice. "A lot has happened, and she just needs a little time to get to know me. We'll just shop, and if you see something you like, then you can just let me know." Catherine was trying desperately to hide her impatience with Ari. She hadn't bargained for the attitude or the pure hatred.

"Is this the first time you have ridden in a limo, Lisa?" Catherine wanted to focus on the positive.

"Oh no, we ride in Uncle Roland's limo all the time. He even picked our friends up for our sleepover birthday party in the limo. We had the party at his house. It's so huge. We had a ball." Lisa smiled broadly as she relayed the story of their first sleepover birthday party.

"Do you spend a lot of time at Roland's house?"

"Not as much as I want. He has everything there. We love the pool the most. He taught us how to swim in that pool. He also taught us how to play basketball. Ari is much better than I am, but we are both on the team." Lisa beamed with pride.

"So if Roland is doing all of this teaching, what is your father doing?" Catherine's tone dripped with sarcasm.

"Daddy teaches us everything. Uncle Roland teaches us a lot of the fun stuff, but Daddy helps us with our homework, and taught us how to sit when we wear a dress. He taught us how to eat with the right forks and how to be young ladies all the time. He told us about our period and not to be scared when it comes. You know, all the stuff your mother normally teaches you." Ari had drawn first blood.

"Well, it does seem that Terrence has it all under control, but wouldn't it be nice to have your mother around more often? We can shop and hang out and just be friends." Catherine was doing a miserable job of remaining civil.

"We do a lot of that with Miss Jackie, and now that she's marrying our dad, I'm sure we'll do a lot more of it. Besides, we don't want to hang out without Ikey and Mikey. If we hang out with you, can they come along too?" Ari looked at Lisa for confirmation.

"I think it would be better if the three of us got to know each other before we brought strangers into this circle. Don't you agree, Lisa?" Catherine mistakenly thought she had an ally.

"Michelle and Michael are not strangers! They're our baby brother and sister, and we don't do a lot of things without them. We wanted them to come with us today, but Miss Jackie said no. Even though Ari begged her." Lisa became defensive for the first time since they had climbed into the limo.

"Momma C says we're a package deal. Our dad, us, and Uncle Roland. If you take one, you take us all. So I guess you need to know we are a package deal. But the package includes Miss Jackie, Momma C, Mikey and Ikey, and Auntie Cedes. If you want to be with us, you have to want to be with them, too." Lisa was the defiant one this time.

"That's right," Ari chimed in.

Stunned by such adult words coming out of the mouth of a child, Catherine simply replied, "I see."

THE PHONE CALL from Roland had done little to cheer
Terry up. He was really glad to hear that Cedes and Roland
were working at starting a relationship. He wondered if his
"brother–best friend–godfather to his babies–playboy" was
capable of doing the main thing required in a committed
relationship—being with *one* woman. Roland had always been
footloose and fancy-free. With his commitments to women last-
ing only a few days—usually a weekend—Roland was clueless
about the inner workings of a relationship. He had watched Terry
with Jackie, but he had no idea how easy Jackie made commitment a way of life.

Terry busied himself with the cleanup and put away the tree or-
naments. Jackie would be over around four o'clock, and he
wanted to spend some quality, uninterrupted time with her. They
had not been alone since he had proposed on Christmas Eve.
Veronica had taken their mother shopping and was taking her to
dinner. Veronica had winked at Jackie when she told Terry they
wouldn't be back until the malls closed.

Terry shook his head as he wondered just how much women
told each other about the intimate details of their relationships.
He quickly dismissed the idea because if he thought of some of

the things Jackie may have told Cedes and Veronica, he would not be able to look either of them in the eyes ever again.

The threat of rain had come to fruition. A pleasurable evening was definitely in the works. It was cold and almost dark as the clock struck four. The fireplace roared as a bottle of champagne chilled. Jazz filled the air. Terry had showered and was wearing the black silk boxers and robe Veronica had given him for Christmas. He wore Jackie's favorite cologne. As he lit the last candle, he heard her key slip into the door. His woman had come home. This was where she belonged.

"Oh my, I would say you are trying to seduce a sistah in the middle of the afternoon if I didn't know better." Jackie's presence sent warmth throughout the room.

"I don't know why you would think such a thing. I am not *trying* to seduce you . . . I *am* seducing you!" Terry met her halfway across the room and pulled her into his arms.

"Well, now that we have that clear . . ." They both laughed, then kissed long and passionately.

It seemed as though they had been apart for weeks when they had actually left each other only a few hours before. Their kiss released all of the emotions they had suppressed since Christmas Eve. Loving was a wonderful feeling . . . being loved was even better.

"Let me take your coat. I've laid out something in the bedroom for you to slip into if you like. Damn, you smell good, baby!" Terry's breath caught in his chest as he unbuttoned Jackie's coat.

"Oh my God." The words were involuntary. Terry had no idea he had even uttered them. He only stared at Jackie. Her face was framed by her curly red hair, her makeup was flawless, and as her coat fell to the floor, she stood before him in the most gorgeous black teddy and robe he had ever seen. She had completed the ensemble with four-inch-high black patent-leather pumps. It was clear he was way out of his league when it came to the game of seduction.

"Merry Christmas, baby! You sho' been good to me." Jackie sang the words from the popular blues Christmas song.

"Come 'ere wit yo' foine ass! Gurl, you tryin' to give a brotha a heart attack." Terry slipped into a rare use of Ebonics to really get his point across.

"No, my darling, you're going to need your heart in good working order." Jackie kissed Terry before he could respond.

The afternoon together was spectacular. Terry left no detail unattended. There were chilled strawberries to go with the champagne and the most exquisite chocolate she had ever tasted. They laughed and hugged and kissed and then laughed some more. They talked about the wedding briefly but in no great detail. The only productive point that was reached was the location—Roland's estate. The date was still up in the air, although they did narrow the window to late June or early July. "Terry, you know what?"

"What, almost Mrs. Winston?"

"I never imagined in a million years that I would find someone who is smart, sexy, handsome, sincere, loving, a good father, and a genuinely good man that could love me the way that you do. I feel so blessed."

"No, Jackie, you don't understand. It is I who is blessed. You have brought so much joy to me. My life was full and good with the twins, but I never knew what was missing until I found the love of a good woman—a beautiful, sexy, sincere, kind woman willing to share all with me. I'm so blessed to have you and both sets of twins in my life. And of course there's your mother. She's the icing on the cake, for sure."

They both laughed and began to kiss, but this time the kiss unleashed the passion that had been perfected between them over the past four years. Their love was true and genuine, and they fell into the natural expression of that love right there on the Persian rug in the den.

Cedes let the hot water cascade over her body as she stood there in a daze. She couldn't believe what a wonderful time she had had with Roland over the past two days. She had fallen asleep in his arms while sitting straight up and fully clothed two nights in a row. He had been the perfect gentleman. She, of course, knew of his reputation from Jackie and never would have guessed that he was capable of such sensitivity.

It was as if she had met a new man. Not the same one who had tortured her for almost four years. What had happened to change all this? Did he feel sorry for her? Was it a game? She just wasn't sure how to take the events of the past two days—and nights.

As she stepped from the shower and wrapped herself in a plush purple terry-cloth robe, the phone rang. She was tired and didn't feel much like talking. She knew it might be Roland checking on her as he had all day, despite his promises to get some sleep. "Hello." Cedes's voice was low and sexy.

"Hey, baby. You been missin' me?"

"Charles!" Cedes immediately stood at attention and pulled the robe tightly around her neck. She had not thought of him once since Christmas Eve. "I've been really busy with family, and now I'm getting dressed to go out to dinner. How was your Christmas with your family?"

"Everything was cool. Would rather have been there with you though. I thought about you a lot yesterday. I called a few times, but kept getting the machine. I thought you were coming home after dinner at your pal's. I called Jackie's place, but her mother said you had gone home. Where were you?" There was a tone in his voice that she did not particularly appreciate.

"Excuse me, Charles, but I don't believe you know me well enough to question where I have been. My plans did change, and I stayed with another friend last night. I had a little too much to drink, if you must know why I didn't come home." Cedes did nothing to mask her anger.

"Calm down, I just was worried. People being on the road during the holidays is always a gamble. Which friend did you stay with? You only ever talk about Jackie."

Why was Cedes uncomfortable telling Charles that she stayed with Roland last night? Did she care what he thought? Was it what she was feeling? Damn, she was so confused. "I spent the night at Roland's. He is a close friend and best friend of Terry's."

There was dead silence on the other end of the phone. "You there?" Cedes knew she should have lied. But why?

"Yeah. I'm here. So you spent the night with another man, and you have the nerve to tell me about it? I gotta tell you, you a bold bitch. But I should have known that, you picking me up in the store and working for the Dallas Cowboys. Yeah, I should have known there was nothing special about yo' ass."

The words stung like a slap on wet skin. "First of all, I do not owe you any explanation for my behavior at all. But Roland and I have been friends for years. I took him home, went in and had champagne, and I wasn't able to drive. We listened to music, and I fell asleep on the couch, fully clothed. End of story. And the next time you feel the need to call someone a bitch, perhaps you should dial your momma's digits." Cedes slammed down the phone.

Her heart raced as the phone rang again. She assumed that it was Charles, calling to get in the last word. She let it ring until the machine picked up. It was Roland. "Hey, pretty lady. I just woke up, and I am a new man. I guess you are napping or in the shower. I'll be by to pick you up around seven-thirty. I thought we could have a drink there and talk before we head out to dinner. You know you have upset my world, Cedes. Until seven-thirty, my sweet. Ciao!" Cedes stared at the machine and wondered if she had done the right thing telling Charles about Roland. She quickly dismissed her misgivings and thought of how easy it was for him to turn on her without the full explanation of what had occurred. She wrote Charles off without a second thought.

She smiled to herself as she thought of how good it felt to be with Roland. None of the normal getting-to-know-you-so-I-gotta-be-on-my-best-behavior bull that usually went along with dating. He had seen her with the flu, with her hair standing ace-deuce, wearing her thick glasses. And he still wanted to be with her. He is the catch of the decade, that was for damn sure. He has it all . . . but can he have it all with just one woman?

There was no doubt they were going to be the best man and maid of honor at the Winston wedding. Would it be a prelude to their own? *Gurl, get ahold of yourself; this is your first date with the man!* Cedes laughed to herself and shook her head. "Slow your roll, gurlfriend, slooooow your roll," she said out loud and threw back her head, laughing as the words filled her spacious bedroom.

2 9

EXHAUSTION ENVELOPED CATHERINE as Ari and Lisa climbed in the limousine for the trip home. Despite their tumultuous start, Catherine felt the day had turned out pretty decently. Ari said very little, but about three hours into the day she seemed much less hostile. Lisa, on the other hand, had been totally caught up in the excitement of the lifestyle of the rich and soon-to-be-famous.

Catherine, who firmly believed that those who fail to plan, definitely plan to fail, was already on to Plan B in her head. She had to undermine Jackie. Lisa and Ari cared just a little too much for this woman with the ready-made family. Who did Jackie and Terry think they were anyway? The Afrocentric Bradys? She had to tread lightly here, but even a mighty oak tree begins with a planted seed.

"So did you girls have fun today? I really enjoyed all this shopping. I was disappointed though. You didn't want me to buy you more things. I have lots and lots of money, and I can buy you whatever you want. But there'll be lots of other shopping trips, and I am sure you'll get more things next time."

Ari stared at Catherine with disdain. "Are you trying to buy our love?"

"Oh, Ari, don't be so mean. She was just buying us Christmas presents!" Lisa defended Catherine.

"Christmas is over!" Ari spat the words at Catherine.

"I know Christmas is over, but you see I wasn't exactly sure what to get for you, and I thought this trip might be nice so I could get to know you better and get you some of the things that you didn't get for Christmas. I am sure your father did the best he could with his meager income, but I can give you *everything* your heart desires. I am a millionaire. Do you know what that means?"

"I do! It's like Michael Jordan. That means you have lots and lots of money." Lisa beamed. Ari stared at Catherine, then her twin. What had happened to Lisa?

"That's right. I have lots of money, and I want to spend lots of it on the two of you. I know your father does the best he can on what he makes, and he has provided a quaint little home for you. And Janice has her own children."

"Her name is Jackie, not Janice! She's a reporter for the Dallas *Herald*. She has her own byline and everything. She's very famous here in Dallas. She makes a lot of money, and our father does not have to give her any money. She owns her own house, and it's even bigger than ours." Ari was on the verge of tears.

"Why are you always so mean to Catherine? She's trying to be nice to us!" Lisa was angry at her sister.

"Why are you yelling at me? You're always taking her side. I've been your sister and best friend all this time, and now you are yelling at me because of *her!*"

Catherine sat back and enjoyed the rift she had caused between the two of them. Conquering would be easier than she had ever imagined.

"I'm yelling at you because you're being mean. Daddy taught us we should always be polite to everyone. And I'm sure that goes double for our mother," Lisa argued.

"She ain't none of my mother. Jackie will be my mother when Dad and her get married," Ari sobbed.

"Oooo, Daddy told you about using 'ain't.' I'm gonna tell!"

Lisa was happy to have something to tell that she perceived would get Ari into trouble.

"Girls, let's not fight!" Catherine said, with a pretense of sincerity. "There's no need to fight. I understand how Ariana feels. I have not been around as much as I would like, and she's come to think of Janice, I mean Jacqueline, as her mother. I'm disappointed that I haven't lived up to her expectations, but I am trying now to make up for it. I am just not . . ." Catherine pretended to be choked up. She searched her Versace bag for a handkerchief to wipe the imaginary tears.

"Look what you did! You made her cry!" Lisa moved from the seat opposite Catherine to her side and hugged her. Dumbfounded by this move, Ari stared. Catherine buried her face in her handkerchief, to hide not her tears, but her smile.

The remainder of the trip was quiet as Ariana stared out of the window. Alisa sat comforting the *deeply hurt* Catherine. As the chauffeur pulled the stretch limousine in front of the Winston house, Ari opened the door. Despite the little talk Catherine had had with them over lunch about the proper thing to do when riding in a chauffeur-driven automobile, she bolted out. Catherine had told her a lady should wait to have the driver open the door for her and always insist a man open doors for her, especially if he was being paid to do it.

"Ari, *wait*! Don't you want your gifts?" Catherine knew that she would never break her gait. "What have I done to make her act this way toward me?" Catherine's pretense at offense was opaque to a ten-year-old.

"I'm real sorry, Catherine. Ari is just mad at you for not coming to see us more. She doesn't mean to be rude." Lisa had played right into Catherine's hands. Catherine had won round one. The sisters, who had not been split on any issue since the womb, were now divided.

"Don't worry about it, Alisa, I'll just have to work really hard to win her over, that's all. I really want to be a mother to the two of you. I know I haven't been around as much as I should have been in the past, but all of that is changing. I am just a short distance away, and I want you to come and visit me. I'm looking at an estate to purchase. I'll have a pool and horses and you will just have a great time. I promise." Catherine pretended to be choked up again.

"Horses?"

"Yes, one for each of you. Do you know what an estate is?" Catherine and Lisa followed the chauffeur, who was heavily laden with packages, up to the house.

"Oh yes, we visit the Carpenter estate all the time," Lisa answered innocently.

"The Carpenter estate? Carpenter, as in Roland?" Catherine was genuinely surprised.

"Yep. Uncle Roland has this really big house and the biggest backyard I have ever seen. It is as big as our whole block, maybe bigger."

"Oh, really?" Catherine cringed inwardly. She knew he was successful, but she had stopped keeping tabs on his ascent to the top when she realized there was a better chance of the L.A. Clippers winning an NBA championship than for her to have a relationship with Roland. Just one more reason she had to bring the great and mighty Roland down.

"Good evening, Catherine. Please explain to me why Ari ran into her room and slammed the door without saying a word?" Terry did nothing to mask his annoyance.

"She has been mean all day to Catherine, and Catherine has only been nice to us. She used the word 'ain't,' Daddy!" Lisa felt relieved to have shared that information with her father.

"Lisa, honey, go on into the den. Jackie, Grandma, and Auntie Vee are in there. I would like to talk to Catherine for a minute." Terry never took his eyes off Catherine.

"Okay, Daddy. Thanks for a great day, Catherine. I'll talk to Daddy about coming to visit you soon. I can't wait to see my horse!" Lisa unknowingly had flawlessly executed Catherine's plan as she reached up to kiss Catherine on the cheek.

"Bye, Alisa. I had a wonderful time today. I'll call you when I get home in the morning, and be sure to send me some of your stories through e-mail. Please tell your sister I'm sorry she didn't have a good time, but I'll try to make it up to her soon." Catherine acted the devoted mother very well.

"Well, well, well. I see you have managed to do what no other human being on this earth could or would want to do . . . drive a wedge between Ari and Lisa. I know the very dangerous game you are trying to play, but Catherine, you can't win. These are my daughters every day, and I will *not* let you do this to *my* family. Have I made myself perfectly clear?" Terry spoke very deliberately into Catherine's face.

"You silly little pathetic man. You won't *let* me? I have already done it, and it was easier than I ever imagined. You don't stand a prayer. Ariana doesn't like me. Fine! I think I have changed my mind; I don't want joint custody of both of them. I want *full* custody of Alisa. My lawyer will be in touch with Roland on Monday." With that, she patted Terry on the cheek, turned on her heels, and was down the steps before Terry could respond.

The cold air rushed past Terry and into the den. He was clueless as to how long he had stared after the limousine before his mother came to ask him why he was standing in the doorway warming the neighborhood. She only had to look in her son's empty eyes to know that Catherine had dropped yet another bomb. She just had no idea that this one was aimed to destroy the Winston family.

"What's wrong, Terry?"

"Catherine wants to split the girls up. She wants full custody of Lisa. Mom, she wants to split my babies up. She's lost her damn mind!"

"What are you yelling about?" Jackie rushed to the foyer with Veronica on her heels.

"Apparently, Ari was a bit of a challenge for Catherine. Now she doesn't want joint custody of both of them. She wants full custody of Lisa," Teresa relayed. Terry had a very faraway look in his eyes; Teresa closed the door and led her son back to the den.

"How could she, Momma?" Terry finally spoke.

"Where is King Solomon when you need him? Damn, this bitch is nuts!" Veronica moved to the bar to freshen her drink.

"Son, I don't know what to say. I guess I'm shocked that anyone could even think of doing such a thing," Teresa said, just above a whisper.

Jackie, Teresa, and Veronica only stared at Terry. All of the women were at a loss for words.

WAIT A MINUTE, chile. Wha' you sayin'?" Momma C stood by the stove waiting for the kettle to whistle for her morning tea.

"Momma, you heard what I'm saying. Catherine wants to split the girls up. She wants to take Lisa full-time. Ari has made no bones about it; she wants little or nothing to do with Catherine. According to Lisa, Ari was not very cooperative during their little outing." Jackie poured herself a cup of coffee.

"Wha' dey Daddy gonna do? I know he ain't gonna stand for dem to be split up. Lawdhamurcy, that woman betta mind. She gonna trip and fall and hurt herself. How can she even have da heart to think of some mess like dat? I have nevah met nobody who makes me wanna cuss like dat Catherine."

"I know, Momma. I wish you could have seen Terry last night. I didn't know what to say to him. He was angry, hurt, and confused."

"Did he call Roland? I knows Roland will know wha' to do!"

"Yeah, he got him, but he was on his way out with Cedes and told him he would be over this morning. I don't know about Terry, but I haven't slept a wink. This woman has cast such a darkness over what should be the happiest time of our lives. Why

doesn't she just go and get her own life? Hell, she can afford to
buy one. Have more babies if she is feeling maternal. Or I guess
she doesn't want the job of raising them, just the reward of having them. Damn! Sorry, Momma."

"I done told ya, baby, dat Catherine makes *me* wanna cuss!"

"I don't think a judge would split the twins up. My God, they
haven't been separated other than the time when Ari was in the
hospital for two days, and even then Lisa slept there one night.
There is no way we can let this happen. Momma, we just can't."
Jackie burst into tears.

"Aw, baby, come 'ere to yo' Momma. We gonna pray on this
thang. God ain't nevah let me down. From the day I started
servin' Him when yo' daddy was so sick 'til this very moment, and
I don't 'spect He gonna start now."

"Oh Momma, I'm so lucky to have you as my mother."

"Yeah, you are blessed, ain't cha." They both laughed and
hugged each other very tightly.

"Now tell me 'zactly wha' happened last night, and don't ya
nevah not wake me up when sum'in this 'portant happens. You
undastan' me, chile?"

"Yes, ma'am." Jackie kissed her mother before she went back to
her steaming cup of coffee.

Momma C poured hot water into her cup and picked a fla-
vored tea bag from the cannister Jackie was always sure to have
filled with her mother's favorites. For as long as she could remember, her mother had never drunk coffee, but she drank two
pots of tea every single day. Jackie had convinced her that herbal
teas were much better for her than black tea—an argument that
Jackie had finally won, though Jackie still thought tea was only
for the infirm. "Now tell yo' Momma 'zactly what happened las'
night, and don't you leave out a thang." Momma C shifted her
weight in her chair trying to find just the right spot.

"Well, the way I understand it, the day with the girls was kinda
rough from Ari's standpoint. She was rude and belligerent with
Catherine. Lisa took Catherine's side, and it hurt Ari more than
it made her angry. Ari thought that Catherine was trying to buy

their love and approval. She wouldn't take any of her gifts willingly. Lisa, on the other hand, was caught up in the whole thing, the limo, the shopping at Saks, and people catering to their every whim. Just listening to them tell the story, I could tell that Catherine played one against other. What a wretched woman!"

"So wha' dem sweet babies think 'bout all dis?" Momma C blew on the steamy hot tea.

"Ari had little or nothing to say. Lisa was the one who relayed the whole story, all the time making Ari out to be the bad one in all of this. Poor thing has no idea what Catherine was doing. She was so glad to report to her father everything she thought would get Ari into trouble. This is so unlike her. They've always had each other's backs. Always the united front."

"And Ari didn't say nuthin' to defend huh'self?"

"You know, Momma, now that you mention it, she didn't. I wonder why?"

"She has no problem tellin' folks how she be feelin' 'bout dem. Dat is da first thing I liked 'bout dat chile."

"She only said that she would rather die than to go live with Catherine, and she couldn't understand why Lisa was so happy to be with her. She said nothing at all about the possibility of the two of them being split up. Neither one of them said anything about the split up, and Terry never mentioned it while they were in the room. I don't believe they know her intent."

"I ain't no psychology doctor, but I know dat ain't no good . . . no good at all. So what did po' Terry say? And Teresa, dat woman is havin' a rough vacation fo' sho'."

"Well, Terry said nothing when Catherine first left. He just had this really faraway look in his eyes. Once he came to his senses, he called Roland. When Roland told him to calm down, and that there was nothing he could do last night, and he would be over first thing this morning to get the full details, Terry swore at him and slammed down the phone. Momma, this is not my Terry. Teresa kept saying how she never liked Catherine even when she and Terry were teenagers. She told us Catherine treated Terry like he had a tail, and he would just make excuses for her."

"You know somebody as nasty as dat Catherine has been dat way from the seed. She was bad when she was still in her daddy's pants. But I tell you dat chile betta mind, mark mah words . . . she betta mind!"

"Momma, nothing bad ever seems to happen to the Catherines of this world. They just go about causing pain and leaving victims in their wake. You know Terry never really told me a lot about his relationship with Catherine, just that she hadn't wanted to raise the babies because she was in college. I guess he was still making excuses for her even after all the pain she had caused him."

"So wha' da story? Why didn't she want dem precious babies?"

"According to Teresa, she made several appointments to have an abortion, and each time Terry talked her out of it. She was actually on her way to the abortion clinic once and her car transmission went out, and she missed the appointment. Teresa had thought all along that Catherine was using the threat of abortion to manipulate Terry until she found out about the missed appointment. Apparently, she never told Terry about that appointment and would have gone through with it, if her car hadn't broken down. It was the last chance she had to have a first-trimester abortion."

"God had it all in His plan, chile, all in His plan. You want some mo' coffee?"

"Thanks, Momma. So after that, she set out to make his life a living hell. She would call him in the middle of the night to go to the Seven-Eleven for a bag of potato chips. Then when he got all the way over there, she would throw them in his face and tell him she had changed her mind because he had taken too long. He would try to tell her how he felt, but then she would only threaten to have an abortion. She threatened him until she was almost six months pregnant. When she had the babies early, she gave him some ridiculous time span to pick up the babies from the hospital or she would sign adoption papers."

"Terry is a good man. There is a lot of men dat would've gone stone gangsta on her ass." Momma C laughed at her own use of the hip-hop term.

"She took his meek spirit as weakness and set out to torture him and has been doing just that for more than twelve years. Well, it is time someone put a stop to her. I have never wanted to do bodily harm to another person in my whole life, but Momma, I'm telling you—"

"Chile, I keep tellin' you, Miss Catherine gonna git hers. And y'all gonna be 'round to see Catherine da Not-So-Great fall. Mah God is too just. So what is Terry gonna do?"

"Well, he's suppose to meet with Roland sometime today. You know Roland and Cedes have been together every day since Christmas Eve. And sistah-gurlfriend hasn't called me. Wait until I talk to her." Jackie and her mother laughed like old friends instead of mother and daughter.

"That chile deserve some happiness. She ain't had no good man in her life, and Roland is a good man despite wha' people thinks about him. He jus' be needin' a good woman. You knows how some black men can't stand a woman wit some success of dey own. Roland gots him 'nough success for four, five men. I jus' wonda if he can be wit jus' one woman. And Cedes will have his nuts if he cheats on her."

"*Momma!*"

"Wha'? Well, she will. You know it, too."

"You do have a point. My sister takes no mess. Her philosophy is a simple one: She don't give none, so she shouldn't have to take none."

"As it oughta be. You sho' have taken yo' share. Lawdhamurcy, it just seems like good people cannot hook up with good people without all dese problems. But you know, my God is gonna give us some answers. Mark mah words, chile, mark mah words."

"I'm markin', Momma, I'm markin'!" Jackie came around the table and hugged her mother. She felt extremely blessed this morning as the sun shone through the kitchen window. It was as though the sun brought with it an answer to the horrendous situation Catherine was causing. She knew now what she would have to do. She would have to talk to Catherine sistah-gurl to sistah-gurl, and perhaps a trip to San Antonio was in order. Her daughters would not be separated. She would not, could not, stand for this madness. But knowing Terry would never approve, she decided she just wouldn't tell him. He was always the one who seemed to have the answers to her problems. He could fix anything for her, but now it was her turn. He was still too much of a gentleman to give Catherine what she deserved, but she, on the other hand . . .

THE ACCELERATION OF the Boeing 737 for takeoff in no way matched the rapidity of Jackie's heart. As the last day of the year dawned, she was convinced she had to confront Catherine. This woman needed to know she would not be allowed to wreak havoc in the Winston family. Lisa had proudly shown Jackie the first letter she had addressed to Catherine thanking her for their shopping trip. Jackie committed the address to memory.

The flight was over almost before it began, and within ninety minutes, Jackie was standing curbside hailing a cab. Despite the cold winter morning, Jackie was sweating. She was nervous and began to wonder if she was in fact doing the right thing. The thirty-minute cab ride gave her time to go over the speech she had prepared in her head. She had taken special care to dress to impress . . . the doorman, that is.

As the uniformed doorman opened the cab door, she let her coat fall open exposing her abundant cleavage. The split in her skirt exposed her beautiful ample thighs. The middle-aged Euro-American man struggled to maintain eye contact as he spoke to her. "Good afternoon, ma'am. How may I assist you?"

"Good afternoon, my good man. I am here to surprise my sister, Catherine Hawkins. She is a penthouse resident. I have just

flown in from Brazil, and I want to surprise her. Please help me."
Jackie struggled to keep her curly red hair out of her face.

"Help you how, ma'am?" The doorman was looking at her like
she was a plate of gravy and he was a biscuit.

Jackie leaned in close and whispered, "I haven't seen Cat in almost two years, with her in Spain and me in Brazil, so could you
please let me up to her place without calling her? It would mean
the world to me." Jackie's breast brushed against his arm.

"Oh, ma'am, I'm sorry. I can't do that. I must announce you."

"Come on, Bill, please." Jackie had read his name tag. This
time she placed her hand on his arm and stared longingly into his
eyes. "Let me give my sister myself as a holiday gift. Please don't
ruin the surprise. I have come so far to do this."

Bill used the time he contemplated his decision to stare at
Jackie from head to toe several times. "How can I deny such a
sweet lady what she wants? Just press P in the elevator. It will take
you up to her penthouse. She is in penthouse four."

"Bill, you are such a dear," Jackie said as she kissed him on the
cheek. She heard him moan involuntarily. She knew her behavior was shameless, but she had to do what she had to do for her
children.

The elevator ride seemed to last for hours. Penthouse number
four was directly in front of the elevator. Jackie knocked softly.

"Come in, Consuella." Catherine's voice was muffled but distinctive. Jackie cautiously opened the French door and stepped
into a room decorated totally in white. It was obvious that no children lived here.

"What the hell are you doing here? Who the fuck let you up
here?"

"Catherine, I didn't come to argue, but to talk woman to
woman. What you're doing is not right! May I please sit down?"
Jackie didn't give her time to respond.

"What a spineless little weasel Terry is. Sending you down here
to do his dirty work. Well, you are wasting your time. I will not reconsider. Those are my children, not yours, and only half his. I

have every right to want to be in their lives." Catherine moved around the room like a lioness about to pounce.

"Terry doesn't even know I'm here. I came here to reason with you. You have turned this family upside down, and quite frankly, I'm not going to stand for it anymore." Jackie sat on the edge of the couch in case she had to move quickly.

"*You* are not going to stand for it! Who the hell are *you*? I am supposed to be afraid because *you* are not going to stand for it. News flash, Jacqueline! This is not about *you*. Watch my lips, these are *my* children. I carried them. I suffered for thirty-one hours and then spit them out, not one, but two of them. So you need to get your fat ass out of my face talking about what you are not going to stand for." Catherine's arms flailed as she yelled.

"Why is everything about you, Catherine? Have you even considered what this will do to Ari and Lisa? Ari is so distraught by all of this, she is not sleeping or eating well. She has never been separated from her sister. But of course you wouldn't know any of this, would you?"

"Look, you busybody bitch, this is not your fight. I'm in this with Terrence. And when I finish telling my attorney about you coming here to threaten me, we'll see how the court feels about this."

"You're wrong. Terry's fights are my fights. I'm going to marry that wonderful man!"

"And y'all are shacking up in front of the children! How do you think a judge is going to feel about that? What a wonderful example that is, you slut!"

"You know, I thought I could appeal to you as one mother to another, but I see there is only one mother in this room. I pity you, Catherine. You'll never win full custody or even joint custody for that matter. You'll end up all alone. And *that* you can take to the bank! When is the last time your money ran up to you, grabbed you around your waist, and told you it loved you? Huh, Catherine? When is the last time your money begged you to crawl into bed with you because it was afraid? When is the last time your money made you so proud that you thought your chest would burst?"

"Get the fuck out of my penthouse *now* or I'll call the police and have your ass arrested for trespassing, invasion of privacy, breaking and entering, and anything else I can come up with."

"I'm going, Catherine, but not because you told me to leave, but because I don't want to be anywhere you are." Jackie got up to leave.

"That doorman will be washing toilets at McDonald's before the clock strikes midnight. I'll see to it personally." Catherine held the door open.

"Don't blame him. I tricked him. He actually thought he was doing something nice for you. Why anyone would want to is beyond me . . ." Jackie walked through the door with her head held high. She knew she had done the right thing. Catherine slammed the door. Jackie knew that she would have to contend with the doorman on her way out. After Catherine, *anything* else would be a piece of cake! As Jackie stepped off the elevator she heard Bill on the phone.

"But Ms. Hawkins . . ."

Jackie stepped quickly toward the door and out of the building. There was a cab waiting. She opened the door, quickly slid in, and spoke to the driver. "San Antonio airport, please." As the cab pulled from the curb, she saw Bill running out of the door.

The trip to the airport did little to calm her. She now had to contend with telling Terry what she had done. He would be livid. She only hoped Catherine didn't get to him first. He was spending the day with the children and dressing for the party at her place. She hoped he wouldn't check his voice mail messages.

3 2

CEDES COULDN'T DECIDE which fragrance to wear. She had the complete collection of all of her favorites, but which one would bring Roland to his knees? Roland had kept his word; he had rocked her world off its axis. The wining and dining had been nonstop since Christmas Eve. She had made it clear that she wanted a man who was willing to give of himself, not his checkbook.

She had seen too many NFL players buy women to want any part of that madness. She had told more than her share of athletes she wasn't for sale. She smiled as she recalled a conversation between herself and an NBA star at the party after a Steelers-Cowboys game a few years before. She told the very handsome, very rich, very tall brotha that nothing was truly a gift, and her reputation wasn't for sale.

"I ain't mad atcha! But my groupie, thinkin'-their-coochie-gonna-hook-ya, hoochie sistahs make me livid!" He had laughed with her and told her he liked her style and the man that landed her would truly have found a treasure. Beauty, brains, and wit were not as plentiful as some other female *assets*.

Roland was not accustomed to women not wanting him to spend his money. He had told her on several occasions that dating her was the biggest challenge of his life. She made the ugliest domestic legal matters look like a day at the beach. But she could see in his eyes that Mr. Carpenter was up for the challenge. Falling in love with Roland had never even been a consideration. His reputation for treating women as paper cups had exempted from contemplation a relationship as anything more than friends. She wasn't sure now why she thought that she had what it took to tame the beast in him, but he had assured her hourly that she had exactly what it took.

Now, for the fifth consecutive year, she was attending the Black Legal Eagles New Year's Eve Ball with Roland. Perhaps the first year didn't count.

With much persuasion, Cedes's mother had convinced her to accept Jackie's tag-along invitation to the black-tie gala filled with eligible, educated, and employed brothas in tuxedos.

"What do you have to lose, girl? What is the worst that can happen? You'll dance until your hair turns nappy and have enough champagne to unwind your tight ass," her mother had quipped.

"But, Momma, I don't want to be at a party with all those couples. I will feel so out of place. I'll be taken as one of three hundred other black women who look desperate enough to be going to a New Year's Eve party alone to find herself a husband."

"Well, Miss High and Mighty, you need to be looking for one yo'self, and if going to a New Year's Eve party looking desperate is what it takes, then I suggest you wear that black dress that is cut low to the waist and split up to your behind like mine."

She had reluctantly agreed to attend the shingdig with Jackie and Terry. Jackie had told her they would pick her up so she wouldn't have to worry about drinking and driving. Much to her surprise, when she answered the door expecting to see her lifelong friend with her newfound love, there stood a uniformed chauffeur.

"Good evening, ma'am. I'm Garrison, and your party awaits you in the car. I'll be transporting you to this evening's gala," the tall woman with the European accent and the deep, dark, rich chocolate, flawless skin and bright smile said as she stood at attention with her chauffeur's cap under her arm. Cedes remembered wondering if Garrison was her first or last name.

As Garrison opened the door, much to her surprise there was not one couple, but two. She had been so shocked that she had paused for a very long time before actually taking her seat inside the poshly equipped vehicle. For a moment, she had considered turning around and walking back into her house and putting on her ugliest pajamas to watch Dick Clark with her mother.

Remembering that night brought tears to her eyes. Oh, how she missed Margaret. She felt so alone this New Year's Eve. Her mother had always been there to help her dress for the ball, like she was a teenage girl heading off to the prom. And now she had no one to fuss over her. Margaret would have decided which fragrance was right! Death was such a cruel thief!

After the polite introductions, Cedes had settled in the car next to Jackie, at whom she shot venomous glances. How dare she not tell her there would be two couples? Now she was a fifth wheel, not a third. *When was the last time you saw anything with five wheels?* she asked herself.

Endurance was the word that came to mind when she thought of the ride to the Ritz that night. Jackie knew better than to look at her. Terry was so pleasant and seemed to genuinely be in awe of her friend. Roland was too cool to be of any earthly good, as Margaret would say, and his date was drinking champagne like it was water after an aerobics class.

She was relieved to find upon her arrival there were several single people in attendance. It never ceased to amaze her that no matter how old men and women got, it was still like being in the gym at a junior high school dance. There was the great divide— women huddled in a group trying to look like they didn't want the men staring at them in their skin-tight, low-cut, split-high, can't-pay-the-rent-on-the-first-because-I-bought-this dress and men on the other side of the room pretending not to notice.

She had to admit that this was one of the most elegant gatherings of her people she had ever attended, and she had attended more than a few. She was impressed. They had arrived at the beginning of the reception hour because Roland was a member of the board of directors and was required to meet and greet. After whispering a death threat into Jackie's ear, she excused herself and began to move around the room. As a public relations person, she was as comfortable at a party with strangers as she was at a family picnic.

There were conversations mainly about points of law and legal fees among the men. Imagine her surprise to find the women plotting which of the presumably eligible bachelors would be picking out china patterns by spring. The evening progressed easily, and Cedes was actually having a decent enough time.

During dinner, to say that Bambi—Roland's date (okay, so her real name was Brenda)—was feeling the effects of the several bottles of champagne she had swigged down would have been an understatement. Halfway through the salad course, she slumped over onto Roland's shoulder sound asleep. After much embarrassment, Roland excused himself and assisted her out of the ballroom. When he returned, he was alone and, without explanation, returned to his salad.

Jackie and Cedes exchanged glances and then stared at the others at the table. It was as though nothing at all had happened. Cedes found out later via Terry that Roland's choices in women left more than a little to be desired. His friends would act as though nothing had happened to save the golden child of the legal field any further personal embarrassment. The one thing that Cedes had learned on her circuit of the room during the cocktail hour was that Roland was *the* most sought-after bachelor in Dallas. Women of all ethnicities sought to be Mrs. Carpenter. Roland began to focus his undivided attention on Cedes, but she wanted no part of this Afrocentric Don Juan.

There were literally a hundred women in that room that would have given their grandmomma's secret fried chicken recipe to change places with her. The champagne flowed, and by the time cream was poured into the coffee being served with dessert, Cedes was having a great time with the handsome, ebony, satin-tongued, and infamous Mr. Carpenter.

Cedes and Roland had danced their way into the new year and brought the sun up with their best friends. They had agreed that until someone special was in their lives, they would always spend New Year's Eve together to spare each other the heartbreak of lottery dating.

Now, some four years later, Cedes was having a date with a man she thought she might be falling in love with. The muffled ring of the phone could hardly be heard over the stereo since it was buried under six dresses, not one of which seemed to be right. She knew she should have gone shopping for a new dress this week.

"Hello."

"Hey, sistah-gurl. So have you decided what you're wearing?" Jackie sounded out of breath.

"Hell no. I've narrowed it down to six dresses. Of course you're probably dressed and having a cocktail by now."

"Gurl, I just got back from San Antonio an hour ago. I'm trying to get my wide hips in these control-top panty hose. I should have stuck to that diet I started in September."

"I can't believe you actually went to see that woman alone. I really wish you had let me go with you. And not to be able to tell Roland what you were doing was so hard. That woman scares me, Jackie. How did it go?"

"You have no idea how wicked this woman is. I have never met anyone who made my blood run as cold as she does. But she has never seen a fight like she is in for this time. She will not destroy my family. I just pray that our confrontation didn't do more harm than good . . . I had no idea I could be that ugly, gurl."

"Why are you telling me this when I have to be ready in fifteen minutes? Roland is coming by early; he says he has to discuss something important with me. Gurl, I am so nervous. He wouldn't give me a hint."

"Gurl, why are you playing naïve? You know good and well what that man wants to talk to you about."

"You know, I think I do . . . I think I do." They both laughed.

"Coming . . ." Cedes said, flying down the stairs with her shoes in her hands.

She slipped her shoes on and took one last look in the hall mirror. She looked fabulous! She paused for a second, just to get her composure before opening the door. "Right on time."

"Hello, sweet—" Roland's word hung in his heart but refused to escape his lips. Cedes had taken his breath away.

"Sweet?" Cedes knew she had worked her magic on him, but she seized the opportunity to tease him. "Is that a new name for me?"

"I'm sorry. I was going to say, 'Hello, sweetheart,' but when I saw you, I couldn't speak. You are so beautiful. These are for you." Roland was as awkward as a schoolboy as he gave Cedes a dozen roses.

"Thank you, Roland. They are beautiful and they smell so good. Please come in."

"No, Cedes, I thought they were beautiful until you opened the door. You are absolutely breathtaking. You always look good to me, but tonight, oh my God!"

"You are so sweet, Roland. You're embarrassing me." Cedes blushed.

"Come here, gurl, and give me a kiss." Roland became lost in Cedes's embrace. "We have a few minutes before we need to head over to pick up Terry and Jackie. Let's have a cocktail and talk for a few minutes." Roland took Cedes by the hand and led her into the den.

"I'll make us a drink while you put those in water," Roland said as he kissed her softly on her forehead.

"So, Roland, what did you want to talk to me about?" Cedes asked as she took a seat next to him on the plush champagne-colored sofa.

"Wow, you get right to the heart of the matter, don't you?" Roland laughed nervously. "You and I have known each other for four years tonight, and during all of that time we have been good friends. Not just tolerating each other because of our best friends, but genuinely liking one another. Of course, we've had our disagreements, but never anything serious. Then, as if someone turned on a light, I really saw you for the first time when you came home on vacation. I've thought of you every waking moment since Christmas Eve, Cedes." Roland looked at the floor as he spoke. "I've fallen head over heels in love with you. I know this because I only want to be where you are. It kills me to be away from you."

"I must confess that I think I'm falling in love with you, too. I can't believe that after all this time, Roland, I yearn to be near you every moment." Cedes spoke barely above a whisper. Her own words scared her.

"What about the other guy, Cedes?"

"I basically told him to forget he ever knew me. He is nonexistent in my book."

"Are you serious? I don't even care why it happened! This is fantastic." Roland put his arms up, making the sign for a touchdown. "Please don't think that I have lost my mind based on what I am about to say. Promise you won't laugh in my face. Promise?"

"I promise! What is it? Dang!"

"Will you marry me, Cedes?"

"What?"

"I know it is wild, but I also know this is right."

"Roland, I know you are an intelligent, levelheaded man. Do you know what you are saying?"

"Cedes, I have never been more serious in my life. I want you to marry me. I will marry you tonight if you say the word."

"Roland, that is probably the sweetest and silliest thing I have ever heard. If this is as right as you think it is, then a year from tonight, let's have this conversation."

"You're right. I don't want to lose you; I just want to be sure that you are my woman for the rest of my life."

"You're not going to lose me if I am the *only* woman you want. But I won't be one of many. I sing solo. Know what I mean?"

"I'll burn the phone book in the morning."

"You are so silly. So can you commit to only dating me, Roland?"

"If you tell me right here, right now, you are my woman exclusively, I will commit to being your man exclusively."

"I'm your woman exclusively."

"I am your man, exclusively. I love you, Mercedes." Roland took Cedes—his woman—in his arms. This was a very happy New Year's.

AIT A MINUTE. Let me understand what you're saying?" Cedes stared at her best friend in the elegantly framed, beveled mirror as she dried her hands on the warmed towel passed to her by the Ritz-Carlton ladies' room attendant.

"You fly to San Antonio, take a cab to her place, convince the doorman you are her sister who just flew in from some foreign country to surprise her, and he lets you up to her penthouse apartment to surprise her? And tell me, was he fired before you reached for the elevator button? You reporters are something else." Cedes shook her head as she continued to stare.

"Well, it is not *my* fault. If he is that gullible, he should not be allowed to guard the door." Jackie checked her flawless makeup in the mirror as she spoke nonchalantly.

"Let me guess, you wore something low, them double D's smiling at him, had that red curly hair of yours blowing in the wind, flashed those stellar, pearly whites at him, and someone should have offered you some cheese to go with that whine?" Cedes checked her perfect figure in the black-lace and sequined see-through dress she had finally decided on and smiled with approval—the dress that rendered Roland speechless earlier that evening.

"Damn, gurl, how did you know? That is exactly what I did!" Jackie laughed as she looked at the woman she could not love any more if they shared the same DNA.

"I've only known you your whole life, remember? So tell me what happened when she opened the door and you were standing there."

Jackie relayed the whole sordid tale.

"Damn, how could you be so cordial? Gurlfriend would have been in for a real beat-down had I been there. And you should have let me go with you. I'm still mad at cha." The two friends took a seat in the lavishly upholstered lounge chairs.

"I had to do this alone, Cedes. Besides, I *know* you would have gotten us arrested for sure. I just hope I didn't do more harm than good. She says she is going to bring up our sexual relationship in court."

"Oh my God! I know that Ho Phi Ho didn't go there! I see what you mean that you may have done more harm than good. When do you plan to tell Terry about this little road trip of yours? You know he is going to be livid, don't you? As he should be!"

"Gurl, I have to tell him in the morning. She may have called him already. He spent the day with all the kids, and then we dressed at my place. I hope I haven't made a very big mistake. I want you to tell Roland tomorrow before he talks to Terry." Jackie glanced down at the beautiful watch she had received for Christmas. "Gurl, we had better get back. We have been gone almost a half an hour. We have left two very handsome black men with skills and benefits alone with a roomful of vulturettes in spandex."

"Gurl, you don't have a thing to worry about. A woman could walk up to Terry butt-nekked, dip and tongue him, and he would break her grip and say: 'Have you seen my fiancée? She is the woman in the black silk dress trimmed in rhinestones with her perfect double-D cleavage showing and wearing the Prudential on her third finger left hand.'" Cedes worked her neck sistah-gurl style.

"You are such a fool, gurl. Just one of the many reasons I love you so much. But you know I see a *real* change in Roland. I guess you don't see the way he looks at you. He has always loved you, but now he is *in* love with you. Don't be too hard on my brother now. Believe me, Roland has made a drastic change in the past seven days. Even Terry mentioned it. Have faith in him. Give the brother a chance. He will prove me right—I am sure of it."

"Well, we'll see. I have to tell you I think I am falling in love with him, too." Cedes smiled to herself.

"I *knew* that. How can you not love him? He is wonderful. He just did not know he had met the right woman until now." Jackie never looked back as she said the words that made Cedes's heart skip a beat.

She had said it out loud. She was in love with Roland. The thought scared her. However, she had read someplace that *fear* was only *False* . . . Evidence . . . Appearing . . . Real.

"Well, we thought we were going to have to send a search party after you two. Where have you been? I know. Some lawyer wanted to show you his briefs." Terry teased them with one of the lamest lines in the legal profession.

"More like some judge wanting to invite them into his chambers. But who could blame him? Look at our women, Terry. They be *foine*! And I have to check my law library, but I do believe both of those dresses break a few laws someplace. Utah is a given!" Roland said as he pulled Cedes closer to him.

"I know that is *correct*. You should see how the other women stared at the two of you when you walked over here. Good thing green goes with black." Terry moved closer to Jackie.

"Well, shall we tell them, Cedes?" Roland smiled.

"Tell us what?" Jackie snapped her neck around to look at her friend, with whom she had just spent more than thirty minutes in the bathroom bearing her soul.

"Tonight, I asked Cedes to date me exclusively. I actually asked her to marry me, but she laughed in my face. But she has agreed that we will take it one day at a time. I don't plan to blow this. My job is to make this woman my wife. And you all know how seriously I take my work."

"Congratulations, my man!" Terry hugged Roland in that fraternal close, but not too close, manner.

"How dare you not tell your best friend whom you have known since the hospital nursery!" Jackie pretended to be angry, but she was so happy and started jumping up and down screaming with joy.

"As he said, we are taking it one day at a time. But he has assured me that I am the only woman for him and I believe him. And, yes, we do love each other." Cedes fought back tears. Her mother would have been so happy.

As the clock drew closer to midnight, each of the friends reflected on the many events of the year that were soon to be a distant memory. A year when . . .

Terry had decided that living another year under a different roof than Jackie, Michael, and Michelle was no longer acceptable. He knew beyond a shadow of a doubt that God was merciful and just and that He would not disrupt his family. His faith was being tested, and he knew now what it meant to lean on God.

Jackie had finally woken up and decided that she could not find a more loving and caring man than Terry, and she would no longer put up the roadblocks that would keep them from making their relationship one that would take them into eternity.

Cedes had lost the one person in her life that meant everything to her, and she had survived. She also knew that her friends loved her as much as or more than her family and that she was truly blessed to have them all. She had learned that she had to trust someone with her heart if she was ever to find true love.

Roland now knew what Terry felt the first time he saw Jackie in that supermarket parking lot. He was disappointed it had taken him all these years to wake his stupid ass up. He also had learned that if he was ever to be healed of his childhood wounds, he had to learn to forgive.

The new year would be born to four people who had made some very important discoveries, four people who each had had a wake-up call.

3 4

YOUR HONOR, THE defense requests a continuance to prepare its case. Truly, Ms. Hawkins and her counsel understand that a case of this magnitude cannot be prepared in little over a month." Roland shot a glance at Catherine and her attorney.

Catherine had been true to her word. She had hired the most expensive law firm in Texas to present her case. The law firm was notorious for high-profile corporate cases. The family law division was small and had only been in existence for a little over three years. Roland's first encounter with Shaw, Rosenberg, and Maxwell would be interesting and long-remembered. However, in the words of that great philosopher Bill Cosby, Terry had retained the best, not the most expensive. The young woman in the black designer suit had her work cut out for her. This was family court, a court where Roland Carpenter reigned as king.

Roland was not pleased with the judge who had been assigned to the case. She was the youngest female judge in all of Texas. She had finished law school at age twenty, passed the bar, and become a licensed attorney by the time she was barely old enough to order a glass of chardonnay. She was elected to the bench by a landslide. She would definitely be sympathetic to a woman who would do whatever it took to pole-vault to the top of her field in record time. Somehow Roland did not believe it was the luck of the draw that Judge Constance Agnew sat staring down at him with raised eyebrows. "Mr. Carpenter, just how much of a continuance do you need?" Judge Agnew inquired in her infamous monotone manner.

"Thirty days, Your Honor," Roland responded with confidence.

"I object, Your Honor. Perhaps if Mr. Carpenter had spent the holiday season preparing this case instead of socializing, he would be prepared. These girls have been kept from their mother far too long as it is, and another thirty days is not acceptable to my client." The razor-tongued, pint-sized advocate, Naomi Sharpe, had overstepped her bounds.

"Your Honor, how I spend my time is none of this court's concern. As far as her client's being kept from her children, we will show in no uncertain terms that it has been *her* choice. She has been basically absent from their lives for almost eleven years except for a few sporadic visits. She could visit them as often as she wished. She just does not seem to wish it to be very often." Roland did nothing to mask his annoyance at the opposing counsel's personal attack.

"That is quite enough from both of you. I will give you ten days, Mr. Carpenter, not thirty. Ms. Sharpe, I trust that meets with your approval. If it doesn't, consider it your payment for the personal attack on Mr. Carpenter. This court is adjourned until January twenty-fourth at nine A.M., and, Mr. Carpenter, I suggest you be prepared." With that, Judge Agnew's gavel let both attorneys know that she was finished with them for today.

"Cheap shot, counselor. Then again, what else should I have expected from this team?" Roland met Catherine's attorney between the plaintiff and defense tables.

"Don't take it personally, Roland. Just doing what I have to do." Naomi Sharpe gave Roland a look that made the hair on the back of his neck stand on end.

"Can we be ready in ten days?" Terry looked nervously at Roland as he packed his briefcase.

"Of course, we'll be ready. We're ready now. I'm just waiting for the private investigator's report. Relax, Terry. I *am* ready for this battle. But believe me, it is going to be a bloodbath."

"You keep telling me to relax, but it is hard to relax when I could be losing two of the most important people in my life."

"I talked to the investigator last night, and we will not lose."

"You keep saying that, but I still don't trust Catherine. And that lawyer of hers is as ruthless as she is."

"Well, my brotha, unfortunately that is why people pay us. To be ruthless. Not a pretty job, but someone has to do it."

"I guess I never really think about what it is you do." Terry looked at the floor almost ashamed of what Catherine had forced his hand to do. Terry had always found his strength in being a solid man with good moral values, and till this point he had never had to fight dirty, but with Catherine he had no choice. When Roland had told him what they were up to, his first reaction was to say no. But Roland convinced him that Catherine would stop at nothing to get what she wanted. Sitting in this courtroom with her today, he knew that Roland had made the right move.

The investigator had filled Roland in on the results of their probe. As Terry sat listening to Roland, it made him sick inside to know that he had once loved Catherine, a woman with a heart of stone, no, make that no heart at all.

"Honey, are you okay?" Jackie's voice had its usual calming effect.

"Yeah, baby, I'm fine. Let's get out of this place." Terry looked to Roland for the sign that his work here had been done.

"Are you headed back to the office, Terry?" Roland held open the swinging gate for him.

"I think so. All of this takes so much out of me. I just want it to be over. Now we have to wait ten more days. Once it all starts, how long do you think we'll be in court?" Terry gripped Jackie's hand as though he were falling from a cliff and she was his only means of survival.

"Probably two to three days. These don't normally take long, but this fight is going to get messy," Roland said, knowing Catherine and Naomi would hear him.

"It doesn't have to be that way. Just give my client what she wants. She *is* their mother, and what judge would deny a mother, a fit mother, custody of her daughter? Hell, I can get a crack addict custody of her child." Naomi displayed that evil smile once again.

"And this is something you are proud of? Lovely clients you have, Ms. Sharpe." Jackie's interjection dripped with sarcasm.

Jackie felt Terry's grip tighten on her hand. He knew she was about to step to Naomi and give her a clear picture of her feelings for both her and Catherine. As much as he wanted to give Jackie free rein to unleash her anger, Terry knew this was not the place. Jackie took his cue.

"Well, we all do what we think is necessary. Don't we, Jacqueline?" Catherine stared at Jackie as if to say, "Watch it or I'll tell Terry you came to see me."

Jackie's mind flashed back to the first few hours of this new year when Roland had dropped them off after the gala. As they strolled hand in hand up the walkway to Jackie's home, she knew that she had to share the truth about what she had done with Terry.

He had always been easy to talk to about problems, but she had never done anything of this magnitude. She still felt the effects of the champagne despite the large breakfast she had consumed at the intimate gathering of the Black Legal Eagles board members and their invited guests following the ball. It had taken the edge off, and she hoped it had done the same to Terry. She asked him to sit on the lovers' bench on the porch before going inside because she needed to talk to him. She explained what she had done and said the previous day. She held her breath, ready for his wrath.

"Do you think I can't handle my own business?" Terry was furious.

"I was only trying to help. I thought I could reason with her," Jackie pleaded.

"Jackie, there is no reasoning with her. Don't you understand that? She will take this and use it against us. I know her! Why didn't you tell me you were going? I thought you were out shopping all day, and you were off on a plane to San Antonio. Suppose something had happened to you? I would never have even known where you were. I can't believe you did this, Jackie!" Terry stood and walked to the other end of the porch. He had never been this angry with her.

"I'm sorry. I was only trying to help. I could no longer sit idly by and watch her drag my man over the coals. Sue me for loving your proud ass." Jackie started to cry.

Her tears weakened his defenses. "Oh, baby, I'm sorry for yelling at you. This whole thing has us all nuts, doing shit we would never do or say to each other." Terry moved back to Jackie's side. "I am still mad at you, but promise me you will talk to me before you decide to help. Deal?"

Through her tears Jackie said, "Deal."

He wiped away her tears, grabbed and kissed her. He told her he couldn't believe she loved him that much. He knew that with her on his side, they would win this thing.

Jackie walked toward Catherine and whispered, "Yes, coming to see you was probably a mistake, but you are right, we all do what we think we have to do." Jackie then moved closer to Terry to show their unshakable solidarity.

Jackie caught Catherine off-guard with her comment. Catherine thought she would be able to hold the threat of exposure over Jackie's head, but Jackie had totally defused Catherine. Honesty and trust had been the foundation of the four-year relationship between Terry and Jackie. She had known all along that she had to tell him what she had done. It didn't matter if Catherine ever told him about her visit or not. She had told him, and that was what mattered. Now their relationship had been even further so-lidified, if that was possible.

Catherine's weak attempt to cause division had failed misera-bly.

Naomi Sharpe shot a questioning glance at her client as if to ask, Is this something I should know about? Catherine stared at Jackie, then at Terry. She thought to herself that she would have the last laugh. She would get her daughter, and there was noth-ing they could do to stop her.

Jackie left the courtroom with a new feeling of victory, one she had not felt since this whole ugly mess began. She turned slightly and smiled at Catherine. Catherine stared.

Catherine needed a cigarette and Wendell, and not necessarily in that order. Wendell had been a breath of fresh air since she had arrived in Texas. Six foot five, two hundred and forty pounds of solid muscle. Muscles that he knew expertly how to use. She would call him to be waiting for her at the airport. It would defi-nitely make for a very pleasant limousine ride back to the pent-house.

As Catherine strolled out of the courtroom, she wondered how much of her life would have to change to indulge this mother-hood madness. If only she had been as smart eleven years ago as she was today, there would have been nothing that her holier-than-thou, Wednesday-night-prayer-meetin'-attendin', Bible-thumpin' mother could have told her that would have convinced her that having a baby was God's gift to her. If her background in-vestigation had not revealed her parental status, this whole mess would not be an issue. She would be president of U.S. operations already. *If snatching one of the brats I brought into the world will ensure that, so damn be it,* she thought.

ONEY, IT'S ALMOST over. I'll be back in less than a month." Cedes lay on top of the custom-made black-and-gold comforter. "This is the first time I have ever hated to go on the road during the play-offs. This is the time that we all work for; all the hype and parties are like drugs to us. You make this so hard for me."

The only light in the room came from the prismed oil lamp Jackie had given her on Friend's Day last year. Roland had met with the private investigator on Terry's case for dinner. The meeting had either gone extremely well or extremely badly because it had not ended until nearly ten o'clock. Roland was careful to explain his whereabouts to Cedes all the time now. She was amused by his overexplanations of any delays. He made every conceivable effort to be the perfect man.

"Let me come to pick you up. You can leave from here in the morning. I miss you and you haven't even left yet. I just need to smell your hair, touch your face." Roland was uncharacteristically pleading.

"Honey, it's almost eleven-thirty. I have a seven A.M. flight, I haven't packed, and you are forty-five minutes farther from the airport. It makes no sense. But you know I do want to kiss those lips of yours though, don't you?" Cedes closed her eyes and touched her fingers to her lips, and moaned at the thought of kissing Roland. The man's lips were magic.

"If you think I am letting you leave town without seeing you, then you are out of your mind. You don't seem to understand; you are my life. It is hard enough that you are on the other side of Dallas, but to be out of the state for a month—I may not survive."

"I'm sure you can find something to occupy your time while I am gone." Cedes regretted the words as soon as they slipped from her mouth.

There was a long pause, a very long pause, on the other end of the phone. Finally, in a defeated tone, Roland managed to say, "I guess I still have a lot to prove. I'll be busy with the case. But I assure you, that is all."

"Honey, I'm sorry. That wasn't fair of me. I am just as upset as you are about leaving. I can fly home on Wednesdays, but I would have to leave on a Thursday." Cedes felt an ache in her heart at the thought of leaving Roland even for three days.

"I guess I haven't been committed long enough to have a proven track record." There was still pain in Roland's voice.

"I am sorry, Roland. I had no right to say that. After we do the wrap of Sunday's game, I'll be home, I promise." Cedes wished she had packed earlier. She really wanted to see Roland before she left.

Since she had been on leave, her first two days back in the office had been stressful, but she loved it. It felt good to be back to her old self again. The counseling had helped, but Roland had been the single most influential factor in her speedy mental recovery. She felt she had buried her only source of unconditional love when they lowered the gold-trimmed, white rectangular box into the ground. This trip home had proven she was wrong. She had friends who loved her no matter how out of control she was. And now, there was a strong black man who loved her. He was not afraid, intimidated, or jealous of her success.

"I love you, Cedes. I need to go; I have to prepare a brief for tomorrow morning. I'll talk to you before you leave in the morning, my love." Roland needed some time to think about Cedes's comment, and the thought of her leaving was more than he could bear.

"I love you, Roland, and I trust you. I honestly do. I need to get up and pack anyway. You gonna miss me?"

"More than you will ever imagine. 'Night, my lady."

"Good night, Roland. Sweet dreams."

As Cedes placed the phone in its cradle, her hand lingered as if it were a mystical connection to Roland. As she sat up on the bed, she ran her hand across the velvety soft comforter. It had been more time than she cared to admit since she had shared this bed with a man. And even then it was someone whom she didn't love. She couldn't remember making love to someone who loved her the way she loved him. Whether it was her loving him more or vice versa. This time would be different, whenever "this time" was.

"Gurl, get up off your butt and pack," Cedes mumbled out loud. Her flight was much too early to leave packing until the morning. Why couldn't Dallas ever play San Diego in the play-offs? But no, she was trekking off to the coldest spot in the United States—Green Bay!

Flipping on the light, she stepped into the closet and her eyes fell on the dress she had worn New Year's Eve. Memories, very pleasant memories, of the most spectacular night she could ever remember flooded back. As Roland's date, she had been the belle of the ball. Roland was serving his second year of a three-year term as the chairman of the Black Legal Eagles—they treated him as if he were the second coming. Consequently, her treatment had been pretty heavenly, as well.

But the perks that were associated with the events paled in comparison to Roland's treatment of her. Regulars to the event had seen them together for years now, but this year, everyone noticed that things were different. He never left her side, held her hand constantly, fed her strawberries, and stared down in her eyes as they slow-danced to fast music. There was not one woman—

with the exception of Jackie—who wasn't at least a tiny bit envious.

- Breakfast had been so much fun. There was nothing greater than being an African-American professional. It was by far the best of both worlds. Whether it was the electric slide or the electoral vote, a juke joint or a judge's chamber, a trip to Boston courtesy of a six no trump or a trip to Brussels courtesy of the White House, they could handle it all! Everyone was tipsy. The event committee had the DJ set up in the banquet room designated for the breakfast, and people were still dancing. The food was endless, and everyone laughed and enjoyed themselves as though it were three-thirty in the afternoon instead of the morning. After the chauffeur had dropped Terry and Jackie off, Roland had had him drive them around until the sun turned the sky royal blue and orange. He had reiterated his love for her countless times. His promise to make her Mrs. Carpenter had almost convinced her of his sincerity. The night had truly been one from a romantic fantasy.

As Cedes packed, she hummed Patti LaBelle's "If Only You Knew." She was trying desperately to keep her cool and not to fall head over heels in love with Roland, but she was failing miserably.

Roland opened his briefcase and strewed papers out on his mahogany four-poster bed to review the brief he needed to dictate, but his heart wasn't in it. The meeting with the private investigator went better than he could have hoped. Their plan had worked flawlessly. It should have been easy to dictate his report. All he could do was see Cedes's face, hear her voice, smell her perfume. He went to the kitchen to get some juice. When he opened the refrigerator, he saw the jar of pickled beets that Cedes had picked up at the market the first time he took her shopping for groceries.

They had shopped and laughed all through the grocery store like two teenagers. He had pretended to gag when she picked up the beets. He would never understand how she could eat them out of the jar. That night had been one of the best dates he had ever had. They drank wine in front of the fireplace, listened to jazz, and finally ate seriously charred steaks and overcooked potatoes around midnight. Once again Cedes fell asleep in his arms. He loved the feeling, one he wanted to experience every night for the rest of his life. It was absolutely amazing how many nights he had spent sitting up "just holding" this woman.

That was it. He knew what he had to do. He slammed the refrigerator shut, grabbed his keys, and headed for the garage. As he backed the Mercedes out of the garage, Kenny G blew, as only Kenny could, "Three of a Kind," and the hypnotic sounds of the saxophone filled the air. He smiled to himself as he thought of a royal flush . . . He had truly drawn the best possible hand life could deal.

As Roland pulled into the circular drive, his heart fluttered. The house was fully illuminated, much to his surprise. He knew he should have called first. He was presuming a little too much by showing up well after midnight. He should have least picked up a rose at the 7-Eleven, but he came only with his heart in his hand.

When Cedes opened the door with no makeup, wearing sweats, and barefoot, she never looked more beautiful. They didn't speak a word. She leapt into his arms. He held her as if they had been separated at birth and this was their first reunion. He stepped in and kicked the door closed behind him. His lips touched hers. An electrical current started in the back of his neck and radiated through his body. When they finally broke their lip lock, tears streamed down Cedes's face. Roland kissed them gently. "Why are you crying?"

"I don't know. I just know that every cell in my body craved to be near you, and as I was getting dressed to come over to your place, I heard you pull into the driveway."

Roland kissed her again, this time lifting her off the floor. This would surely be another night when they would bring the sun up together.

WENDELL STOOD AT the gate holding a perfect red rose and looking like a home-cooked meal to a student coming home for Thanksgiving. Catherine smiled. She was so glad she had left him a voice mail message instructing him to meet her at the airport. She was tired, and the man had hands from God. He could massage her woes away with a simple touch. He was a professional masseur, but she refused to let him see other clients. She paid him handsomely for being hers exclusively.

A month before she had been walking and reading the morning stock report when she collided with Wendell. As she looked up at his massive form, she saw the most brilliant smile she had seen since Roland Carpenter had crossed the quad with Terry their freshman year of college. "Excuse me, I shouldn't have been reading and walking." Catherine was much more polite than usual.

"I must confess that I saw you coming toward me and let you walk into me. I wanted to know if you felt as good as I thought you would." The stranger's voice made her think of hot caramel being poured over vanilla ice cream.

"And do I?" Catherine boldly looked straight into his green eyes.

"Much better than I ever imagined. Wendell—Wendell Johnson at your service." He extended his hand.

"Catherine Hawkins, Wendell Johnson. I must say you have very large, I mean strong, hands." Catherine had to get to know this man much better.

"It is a pleasure to meet you, Ms. Hawkins. I must say you are absolutely striking. A man of my size rarely finds a woman who is so physically *compatible*. Do you work here in the building? I have never seen you before."

"I'm new. I've only been here a few weeks. And I certainly would have remembered seeing you." Catherine felt hormonal stirrings as she stared into his eyes.

"May I buy you lunch today, Catherine? I have a meeting at ten. How does one o'clock sound?" Wendell's green eyes stared right back at her.

"And after we have lunch, how is the rest of your afternoon?" Catherine literally salivated.

"Should I clear my calendar?"

"I would strongly suggest it!" Catherine felt like a cat prancing around waiting to be stroked.

"Then consider it cleared."

"I like a man who can think on his feet and make decisions. I am in suite twenty-six hundred."

"Oh, El Salvadore de Casa. Very impressive."

"You know it?"

"There is no one in this building who doesn't know the twenty-sixth floor. I'll pick you up at one."

"Until one, Mr. Johnson."

Wendell arrived promptly at one with a dozen roses in hand. There was no doubt that the gray pin-striped suit had been custom-made to enhance his muscular, rock-hard body. Perfectly manicured hair framed his gorgeous, exotic features. When he smiled, his eyes sparkled like emeralds.

Catherine immediately walked to the front desk. "I am out for the remainder of the day. I'll see you in the morning." Catherine spoke very matter-of-factly to the receptionist without waiting for a response.

"I took the liberty of booking reservations at a great Italian restaurant. I hope that meets with your approval." Wendell held the door as Catherine took command of the doorway space.

"I would prefer something a little more intimate. I have taken the liberty of having my chef prepare a gourmet lunch at my place. I was certain you wouldn't mind." Catherine's tone left no room for objection.

"Your chef? *Wow*. I must tell you, I'm not a pauper, but I may be a little out of my league here. I enjoy the finer things in life, but I suddenly realize that the term is very subjective. I expect to hear Robin Leach's voice at any moment."

"Please don't tell me you're one of those brothers intimidated by the wealth and power of a woman. I'm so bored with those types. It is only lunch, not a marriage proposal." Catherine's sarcasm masked her disappointment that he was yet another man who would be intimidated by her success.

"No, I'm sorry. You're right. It *is* only lunch. Your place it is. Should I follow you?"

"My driver will bring you back to your car later." *Maybe*, Catherine thought to herself.

"I am your humble servant, Ms. Hawkins." Wendell bowed, seemingly impressed.

"Now, that is more like it. You'll enjoy the afternoon, I assure you, Wendell. I suggest you give your heart to God, because all else is going to be mine."

"Oh *my*!" They both laughed, though Wendell's was a nervous one.

That had been the beginning of an affair to remember. Wendell and Catherine became lovers on that fateful day. Wendell was Catherine's drug of choice. She could not get enough of him. He would meet her for lunch, and food would never touch their lips. She would claim to have meetings, but would go home to spend the afternoons with him in bed or on the floor, or on the sundeck, or in the pool. She had never been so irresponsible in her entire career. The man brought alive physiological urges in her that she had only read about. Now here he stood with a rose looking and smelling better than he had when she had left him reluctantly that morning.

Wendell had spent almost every night at the penthouse since they met. He had been an administrative assistant for an attorney in the twin tower adjacent to her building. She had begged him to quit the law firm and come to work for her. His explanation of his total lack of self-control where she was concerned had left her no alternative but to offer him a position as her *personal* trainer at whatever cost he demanded. He accepted.

When Jackie had arrived unannounced, she had missed Wendell by less than twenty minutes. While she was not ashamed of her relationship with this hunk of burning love, she did not want to expose him until after the custody hearing.

"Hey, baby! How did it go?" Wendell lifted her off the floor as he kissed her, something no other man had ever even attempted to do.

"It was continued for ten days. They weren't ready. Imagine that. Roland is so smug, just wait until we finish with him. I have hired the best money can buy. We'll see if his reputation will withstand the beating he is going to take at my hands. And believe me, we will have media there to cover it all."

"Well, we had better get plenty freak on before you're Mother of the Year." Wendell kissed her again.

"Wendell, my love, you needn't worry your ultra-foine self about that. Alisa will be whisked off to boarding school before her little luggage hits the white carpet. There won't even be any need to take it out of the trunk of the limo."

"Hmmmm, don't say carpet after what you put me through last night on the floor in your office. You are such a bad girl. What if the cleaning crew had come in?" Wendell teased her as he took her briefcase.

"Well, if it had been that cute little Carmen, we could have asked her to join us." Catherine studied his reaction.

"Damn, baby, you never cease to amaze me. But I think that's something we can have arranged. I don't know how you're going to settle down to motherhood though. From jetting all over the world at the drop of a hat to freaking with me. All of that is going to have to come to an abrupt end."

"Nothing is going to change. I told you that brat is not going to upset my life, especially what we have. Now let's get to that limo. I have something for you to do with those wonder lips of yours."

"If your daughter was getting off the plane with you now, there is no way we would be doing anything in that limo except riding, and you know this. I most likely wouldn't even be here. I'm not sure if I want things to change between us, baby." Wendell didn't look at her as he spoke.

"Look at me, Wendell. I need you to listen and listen good. I am indulging this little inconvenience to get what I want from El Salvadore. Once I am securely president of North American operations, we'll ship Little Miss Alisa back to daddy dearest. He'll be so pleased to have her back, he won't even question what I've done. And while she is here, she'll be at boarding school, computer camp, space camp, any kind of camp I can possibly find to keep her out of my hair so that you and I can still be together. On the rare occasion when I can't find somewhere to send her, I'll hire someone to stay with her and we'll be at your place or anywhere in the world for that matter."

"I'm glad you weren't my mother. Damn!"

"Your mother probably loved *you*." Catherine's words shocked her almost as much as they astounded Wendell.

"I sure hope you never grow tired of me." Wendell was trying to get his emotional footing after such a revealing jolt.

"As long as you are serving my purposes, there is a place for you, my sweet. But remember, everyone is expendable." Catherine's cold stare made Wendell want to cut and run. That is what a smart man would have done, but maybe he wasn't so smart after all.

37

I T'S GONNA BE alright, baby. Has Momma evah lied to you
befo'?" Momma C tried to calm Jackie down, who was trying to
calm Terry down, who was beyond help.

"Momma, I know it's going to be okay. I am just really upset
that Catherine insists we bring Lisa and Ari into court today.
Terry hasn't slept a wink since he got the word three days ago.
Even Roland is livid." Jackie hugged her mother more out of
habit than anything else. There was something very therapeutic
about Momma C's hugs.

"Are you scared?" Ari asked Lisa. They were holding hands.

The dissension between them had ended the moment they
found out Catherine's plan to separate them. Lisa had cried and
begged Ari to forgive her for the way she had acted and for taking Catherine's side against her. She told her she never wanted to
be away from her *ever*. They agreed they would get married on
the same day and that they would marry twin brothers because
only twin brothers would understand how they felt about each
other.

Ari had said she would not go to court and promised to run
away. Lisa had talked her out of it by saying she would not go with

her. Each agreed they had to be brave and let the law protect them, which was a direct quote from their Uncle Roland.

Now they sat outside of a room where their futures would be decided for them. *Why are strangers deciding if we should live with our father?* they each wondered. *Why can't love decide that?* The same way selfishness had decided that they had had to live all this time without their mother.

They were both frightened. As they sat comforting each other, Catherine and her attorney stepped from the elevator. Catherine wore a full-length mink coat, mink hat, and mink-lined designer boots. This in itself would not have been so conspicuous if the weather prediction had not been sixty-five degrees.

Roland spoke politely to Naomi and asked if he could talk to her alone for a moment. Catherine made no effort to hide her annoyance at his request. As they stepped around the corner, Catherine was overheard saying she did not pay four hundred dollars an hour to have secrets kept from her. Everyone, including Naomi, ignored her.

"Look, Naomi, this is getting way out of hand. You know as well as I do the judge is not going to split up these girls. The best you can hope for is a fifty-fifty arrangement. Your client wants to have these girls every other week like I want to have a tooth removed without novocaine! Here's our offer: Three months in the summer. Every other Christmas and every other holiday. She can even take them abroad if she wants, though I don't think her interest will last long enough for them to process the passport application. We will have ourselves right back in here seeking an amendment within three weeks of her parenting full-time." Roland towered over Naomi.

"Mr. Carpenter, your offer is unacceptable to my client. She wants to be a full-time parent. Now, if your client doesn't want them split up, perhaps they can both live with her. After all, he has had them for almost eleven years. She misses them and feels she has waited much too long to take her rightful place in their lives."

"Naomi, even you don't believe what you're saying. We tried to play fair, but you've left us no choice. You want a fight. Well, you betta call Don King because we're getting ready to rumble." Roland walked away before Naomi could respond.

Roland looked at Terry and shook his head, which told him they had rejected his offer—an offer that Roland had adamantly objected to putting on the table. It wasn't necessary. They had her. Roland was certain of it. But now Catherine had rejected their last offer to save face.

The bailiff opened the doors to the courtroom, and true to form, Catherine barged her way through the others to enter the courtroom first. She even knocked Momma C off balance. Momma C had to grab Jackie's arm to keep her from attacking Catherine from behind.

"Leave her be, chile. She didn't do me no harm. Let's jus' go in here and win dis here case 'cause we got us a weddin' to plan. A June garden weddin' at dat big ole place of Roland's is what I gots in mind. What chu think?" Momma C placed her arm heavily on Jackie's.

"That sounds wonderful, Momma. I do love you, you know."

"You betta! I's the only momma you gots."

Terry helped Momma C into her seat and kissed Jackie as she took her seat behind the defense table. As Terry took his seat, he turned to Jackie and mouthed the words "I love you." Momma C touched her child's arm as Jackie mouthed the same words back to her future husband.

The court reporter took his seat, and the clerk entered the courtroom. Judge Agnew would not be far behind. The tension was so thick it would have taken a machete to cut through it.

"All rise. The twelfth district court of Dallas County is now in session, the Honorable Judge Constance Agnew presiding. Please remain standing to be sworn in. Raise your right hand. Repeat after me. I do solemnly swear or affirm all statements presented by me in this court to be the truth, the whole truth, and nothing but the truth, so help me God." The bailiff spoke in a monotone, routine manner.

The gavel signaled for everyone to be seated. The hearing was under way. Judge Agnew asked both attorneys if they were ready to proceed. Both affirmed they were.

"Are there any motions for settlement without my ruling in this case?"

Neither attorney said a word.

"I really hoped that you two could settle this case before now. Ms. Sharpe, you may proceed," Judge Agnew said with a rare display of emotion.

Naomi Sharpe stood behind her table and began to orate in a fashion that might have been envied by Johnnie Cochran. She told of the pain and suffering endured by her client over the many years she had been separated from her daughters. She felt that what her client asked for was fair since they could each have one of the children and because the defendant had been sole parent for nearly eleven years. She ended by saying that she was sure the court would rule in favor of her client.

Roland stood and walked around in front of the defense table, turned and looked at Terry, then the girls, Jackie, and Momma C. "Your Honor, a picture is worth a thousand words. This is a family in every sense of the word. Taking away any member of this family would be like removing a piece from the puzzle. It completely destroys the picture. We plan to show this court that it is in everyone's best interest to keep all of the pieces of this puzzle in place."

"Well, I guess we will proceed then. I will not tolerate any nonsense with these children present. Is that clear?" Judge Agnew leaned forward for effect.

"Clear as a bell, Your Honor." Roland smiled.

"Yes, Your Honor." Naomi's tone was hard to read.

All of the preliminary documentation was presented in the morning session. Reports submitted by family services included financial statements from both Catherine and Terry. Catherine's net worth was in excess of ten million dollars. At this revelation, the look of smugness on her face as all eyes in the court were on her, including the bailiff's, was unmistakable.

Momma C gasped audibly. "Money don't make her no good momma, though."

Jackie touched her hand, and Momma C pulled it away. She was visibly angry. *How dare dey even think dat money made a good momma,* she thought.

The reading of documents seemed to go on for hours. As the clock approached noon, the judge called a recess for lunch, but asked the attorneys to approach the bench first. She asked them one last time if they wanted to continue this case and to call these children as witnesses.

"Your Honor, we intend to prove that these girls have been prejudiced against my client, their mother. Also, that she is able and, more important, willing to provide a loving home for Alisa Winston and Ariana if she is willing to reconsider. In time, she's hoping Ariana will come around and choose to spend more time with her." Naomi's voice was raised above the traditional whisper that was embraced at the bench.

"Your Honor, these girls are happy, productive, and developing well under the guardianship of their father, as they have for the past eleven years. We will show beyond any doubt that it is in the best interest of Ariana and Alisa to remain in the loving and caring home where they have grown up." Roland felt far too emotional.

"Let me warn you both: For the sake of these children, you had better not try any showcasing this afternoon. Call your witnesses, ask the necessary questions, and get this over with. If I have to watch the petrified look on those precious faces for more than this afternoon, I will not be happy. Is that clear?"

"Yes, Your Honor." They spoke in unison.

"This court is in recess until two o'clock. Counselors, I would suggest you use the two hours to hammer out an agreement."

Catherine approached Terry. "Give it up, Terry. Don't put them through this. Give me what I want. You know I always get it. I'll even buy your little family lunch. After all, I can afford it." Her laughter resounded as she left the courtroom.

Those left behind looked from one to the other, unable to

comment on what had just occurred. Naomi had a pleading look that begged Roland to make her another offer.

Roland grab his briefcase and asked, "Chinese, or shall we go to Dick's and get burgers?"

"DICK'S!" the twins yelled.

"Dick's it is! Let's go!" Roland turned to look at Naomi. "Have a good lunch, counselor."

Dick's had been just what the doctor ordered. The sawdust on the floor, the rude servers, and excellent food had lightened the mood of almost everyone. Lisa and Ari seemed almost animated. Chuck, their server, made such a big deal about their duplicate identity and teased them mercilessly. For their good-natured acceptance of his teasing, they had been rewarded with free dessert. Everyone was having a good time, except Terry.

He picked at his food and gave only one-word answers to Jackie's pathetic attempts to draw him out of his mood. He and Roland argued over who was going to pick up the check. Terry finally won. The ladies stepped out onto the landing while Roland remained behind with Terry to pay the check. "Terry, we have no choice. We've given them every opportunity. We'll have Jackie take the girls out of the courtroom after their testimony, but we have to do this."

"I know, man, I know. But even if they leave the courtroom, I know this will get back to them, and I would do anything to shield them from any further hurt. But we have to do what we have to do. I just don't understand how she could be the way she is." Terry spoke in a defeated tone.

"You would not believe the types of people I have encountered in this business. Some of them make Catherine seem like Mother Teresa for sure. But it'll all be over soon, I promise you. The judge is pissed because we can't settle this. She has told us in no uncertain terms to get to the point. She wants this over by this afternoon."

"Let's do it!" Terry reached deep inside himself to find a renewed strength. This was for the good of his family. He was not the one who had waged this war, but he would walk away victorious, though slightly wounded.

The day was clear and warm. A slight breeze made it a perfect day, unseasonably warm for January. Everyone was happy they had decided to walk back. They reached the court just a few minutes before the doors would be opened and lives would be forever changed.

Naomi and Catherine were already waiting. This time Naomi asked to speak to Roland.

"I just wanted you to know that I tried to reason with her over lunch. She won't budge. I also told her that Judge Agnew will not stand for any drama queens in her courtroom. She is determined to have her day in court. Just so you know, she has called the press. None of this is my idea." Naomi's sincerity didn't phase Roland in the least.

"Thank you for the heads up, counselor. Your client will get everything that is coming to her today, I assure you. Shall we?" Roland stepped aside to allow Naomi to enter in front of him.

The courtroom doors opened and the afternoon session was set to begin. Just as the Winstons were about to step through the doors of the courtroom, the elevator doors opened and with much flurry a short, unassuming man with a very large camera stepped out, followed by Michelle Monty, one of Dallas's top reporters.

"Jackie, what are you doing here?" Michelle asked her longtime colleague.

"This is my fiancé, Terry Winston, and this is the custody hearing for his, I mean our, daughters. What are you here covering?" Jackie was surprised.

"Winston? As in 'Hawkins versus Winston'? That's why I'm

here. You and Terry are engaged? Congratulations, Jackie!" Michelle hugged her.

"Thank you. We got engaged Christmas Eve. Yes, one and the same. Why are you here to cover this small-time matter?" Jackie couldn't even relish this congratulatory moment.

"I really don't know. Steve just told me to get down here. Does he know that you are involved?"

"I don't believe so. My name didn't appear in any of the filings. This is rather strange, don't you think?"

"I agree. I asked him if it was a slow news day." Michelle laughed.

Jackie didn't think it was a slow news day at all. Catherine must be responsible for this! But why? Michelle was making small talk, but Jackie's focus was elsewhere.

"Honey, we have to get inside. Are you okay?" Terry touched her arm.

"Why did Catherine call in reporters?" Jackie was angry. She knew what it would take to get a reporter of Michelle's caliber.

"How do you know Catherine did it?" Terry didn't understand Jackie's anger.

"Michelle is a top staff writer. She covers only high-profile stories. This is high profile to us, but come on, to the rest of Dallas?"

"If she in fact called them, then she will be sorry. We need to get inside." Terry gently steered Jackie toward the open courtroom doors.

"What do you mean?" Jackie looked at her fiancé strangely.

"Honey, this is not going to be pretty. After Lisa and Ari take the stand, I want you to take them out of the courtroom." Terry looked directly into Jackie's eyes.

"What is going on here? First the reporter, and now you're telling me things are going to get ugly. Did Roland ask the reporter to be here? You're keeping secrets from me. I don't like this!"

"No, honey, we have nothing to do with the reporter. But Catherine's character will be entered as testimony, and I don't want Ari and Lisa to hear that about their mother. Even if it is true. Just trust me, please." Terry kissed her forehead.

"I do trust you. This thing is breaking me down. I don't know what to feel or think. I'll do whatever you need me to do, but I'll have Momma take them out. I want to stay with you."

"Oh, honey, that's why I love you. You're always looking out for your man. Now let's go kick Catherine Marie Hawkins's uppity ass." He kissed her again and led her into the courtroom.

There were a few spectators seated near the back of the court. Some were young and presumed to be law students. Others were older and presumed to be without a life and living through the drama of others. Jackie wondered why the thoughts were even in her head. Why did she even care?

"All rise. The twelfth district court of Dallas County is now in session, Judge Constance Agnew presiding. You are still sworn in. You may be seated." The bailiff passed a piece of paper to the judge.

"Ms. Sharpe, are you ready to proceed?"

"I am, Your Honor. We would like to call Alisa Winston to the stand." Naomi moved toward the railing.

Lisa took the stand and looked straight at her dad. Her eyes pleaded with him to save her from this ordeal.

"Lisa, my name is Naomi Sharpe, and I am the attorney for your mother, Catherine Hawkins. I just have a few questions so that your statements can be a part of the court records. Do you understand?"

Lisa nodded.

"You will have to speak out loud so that the gentleman here can record your answers, okay?" Naomi leaned in close to Lisa and almost whispered.

"Yes, I understand. Uncle Roland told me that part. I am sorry, but I forgot."

"Now, Lisa, for the record, please tell the court your name."

"Alisa Terri Winston."

"How old are you, Alisa?"

"Almost eleven."

"So that means right now you are ten?" Naomi smiled.

"Yes, ma'am."

"And for the past ten years, with whom have you lived?"

"My dad, Terry Winston."

"Has he been a good dad?"

"He has been the best dad. He does everything with us. He does everything for us."

"Do you miss having a mother around like your girlfriends do?"

"Yes." Alisa dropped her head.

Terry's heart sank.

"But when Daddy and Miss Jackie get married, we will have a mother all the time. We'll have a brother and another sister, too. They're going to buy a bigger house and move us all into it." Lisa beamed.

"Do you like spending time with your mother, Catherine?"

"Yes, she takes us shopping, and she's going to buy a ranch and give us each a horse. I have a lot of fun with her."

"Now, Alisa, wouldn't you like to live on a ranch all the time with your own horse?"

"I would love to live on a ranch. I really like being outside all the time."

Terry looked desperately at Roland. This was not going the way he thought it should. Catherine looked over and flashed a bone-chilling smile.

"But I can't go live there because Ari doesn't want to. I'll never leave my sister. *Never!* And I don't care how nice the ranch is. If my dad isn't there, I don't want to be there, anyway."

"Tell me something, Alisa. You said that your Uncle Roland told you about shaking your head in court. Did he also tell you what to say when I asked you questions?"

"Yes, ma'am. He did."

Terry sank lower in his chair. Roland stared at Alisa and nodded. Jackie sighed and hid her face in her hands. Catherine smiled.

"And what exactly did he tell you to say."

"Well, he told me to only answer the questions you asked. Then he told me to tell you the truth about how I felt."

"I see. One last question. If Ariana wanted to go live with Catherine, would you feel differently about it?"

"You mean would I want to go?"

"Yes."

"I don't ever want to live away from my dad. It's okay to go visit Catherine—she is a real nice lady. But our father is our daddy. He takes care of us when we're sick. He helps me with my homework. He lets us help him cook dinner. He wrestles with us. He cries with us. He loves us."

"No further questions, Your Honor." Naomi took her seat next to Catherine, who immediately began whispering to her lawyer.

"Mr. Carpenter, any questions of this witness?" Judge Agnew looked stoically at Roland.

"Just a couple, Your Honor. Alisa, has your dad ever tried to stop Catherine from visiting or you from visiting her?" Roland moved very close to the witness box.

"Oh no, Uncle Roland. There have been so many times he would ask her when she was going to visit or allow us to visit, and she would never have time. She made a lot of promises, but something always happened and she had to cancel."

"And whenever she canceled, how did you and Ari feel about that?"

"I object, this witness can only testify as to how she feels, not her sister." Naomi was on her feet instantly.

"Your Honor, in most cases I would agree, but these twins share everything. Surely, they would share with each other their innermost feelings." Roland turned his body so that he could see the judge, Catherine, and Alisa.

"I will allow it, but tread lightly, Mr. Carpenter."

"I will rephrase the question. Alisa, tell me what you felt about her canceling so many times, and then tell me what Ariana told you she felt."

"I would be disappointed, and then after a while I would not even get excited anymore. But Ari would get mad every time. She would sometimes cry and say that she hated Catherine."

"One last question. Would you like to visit Catherine on her ranch on weekends and holidays?"

"I sure would. I have always wanted to go visit her. She just never had time for us. But we have to be with my dad and Miss Jackie on Christmas. We don't want to ever be away from home on Christmas."

"Thank you, Alisa. No further questions, Your Honor."

"Alisa, you did very well. You may go back to your seat now. Please call your next witness, Ms. Sharpe."

"We will call the petitioner in this case, Catherine Hawkins, to the stand, Your Honor." Naomi stepped aside to let Catherine pass.

Naomi began her interrogation. "For the record, please state your full name."

"Catherine Marie Hawkins."

"Ms. Hawkins, please tell the court why you are asking for sole custody of Alisa and not joint custody of both girls."

"I have so selfishly pursued my career and never realized what I was missing as a mother. I have missed their first steps, their teething, kindergarten graduations. There has been a void in my life, and I have sought to fill it not realizing that it is a void that can only be filled by my children. I have returned to the United States for the sole purpose of forming a mother-daughter relationship with Ariana and Alisa. I love them so much. I am so very disappointed that Ariana doesn't want to come live with me. But I understand. I will have to prove my love to her, and in time she will see that I am sincere, and she will come around. She just has to." Catherine had missed her calling. She should have been an actress.

However, no one was fooled by the performance.

"Now tell the court what you plan to do to make up for your absence all these years."

"Time once gone is lost forever. I can never get those moments back. But I will make the absolute most of every second of every minute of every hour of every day God allows me to share my life with my children. It will take time, but we will have a mother-daughter bond. All three of us." Catherine looked compassionately at Ariana and Alisa.

"No further questions. Your witness." Naomi looked directly at Roland.

"Your Honor, I do have a few questions of this witness. But I would like the court's permission to have Ariana and Alisa removed by their grandmother." Roland refused to look at Catherine.

"Very well, Mr. Carpenter. You have five minutes."

Momma C gathered Ariana and Alisa, along with her purse, and headed for the door. Ariana turned and waved to her father. He blew her a kiss. As Momma C held the door for the twins, a very tall, very handsome man took the door from her. He entered the courtroom as they exited.

Your honor, the defense is ready." Roland acknowledged the newcomer's presence in the courtroom as he took the seat that Momma C had vacated next to Jackie.

"You may proceed, Mr. Carpenter." Judge Agnew stared at the man who had entered her courtroom.

"Ms. Hawkins, tell the court, if you will, when you deserted your children."

"I object, Your Honor. My client did not desert her children. She relinquished custody to their father." Naomi was on her feet again.

"Sustained. Watch it, Mr. Carpenter," Judge Agnew warned.

"Tell the court then, Ms. Hawkins, when did you relinquish custody of the twins to Terrence Winston?"

Catherine stared past Roland to the handsome newcomer to the proceedings. She never heard the question.

"Ms. Hawkins, do I need to repeat the question?"

Still no response.

"Ms. Hawkins, you are required to answer questions presented by the defense. Do you understand?" Judge Agnew was becoming agitated.

"I'm . . . I'm sorry, Your Honor. What is the question?" Catherine's eyes never left Wendell.

"I repeat, Ms. Hawkins. When did you relinquish custody of your twin daughters to their father, Terrence Winston?"

After a very long pause, Catherine managed to tear her gaze from Wendell. "In the hospital when they were born." Her line of sight went back to Wendell.

"In the ten years, nine months, and eleven days since that memorable day, have you had custody of Ariana and Alisa Winston?"

"No." Catherine could not comprehend why Wendell was in this courtroom and sitting next to Jackie.

"Have they ever spent an extended vacation with you in those ten-plus years?"

"No."

"Have they ever spent a weekend with you in almost eleven years?"

"No, they haven't, Mr. Carpenter. I have been out of the country for the past three years. I am here today to rectify some of my shortcomings as a mother." Catherine's attention returned to Roland. Her gaze wandered back to Wendell immediately after she answered.

"So, Ms. Hawkins, could you please help the court to understand why you want to leapfrog from totally absent parent to Clair Huxtable in one swift movement?"

"I object!"

"Overruled. Please answer the question, Ms. Hawkins. Mr. Carpenter, I will not warn you again."

"I have missed my children. I have had a longing to be near them. I was caught up in a corporate position that did not afford me the opportunity to spend the time with them that I wanted to. I asked the company to transfer me back to the United States so that I could be near them. I am not saying that I was right in the path I chose, but I can say that I am sorry. I want to be with my children. Even if one of them doesn't want to be with me, Mr. Carpenter." Catherine spat the words at him.

"So, let me understand. You are in this court today to seek custody of Alisa because you love and miss your daughters and now after ten years are feeling very maternal. Was there an occasion during this past holiday season when you did not know Ariana from Alisa?"

"I made a mistake. Is that a crime?"

"No, Ms. Hawkins, but wanting to split up two sisters who have been together since conception should be. So there is no reason other than your need to fulfill your maternal instincts for your seeking custody of Alisa?"

"What other motive could I have? She is my child, and I want to be with her. It is that simple."

"Only her, not Ariana. Are you not equally both their mother?"

"Of course, I am, but Ariana wants nothing to do with me. I can't force the child to come to live with me."

"But you are trying to force Alisa to come and live with you?"

"She wants to come and live with me. She said so here in this courtroom."

"No, Catherine, she said she would come to visit you, which is what we have offered you from the beginning. So which is it, do you or don't you want the children to be able to choose their living arrangements?"

"I want Alisa to choose to live with me. And she will, if you and Terry stop poisoning her mind against me!" Catherine's true persona began to shine through.

"Your Honor, I have no further questions."

"Any redirect, Ms. Sharpe?"

"Just one question, Your Honor. Catherine, if Ariana were willing to come to live with you part-time, would you be willing to accept joint custody?"

"Absolutely. In an arrangement that works for everyone!"

"No further questions, Your Honor."

"You may step down, Ms. Hawkins. Any other witnesses, Ms. Sharpe?"

Catherine stepped from the witness box, never taking her eyes off Wendell, who met her gaze uncompromised. She immediately began whispering to Naomi. Naomi snapped her neck to see who Catherine was referring to in her rapid description of the recent weeks' escapades with Wendell. When Catherine finished, Naomi stared at her client in disbelief.

"No, Your Honor." Naomi's voice faltered.

"Mr. Carpenter, would you like to call any witnesses?"

"Only one, Your Honor. We call Mr. Howard Michelson."

The tall, large, very handsome man with the green eyes stood and headed toward the witness box. Catherine began to feel as if she were in a dream. *Who the hell is Howard Michelson? This man's name is Wendell Johnson,* she thought.

"Your Honor, this witness will need to be sworn in."

Roland smiled at Catherine, who stared from Roland to Wendell. The bailiff handled the swearing-in process promptly.

"Please state your name and occupation for the record." Roland strutted like a peacock.

"Howard Michelson. I am a licensed private investigator with Michelson and Michelson."

"Mr. Michelson, has your agency been retained by the law firm of Carpenter, Pickford, and Harper in the Hawkins versus Winston child custody suit?"

"Yes, we have." Howard stared directly at Catherine as she shrank further and further into her chair.

"Who in your firm was assigned to this case?"

"I handled it personally."

"Please tell this court what you were assigned to uncover."

"I had been asked to gather any adverse information on Ms. Hawkins that would prove to this court that her intent was to destroy the Winston family."

"In your professional opinion, were you able to gather substantial information about the plaintiff that will be beneficial to the defense in this proceeding?"

"Yes, we have submitted a ninety-four-page report to your office outlining all the information we gathered."

"I hope your report outlines how you have been fucking me senseless for the past six weeks, you lousy son of a bitch," Catherine screamed out in the courtroom.

"*Order!* Ms. Hawkins, I will have you removed from this court and will slap you with a contempt charge if you use that type of language in my courtroom."

Naomi tried in vain to calm her client.

"Please, Mr. Michelson, tell us how you gathered the information used in your rather lengthy report."

"I befriended Ms. Hawkins with the intent of gaining her confidence in hopes of striking up a romantic relationship with her. By doing this, it was my intent to see if she was serious about her motherhood role."

"And were you successful?"

"I'll say I was. We were together constantly from the day I staged our meeting until this morning when she left for this hearing."

"When you say 'together,' please explain what you mean to this court."

"The first day we met, she invited me to her penthouse for lunch. We became lovers that afternoon. She begged me to quit my job and be her personal fitness trainer for a very handsome rate. I spent most nights at her place. We were lovers. I was her paid lover."

"Now, as lovers, as you put it, did you have occasion to question Ms. Hawkins about her daughters?"

"On many occasions I told her that I did not want things to change between us. She assured me that they wouldn't. That as soon as her presidency with El Salvadore de Casa was confirmed, she would send Alisa back to Dallas. But in the meantime, she would be in boarding school and various camps, which would ensure us that we would have our time together.

"On one occasion in particular, she spoke with such callousness that I commented that I was glad she was never my mother. She responded that at least my mother had loved *me*."

"As I understand it, Mr. Michelson, Ms. Hawkins only wanted

to pursue custody to advance her career. She had no intention of keeping Alisa after her promotion and was simply disrupting this family for her own personal gain?"

"That is correct."

"I HATE YOU, WENDELL! How dare you? You are lying! You will never prove anything you're saying!" Catherine screamed, refusing to take direction from Naomi.

"Either calm your client, or I will have her removed from this court." Judge Agnew hammered her gavel.

"I'm sorry, Your Honor. She will not do it again," Naomi addressed the court, then whispered loudly to Catherine, "Sit down and be quiet. I will get a chance to refute his testimony. What he did was unethical. His behavior has prejudiced his testimony. Please just let me handle this. Why didn't you tell me you were involved with someone?" Naomi was angry.

"It's none of your damn business who I am involved with. This is my life. That son of a bitch tricked me. You get his ass. Do you understand me? Get his ass, or I will get yours." Catherine spoke through clenched teeth.

"Mr. Michelson, do you in fact have proof of what you are saying?"

"Yes. Ms. Hawkins has been under surveillance the entire time. The conversations have been recorded."

"Are you prepared to produce the recordings for this court?"

"Yes, we have several volumes."

"No further questions, Your Honor."

"Ms. Sharpe, your witness."

"Your Honor, may we approach the bench?"

Constance Agnew had been waiting for this request. She beckoned them forward.

"Your Honor, in light of this testimony, I need to confer with my client. She clearly needs to get herself together," Naomi pleaded.

"I have no objection, Your Honor. I would recommend that you convince her to drop this petition and take the visitation offer we made from the beginning. With the press here, she does not want these tapes played in this courtroom." Roland was sincerely trying to save Catherine any further embarrassment.

"You have ten minutes." Judge Agnew was running out of patience.

"Thank you, Your Honor."

Naomi took Catherine by the arm and led her from the courtroom. She had to talk some sense into her before she lost all visitation with her children, which Naomi wasn't even sure that Catherine really wanted. When she was in law school, she wanted to make a difference in family law. How in the hell had she gotten here?

Howard had stepped down from the witness box and joined Roland, Jackie, and Terry at the defense table. He shook hands with Terry and Roland.

"Excellent job, Howard. I think they'll return with an acceptance of the visitation proposal. Sounds like this assignment wasn't all work." Roland smiled at Howard.

"It did have its perks, but I gotta tell you, that woman is as cold as anyone I have ever encountered. Some of the things she said made my blood coagulate. She needs to get some psychiatric help," Howard said, embarrassed by Roland's implication in Jackie's presence.

"Thank you for a job well done. You know, I owe you for this one, my brotha. You need to hang around in case they want to cross, but I seriously doubt that will be required. We'll take care of your expenses right away, since you didn't charge us."

"Roland, that woman gave me so much money, I'll deduct my expenses and the rest I'll forward to Terry to put in a trust fund for Ariana and Alisa. I'd do anything to keep those precious kids away from that evil woman." Howard shook Terry's hand again.

"You better watch your back, Howard. You have scorned her. Hell hath no fury . . ." Jackie smiled as she thought how men could separate sex from emotion.

The door to the judge's chamber opened, and Constance Agnew stepped to her bench. This mess was almost over.

Naomi Sharpe entered the courtroom alone.

THERE IS NOTHING as beautiful as the sunrise in the Caribbean. The white sandy beach against the crystal blue water and the sun peeking through the lush green hilltops make a perfect backdrop for the early morning exchange of wedding vows.

The decision to get married on the beach at sunrise had been an instant hit with everyone. Ariana and Alisa looked absolutely beautiful in their white sundresses with lilies in their hair. Michael and Michelle wore white shorts and tops, and they each carried a pillow with a wedding band.

Veronica had bloodshot eyes from the party the night before at the local bar. She had not even slept. But to everyone's pleasure, she was not hung over. Terry, Teresa, and Roland had confronted her about her drinking and voiced their concerns. They explained they loved her too much to allow her to continue on this destructive path. With much persuasion, she agreed to get help. She had been sober for one hundred and fifty-nine days.

Momma C and Teresa held each other's hands as the bride and groom, along with their best friends, approached the minister.

A reggae band played softly in the background. The day was perfect. The bride wore a very simple white crinkle-cloth dress with white sandals. The groom wore a white silk shirt and white linen pants with no shoes. The maid of honor wore a bright floral sundress with white sandals; the best man's shirt matched the maid of honor's dress. He wore white linen pants, and like the groom, he was barefoot. Not the typical African-American wedding attire, to say the least.

"Dearly beloved, we are gathered here on this your glorious morning to join this man and this woman in holy matrimony. As they enter into this sacred state, we ask your blessing on them and their family. For today truly two families become one." The minister with the dreads spoke in an accent so thick it was almost difficult to understand him.

"Do you, Roland Alexander Carpenter, take Mercedes Harper Marshall to be your lawfully wedded wife, vowing your undying love and lifetime commitment?"

"With all that is within me, I do."

"Do you, Mercedes Harper Marshall, take Roland Alexander Carpenter to be your lawfully wedded husband, vowing your undying love and lifetime commitment?"

"With all that is within me, I do."

As the soft breeze blew a sea mist across her face, Jackie thought back to three days earlier when she and Terry had said those exact same words. Their garden wedding had been the social event of the season. Roland had made sure of it. Musicians, caterers, photographers, and coordinators seemed to be everywhere. What had started out as an intimate gathering of a few friends had turned into a major production.

Jackie loved every moment of it. Terry flowed with whatever made Jackie happy. He would just shake his head at the arrangements and say, "Whatever you want, baby."

Judge Agnew's ruling had realigned everything in Terry's universe. Naomi Sharpe had returned to the courtroom and withdrawn the petition for custody. Constance Agnew, with a swift pounding of her gavel, had declared Terrence Winston sole custodian of Ariana and Alisa Winston.

In the hallway outside the courtroom, Catherine had looked Ariana and Alisa in their faces, faces so much like her own, and told them that she did not love them, never had, and never could. She would have to make president without having to endure such an inconvenience as motherhood. She wanted them to have a good life, but told them to never expect to hear from her again. Momma C asked Catherine how she could be so cruel and heartless. Catherine simply turned and walked into the open elevator and out of their lives.

Terry had received a document from Naomi Sharpe with Catherine Marie Hawkins's notarized signature relinquishing all parental rights to Ari and Lisa. Included in the envelope was a certified check for one million dollars. He placed the document in the safe-deposit box at the bank. Though the women in his life couldn't understand, Terry's first instinct was to return the check. Catherine tried to buy a clear conscience; Terry wasn't selling. Roland convinced him to set up an irrevocable trust to cover college, with the balance to be disbursed when the girls turned twenty-five.

At the lavish Winston wedding reception, as Roland proposed a toast to his best friend and his friend's new bride, he thanked Terry for their lifelong friendship and for bringing Jackie into his life, because Jackie had brought Cedes along with her. The only thing that would make him happier than he was at that moment would be Cedes's accepting his proposal of marriage.

Cedes in turn offered a toast to her best friend and sister, thanking her for bringing Terry into her life because along with Terry came Roland and she would be honored to become his wife. There was not a dry eye under the massive tent, which held three hundred guests. Cheers resounded for both couples.

The day after the wedding, a private breakfast was held for the newlyweds, the family, and the wedding party. As everyone reflected on the events of the previous day, Ariana casually mentioned that Cedes and Roland should get married on the beach in the Caribbean and that they should all go on her dad and new mom's honeymoon with them.

Everyone laughed except Terry. "Roland, you are the master at pulling things together at the last minute. Can you arrange to have the entire family on the plane with us tomorrow morning? Cedes and Jackie can plan a small wedding on the beach. You can throw one of your big hoedowns later. What do you say?"

"Honey?" Roland's eyes begged Cedes to agree.

"One major matrimonial production in a lifetime is more than enough for me. Let's do it!" Cedes leapt into Roland's waiting arms.

"Well, jus' praise da Lawd. Margaret is so happy. I is pretty happy mahself." Momma C wiped tears with her napkin.

"Are you sure you want all of us on your honeymoon, my brotha? It is a pretty special time in your lives," Roland earnestly inquired.

"Roland, I am going to be with Jackie for the rest of my life, which I pray will be a very long time, and I plan to make every day our honeymoon." Terry kissed Jackie on her forehead.

"I couldn't agree more. Cedes, if I gotta share my honeymoon with people, why not the people I love most in the world?"

Now here they all stood at sunrise on the beach on a Caribbean island with everyone they loved in the world around them. Life just didn't get much better than that.

TERRENCE AND JACQUELINE Winston sat across from Judge Constance Agnew for the last time. Jackie was so nervous she felt light-headed. She sat between Roland and Terry holding their hands.

"Mr. and Mrs. Winston, it is with great pleasure that I sign the adoption decree for Alisa, Ariana, Michelle, and Michael Winston. I have sat on the bench in family court for a lot of years, and it is times like these that make up for those when my heart was broken by some of the decisions made within these walls." Judge Agnew smiled broadly.

"We never thought we could be happier than we were the last time we were here, but I guess we were wrong." Jackie flinched as the baby kicked with a fury.

"When is the baby due? And do we know what this one is? Or is it two?" Judge Agnew laughed at her own rapid succession of questions.

"The baby, I repeat, *baby*, singular, is due in five weeks, and it is a boy. Terry threatened to build a guest house and move into it if it was another girl." Jackie and Constance laughed as though they were old girlfriends.

"And Roland, I understand there's a future lawyer to be roaming the Carpenter estate soon."

"Constance, it can't be soon enough for me. We are only seven weeks along, but yes, we are very excited, too."

"I sure hope that this doesn't mean I can't still get Cowboys tickets." Constance pretended to be concerned.

"Now Constance, you know Cedes as well as anyone. Do you think a baby is going to slow her roll?"

"Yeah, I guess you are right. Are we still on for whist this Sunday?"

"You betcha, Your Honor. And I suggest packing your luggage before you leave home this time . . . 'cause ya goin' to Boston!"

"Terry and Jackie, I sure hope you are going to be there. I owe Terry from the last time. I am going to whip you like you stole something." The Honorable Constance Agnew was now just Connie, as she relaxed into an entirely different persona.

"Connie, considering all that you have done for us . . . I'd gladly give you the shirt off my back."

Reading has been my life's passion since the days (actually nights) I had to hold a flashlight under the covers while I was supposed to be sleeping. When I first discovered African-American fiction, I knew I had died and gone to literary heaven. As the years passed, I found that novels penned by African-American female writers had a single common denominator: the brothers were all less than desirable characters. I was so disappointed not to find my male friends represented on any of those pages.

Imagine the disappointment experienced by the more than ten million adult African-American males each year when they attempt to uncover fictional material that is entertaining but not demeaning to them. I knew in my heart that it was time for a change. *The Shirt off His Back* is a novel about the real African-American man—the good husband, good father, good son, good friend. So this work is dedicated to all the brothas who do the right thing, even when no one is watching!

Parry "EbonySatin" Brown

1. Alisa's and Ariana's contrary behavior with their mother during Christmas reflects the twins' mixed feelings about her sudden reappearance. Their excitement at seeing her and their anger at her neglect are expressed by each twin; Alisa can't wait to see Catherine, while Ariana can't stand to be around her. Why do the twins have such different reactions? How much does their father influence their feelings about their mother? Which twin do you most sympathize with?

2. In many ways Terry's children have helped make him who he is; likewise for Jackie. Their children, they admit, are the best things that have happened to them. How have their children shaped their lives? How different would they be had they not had their twins?

3. It is clear Jackie and her girlfriends think Terry is great husband material; after all, not only is he a single father who cares deeply for his children, he is exceptionally kind to family and friends alike. Is Terry unusual? How easy would it be to find Terry's equivalent in the real world?

4. After Catherine threatens to take Alisa and Ariana away from him, Terry's contact with her is, at times, unyielding and bitter. His initial reaction to her request to see the twins on Christmas is outright refusal. Is Terry right to treat Catherine the way she treats him? Are his actions justified, or is he stooping to her level? If she had been a more sympathetic character, do you think Terry would have been more willing to share custody?

5. Despite Terry's clear preference for her size, Jackie often feels unhappy about her weight. Her obsession with it increases during times of stress—when she seems to feel particularly insecure. Should she lose weight? What is holding Jackie back from accepting herself as she is? What is Brown showing us about our obsession with weight?

6. Although Catherine makes it clear she is only seeking custody of the twins for professional gain, she displays a few instances of motherly concern. Do you think Catherine regrets her ruthlessness in any way? Do you have any sympathy for her character? Why does she choose to sever all ties with her daughters at the end?

7. While Roland and Cedes have known each other for years, it is not until Roland sees Cedes's vulnerability that he becomes attracted to her. Why is this? What does he finally come to understand about her? About himself?

8. Cedes envies Jackie and Terry's relationship but has been unable to replicate it for herself; she has not been able to find a man with whom she can have a long-term relationship. What changes in Cedes allow her to see Roland in a new light? Had she pursued a relationship with Charles, do you think it would have been successful?

9. Roland and Terry employ some pretty dirty tactics to expose Catherine's vicious nature. Is this fair? Could they have won the case without Wendell/Howard's "undercover" work?

10. Together with their grandparents, siblings, and friends, Jackie and Terry's extended family form a strong, supportive unit. How do different family members step in to help one another? How important is family in providing support when times get tough?

11. As the matriarch of Jackie and Terry's family, Momma C dispenses wisdom and love with her own special way with words. What are some of her more memorable "proverbs"? How essential is she in the lives of her children and grandchildren? Describe the differences between Momma C and Catherine.

12. Even though Jackie and Terry are deeply in love with each other, Jackie seems apprehensive about accepting Terry's marriage proposal and Terry is equally shy about asking her. Why is it so difficult for them? Have their past relationships with the parents of their children affected them? How hard is it to enter into a new relationship after leaving a bad one?

13. Love is one of the central themes of *The Shirt off His Back* and it takes many forms: fatherly and motherly love, romantic love, brotherly and sisterly love. Those who do not experience these kinds of love are unable to do so because of selfishness and distrust; we see this mostly in Catherine and, to a much lesser extent, in Roland and Cedes. What emotions are necessary for love to flourish? What is Brown telling us about love of self and love for others?

PARRY "EBONYSATIN" BROWN is the co-producer and host of the radio talk show *Single Black Mom Parenting Magazine,* which airs in Georgia, and is an internationally renowned motivational speaker.

She is also president of ShanKrys Publishing, Inc., and chairperson and founder of Los Angeles Ebony Online People, a nonprofit organization dedicated to placing Internet-ready computers in the homes of deserving, yet economically challenged, young people.

She is the author of *Sexy Doesn't Have a Dress Size* and is currently working on her second novel. She invites you to visit her website, www.parryebonysatinbrown.com, and to e-mail her directly at ebonysatin @aol.com.